GEOMANCER'S BARGAIN

THE WESTERN GEOMANCER

BOOK ONE

DANIEL R. MARVELLO

 Published by Magic Fur Press
An imprint of Logical Expressions, Inc.
P.O. Box 383, Ponderay, Idaho 83852, USA

This is a work of fiction. All names, characters, places, and events are either the product of the author's imagination or are used fictitiously. Any resemblance to actual persons, living or dead, business organizations, events, or locales is purely coincidental.

GEOMANCER'S BARGAIN

Copyright © 2016 by Daniel R. Marvello
All rights reserved.

ISBN: Print: 978-1-61038-041-6
       EPUB: 978-1-61038-042-3

Cover design and print layout by Susan C. Daffron
Ebook formatting by Logical Expressions, Inc.

Geomancer's Bargain is dedicated to my lovely
and talented wife.
She is the real magic in my life.

Books by Daniel R. Marvello
<u>The Vaetra Chronicles</u>
Vaetra Unveiled
Vaetra Untrained
Vaetra Unleashed

<u>The Ternion Order</u>
First Moon

CHAPTER 1

Munsey Gang

Carleton Kazimer strode down the Baltimore sidewalk, stepping over puddles formed by the light autumn rain. Tipping his head forward slightly, he shed the water that had collected in the brim of his bowler. He kept a watchful eye on the street traffic, ready to dodge the next splash of muddy water thrown up by a horse-drawn carriage.

As he walked, he mentally organized the clues he had collected from his latest inquiries. Consulting with the U.S. Marshals Service had turned out to be much more exciting and satisfying than he'd expected it to be when he first received the short-term assignment from the Wizard Guild. He expected his involvement to end after he helped apprehend the murdering fugitive Theodore Munsey, but the investigation had exposed a nest of criminals on the federal government's Most Wanted list. The Munsey Gang, as they had come to be known, had scattered like the rats they were. The marshals invited Carleton to help track them down, and he was determined to do so.

Carleton took little notice of the man leaning against the side of the building until the fellow stepped forward and shoved him into the alleyway. Shaken from his ruminations, Carleton stumbled several steps away from his assailant before coming face-to-face with three men, all slapping billy clubs into their hands. It seemed some of the rats hadn't scattered very far.

The thug who had shoved him probably meant to send him sprawling, but Carleton's tall, wiry build was misleading. His balance and stability were strong even for an earth mage.

As the men with billy clubs advanced on him with feral grins, Carleton's training took over. He stretched his left arm forward, exposing a leather bracer around his wrist that was studded with gemstones. Touching one of the stones, he drew the magical essence of swi from within himself and energized it. "Away!" he shouted, invoking the power of the stone.

The eyes of largest man who faced him widened with alarm the moment he spotted the device on Carleton's arm, but he didn't have enough time to close the gap between them. The force of Carleton's spell slammed into him and his companions, throwing them into the air and backward at least ten feet. One of the trio slumped to the ground unconscious while the other two groaned and put their hands to their heads.

The force of his spell had pushed backward as well as forward although not quite as strongly. Carleton turned around as the thug who had pushed him rose from the ground with a growl, his teeth bared in fury. That one was going to be real trouble.

Closing his right hand into a fist, Carleton used his left hand to activate the ring he wore on his third finger. A reddish-orange glow sheathed his right arm from his elbow to his fist. He stalked toward the thug, feigning more confidence than he felt.

The man glanced at Carleton's glowing arm with narrowed eyes but stood his ground. He pulled out a knife from behind his back and dropped into a crouch.

Carleton didn't slow his advance, which startled the knife-wielding thug into slashing haphazardly at him. The blade sparked and clanged off Carleton's glowing arm, which his magic had turned as hard as stone. As the thug hesitated with surprise, Carleton crashed his augmented fist into the side of the man's head. The knife clattered to the ground and the thug went down in a heap.

Carleton turned toward the other attackers just as the big one got to his feet. With a wary glare at Carleton's still-glowing arm, he dropped his billy club and withdrew a pistol from under his jacket. His voice was cold and harsh. "The boss will be disappointed that I didn't bring you to meet him personally, but one way or another, you'll not be troubling the Munseys again, wizard."

Carleton dodged to the side and ran to escape the alley as the shot rang out. As luck would have it, the bullet slammed into Carleton's right forearm where it did no damage, but luck didn't stop the ricochet. An explosion of stars eclipsed his vision, and he fell to the ground, clutching at the searing pain in his head. Lying on his side, his vision swimming dizzily, Carleton's strength faded and his hand fell limply to the ground. Blood coated his palm.

A woman's scream penetrated the fog of his fading consciousness, but he couldn't move or respond. An urgent command and pounding footsteps signaled the departure of the Munsey men. Some moments later—it might have been seconds or hours—a pair of hands carefully turned him over and cold fingers checked for a pulse at his neck. A voice said, "Get a doctor. This man's still alive."

~

Deputy U.S. Marshal Marcus Keenan leaned back against his desk with his arms folded. The badge pinned to the lapel of his dark gray suit had been polished so that it sparkled in the light coming in through the window. An unlit cigar bobbed up and down below his reddish-gray mustache as he gave Carleton the once-over. He took the cigar out of his mouth and spoke. "You look like you could use a few more days of rest."

Carleton rubbed at the bandage on the side of his head self-consciously. According to the doctor, the wound from the bullet that had grazed his skull was healing nicely, and his mop of dark curly hair would eventually cover the scar. The headache from his concussion was mostly gone, although it tended to return with little provocation. Still, as everyone kept telling him, he was lucky to be alive.

"The doctor says I'm fit for duty, sir, and I'm tired of resting."

Keenan chuckled, the lines at the corners of his blue eyes crinkling to reflect his mirth. "So, you're ready to dodge some more bullets?"

"I think the Munsey clan is getting desperate, sir. Attacking me so boldly was risky. We must be closing in on them."

"That's one explanation. It's also possible that the attack was personal. Thanks to you, Ted Munsey is behind bars again."

Carleton straightened his back and shook his head. He didn't deserve all the credit. "But sir, I was only one member of the team that made the capture."

"I appreciate your modesty," Keenan said with a nod. Then he pointed his cigar at Carleton. "But everyone knows it was your skills that made it possible. *Everyone* knows. Including the Munseys."

Carleton wasn't sure what his boss was getting at. "Sir, I knew the risks of this assignment when I accepted it. We can't run and hide every time a crook threatens us."

"No, we can't," the deputy marshal agreed as he stood and walked around behind his desk. To Carleton, the man always moved with speed and purpose, making him seem imposing in a way that could not be attributed to his heavy build and average height. He snatched up a sheet of paper and held it out toward Carleton. "But you're technically a civilian, and sometimes it's best to get out of the line of fire."

Carleton's heart sank as he stepped forward to accept the paper. The official seal of the U.S. Marshal's office was embossed at the top. "Are you canceling my contract, sir?"

Keenan's face softened in sympathy. "I'm sorry, Carleton. You've done a good job for us, but we need to get you out of Baltimore quickly for your own safety."

The timing was rotten. In another month, Carleton would have completed his second year with the marshals and qualified for a Guild promotion from apprentice to journeyman. As a journeyman, he would have been able to work his next contract without supervision, giving him a much wider range of assignments to choose from. As it was, the promotion would have to wait until he completed his next contract. That probably meant another three months to a year, assuming he could start right away. His plans to reach senior journeyman rank before he turned thirty at the start of the twentieth century weren't looking promising. Could he still make it happen within the next five years in spite of the setback?

Keenan interrupted Carleton's despairing thoughts by tapping the edge of the paper with his cigar. "Read it, Carleton."

Carleton's eyes scanned the document that terminated his contract between the Marshals Service and the Wizard Guild of the United States. Keenan had given him a performance rating of Excellent, which would bump his pay on the next apprentice contract he took. But what made his pulse quicken was the line that strongly recommended Carleton's immediate promotion to journeyman.

The Guild wasn't known for bending promotion rules, but for a man of Keenan's stature, they'd at least consider it.

In addition to being a Deputy U.S. Marshal, Keenan was a Senior Journeyman Hydromancer in the Guild. Keenan had mentored Carleton from the day he'd joined the Marshals Service as an inexperienced wizard fresh out of college. He'd helped Carleton become a confident and productive member of the investigative team.

Carleton looked up at his boss. "Thank you, sir. This is very generous." Maybe he wouldn't have to take another apprentice contract after all.

Keenan gave him a lopsided grin. "It gets better. I took the liberty of negotiating with the Guild on your behalf, so they've already approved the promotion. I also found a new assignment that will put some distance between you and the murdering Munseys."

"That's excellent news, sir. Thank you again. May I ask about the assignment?" Carleton was careful to keep his disappointment to himself. The promotion was wonderful, but he'd hoped to have some choice in his next assignment.

Keenan motioned for Carleton to close the door. After Carleton had done so, his superior set his cigar down on an ashtray. Even though the door was closed, he spoke quietly. "I found you a three-month contract in the Arizona Territory. It will be mining work, quite different from what you're used to, but I'm sure you'll rise to the challenge. In the meantime, we'll try to round up the rest of the Munsey gang so you can come back home safely."

Carleton blinked in surprise. The Arizona Territory? That was indeed some distance from Baltimore. About 2,000 miles worth of distance. He wouldn't know anyone out there, although maybe that was the point.

It was all happening too fast. Carleton hated the idea of leaving his home town. Some people might love the opportunity to get a fresh start in the West where land was plentiful and available for the taking. Carleton wasn't one of them. He'd heard nothing appealing about the Western Frontier.

He wasn't reassured by the fact that the assignment was temporary. Life experiences had a way of taking a direction and gaining momentum. If he went to the Arizona Territory, he might never return.

"It's so far away," he finally said, unable to keep the dismay from his voice.

The marshal patted his shoulder. "I know. But if you stay in Baltimore with the Munseys out for your blood, your next journey might be to the cemetery." Keenan let him think about that for a moment before he went on. "Besides, I didn't suggest this contract just because it's far away."

The tone in his voice made Carleton perk up. "You didn't?"

"It caught my eye because the mine is located near a town named Pearce, and I know someone who lives in that area." Keenan picked up his cigar and leaned back against his desk. "My wife's younger brother went west some years ago. He was a deputy marshal for a while, and then he bought himself a small ranch. I'm sure he'd be happy to help you get settled."

"How should I contact him?" Carleton asked.

"I already sent a telegram to let him know you're coming. Your train leaves tomorrow, and your new client is picking up the fare although you'll have to cover expenses along the way. When you arrive in Cochise, go ahead and check into the hotel. Keep a watch for a sandy-haired fellow named Peregrine Maine."

Peregrine Maine. What an unusual name. It would be nice to know *someone* in the area, and if Peregrine Maine was a former marshal, he was probably a decent man.

"You seem to have thought of everything, sir," Carleton said sincerely. "I appreciate how much effort you've put into this."

Keenan waved his hand dismissively. "You're welcome, Carleton, but it wasn't any trouble. It was the least I could do, considering I'm the one who got you into this mess."

Carleton looked down at the contract termination paper and sighed. "It's not your fault, sir. We were all just trying to catch the bad guys."

A deputy knocked on the door and suddenly Deputy Marshal Keenan had a new crisis to deal with. The marshal shook hands with Carleton, ending their meeting. "Let me see who's on roster that can walk you home and keep an eye on your place tonight."

"That's okay, sir," Carleton protested. "The officers who patrol my street have been extra vigilant since the attack, and I promise to stay alert." The marshal's office was chronically short-handed, and Carleton didn't want to waste a valuable resource on babysitting duty.

Marshal Keenan looked like he might insist, but then he pressed his lips together and nodded once. "Then be careful, and good luck."

Carleton left the marshal's office for what he realized might be the last time. Neatly folding the paper that ended his time with the U.S. Marshals Service, he slipped it into his breast pocket as he went down the stairs to the bottom floor. Working for the marshals had been interesting and satisfying, if dangerous at times. As nice as it was that Keenan had set up his next assignment, he couldn't help but feel rushed. Was it really necessary to leave so soon?

～

Carleton left the building and started toward home, the light drizzle tickling his scalp and making him miss his bowler. The bullet that had nearly killed him had torn a ragged swath through his poor hat. He'd have to acquire a new one before leaving Baltimore, although the bandage on his head might make that a painful challenge. Flipping up the collar of his jacket, he huddled into himself and shoved his hands into his pockets.

After his near-death experience, he had convalesced in the small apartment he rented a few blocks from the office. Being outdoors again was a treat, although he couldn't help but feel he had a target painted on his back. His eyes carefully took in every movement of each person on the streets and the sidewalks.

He was only a few buildings away from his home when he spotted a man leaning against a wall several paces ahead, posed exactly like the ruffian who had shoved him into the alley. Carleton came to an abrupt stop as his heart leapt into his throat. He stared at the man, mentally preparing himself for another fight.

A young couple holding hands went around Carleton, looking at him curiously. A moment later, an old man wearing several layers of poorly-fitted clothing limped past. The fellow slowed down and half turned with his hand out as if he might ask for money, but he curled his lip and threw his hand in disgust when Carleton failed to acknowledge his presence.

The man leaning against the wall glanced Carleton's way and froze when he saw Carleton staring intensely at him. Looking more confused and uncomfortable than suspicious, the man threw the remains of his cigarette to the ground, smashed it with his boot, and walked in the opposite direction.

False alarm.

Carleton took a few deep breaths to calm himself and resumed his trek to his apartment.

Maybe getting out of Baltimore for a while wasn't such a bad idea after all. Eventually, the Munseys would figure out that he had survived their attack, and they might try again. Meanwhile, he would be jumping at every shadow.

If only the new contract weren't so far away and in such an inhospitable place. But then, a couple thousand miles or so would probably give him plenty of distance from the Munseys. Who in their right mind would want to follow him into the primitive and barren southwest desert? By the time he completed the contract, the marshals would probably have the whole gang rounded up. He could return home, and his life could get back to normal.

Carleton opened the door to the small foyer of his apartment building. He turned his mind to what he'd need to gather for an extended stay in the Arizona Territory.

~

Carleton dodged the other passengers scurrying around the Baltimore train station and hurried toward the car that would carry him on the first leg of his trip westward. Bells, whistles, and the hiss of pressurized steam overrode the monotonous hum of conversation that floated around the busy train yard.

After handing off his steamer trunk to the porters, he went in search of provisions. The long trips between Baltimore and Cambridge to attend Harvard had taught him that decent meals were not always available along the way. As he left civilization behind and traveled into the sparsely populated wilderness of the West, the food situation would undoubtedly get much worse.

Carleton gritted his teeth as he anticipated the upcoming ride. He had been unable to purchase a first-class ticket, so he would have to share a coach seat with a stranger who would probably fill the time with meaningless chatter. The illustrated booklet he'd found about the curiosities of the West would probably have to wait for a while.

As he neared his coach, the crowd thickened with other passengers sharing farewell hugs with loved ones and gathering their possessions before boarding. Carleton fell in behind a tall man whose gaze shifted among the people, the train car windows, and something he was holding. His size was imposing enough that the other passengers made room for him to pass after a single glance in his direction.

Glancing around the man's shoulder, Carleton came abruptly to a stop and let other passengers flow around him. The paper in the man's hand showed the name and a reasonable likeness of one Carleton Kazimer. The Munseys were looking for him, and all their agent had to do was turn around.

Several courses of action ran through Carleton's head. He could wait until the man moved on and then slip aboard the train, but he'd be trapped if the thug returned and spotted him in the car. For one crazy moment, he considered an ambush, leaving the man unconscious around a corner somewhere. But that would take planning and time he didn't have. Besides, anything he did to interfere with their agent would let the Munseys know they were on the right track, so to speak. His best bet was to get out of town without anyone knowing how he'd left or what direction he'd gone.

Spotting the Munseys' man first gave Carleton the advantage. The most sensible plan was to stay out of sight and board at the last minute.

Carleton clambered up onto a coach platform and crossed to the opposite side of the train, away from the terminal, trading the cover of milling passengers for freedom of movement. Carleton trailed the Munsey man, catching glimpses of him between cars as the fellow progressed through the crowd on the other side. A conductor called "all aboard," but Carleton chose to continue his surreptitious vigil until the last moment.

He was about to move on to the next gap between cars when something cold and hard poked him in the back. "Not so fast, Mr. Kazimer. Drop your luggage and put your hands up."

Carleton's jaw clenched in bitter disappointment. The Munseys had found him after all. Angry with himself for failing to watch his back more carefully and certain his future in the hands of the Munseys would be short, Carleton reacted instinctively and desperately. He whirled, swinging his sack of provisions like a weapon.

The gunman had stepped back, but not far enough. The sack made contact with the assailant's forearm and knocked the pistol from his hand. The gun spun across the ground, hit a crack in the concrete, and flipped under the rail car.

Pressing his advantage, Carleton dropped the sack and used both hands to ram his equipment case into the shorter man's angry weasel face. The man staggered back, but managed to shove the case aside and jab a quick punch at Carleton's head. The glancing blow burned Carleton's cheek but did no real damage.

Recognition dawned as Carleton looked into the flat green eyes of Conlon Munsey, and his throat tightened with fear. Conlon was a Munsey clan enforcer with a reputation for cruelty. Carleton was badly outclassed.

Understanding the extent of his peril, he nearly dropped his case and apologized. But it was too late to beg for mercy. No one was known to survive Conlon's rage, and the look he gave Carleton promised a painful death.

The assassin was too close and too dangerous to try using magic. The train whistle blew, galvanizing Carleton into action. He stepped back and heaved his equipment case at Conlon as hard as he could before running the few steps toward the train coach and diving under it to retrieve the gun.

A firm grip on his ankle turned into a sharp pull as Conlon tried to drag him out from under the car. Carleton reached frantically for the gun, but his fingers fell inches short as Conlon gave another tug.

Carleton tried to kick himself free, but only managed to hasten his slide into the open. He looked up to see a gleaming knife in Conlon's hand and the twisted smile of a killer enjoying his work.

In a smooth, practiced motion, Conlon cocked his arm back and bent toward Carleton to deliver a mortal blow. Carleton raised his hands to block but doubted the attempt would be effective. The Munseys were about to have their revenge.

A shot rang out, startling both Carleton and Conlon. Carleton turned his head toward the origin of the sound to see Marshal Keenan with a deputy at his side. A wisp of smoke curled from the barrel of the deputy's raised service pistol.

Conlon dropped his knife as he stood and turned toward the marshals. He stumbled back a step, a look of confusion crossing his face. His knees buckled, and he collapsed to the ground.

A woman on the train screamed and Carleton turned to see several faces peering down at the scene. The noise and commotion would probably bring the other Munsey man to investigate before long.

The first huff of the engine started the train rolling as Carleton sat up to accept the hand of the deputy marshal. The man helped Carleton to his feet while Keenan checked on Conlon.

"Sorry for the late arrival," his former boss said with a grin. "We got word Conlon Munsey was seen staking out the station, and we came as fast as we could. Thanks for flushing him out."

"Glad I could be of service," Carleton said as he brushed the dirt off his clothes. "The Munseys have another man on the other side of the train."

Marshal Keenan hefted Carleton's equipment case and handed it to him. The deputy had retrieved the provision sack. "Aye, we have two men on him. Let us worry about the Munseys. You have a train to catch."

The train had already accelerated to the speed of a slow walk. If Carleton was going to jump aboard, he'd have to do it soon. He tilted his head toward Conlon. "Do you think I've blown my cover?" Although Carleton was traveling under an assumed name, it wouldn't help much if the Munseys knew his exact departure time and destination.

Keenan looked down at Conlon with a raised eyebrow. "Dead men tell no tales. Conlon Munsey is high on our Most Wanted list, so we had plenty of reason to nab him here. It's a shame he had to go and pull a knife on us," the marshal added with a wink. "Now get going, and that's an order."

Carleton smiled at his former boss. The man no longer had the authority to give him orders, but he appreciated the sentiment. "Thanks for everything, Marshal." He gave the deputy a nod as the man handed him the provision sack. "Nice shot. My thanks to you as well."

Carleton waved and turned to the departing train. He jogged to match its speed, his equipment case tucked under one arm. The train continued accelerating until the cars started to pull ahead. As the rear platform of the last coach came alongside him, he leaped up and grabbed the handrail, gaining a perch on the hanging metal step. Panting from the exertion, Carleton clung to the side of the train while he tried to catch his breath.

A conductor appeared at the rear door and shook his head with a disapproving frown, but he was quick to help Carleton get onto the platform.

While Carleton thanked the conductor, the coach rolled past the thug who had been searching for him. Fortunately, the Munsey man had his back to the train and was distracted by an argument with two deputy marshals.

"Ticket, please," said the conductor with his hand out. Carleton dutifully reached into his vest pocket and gave the man his ticket. The conductor nodded approvingly and handed it back. "Thank you," he said, stepping clear of the doorway. "Your seat is three coaches forward."

Taking the hint, Carleton entered the car and staggered up the aisle toward the other end. It was difficult to maintain his balance while carrying his luggage and food, but he managed not to whack anyone as he made his way toward his coach.

The rhythmic side-to-side motion of the cars was consistent, but not entirely predictable. With every variation in the tracks, the cars would swing from one side to the other until they reached the limit of their suspension. The sway wasn't a problem—it was the bump at the end that tended to knock him off balance.

When he finally reached his coach, Carleton discovered that nearly every bench was occupied. The nearest available seat was next to an elderly woman dressed entirely in black. She was leaning against the window with her eyes closed, using a sweater as a pillow. At least she'd be a quiet travel companion.

An empty space on the luggage rack above the bench settled the matter. Carleton heaved his equipment case up, and it slid into place with a clang. His seat mate didn't stir at the noise, so the apologetic glance he sent her way was wasted.

He sat down, careful not to disturb the sleeping woman. With a smile, he tucked his food sack under his seat. Maybe he'd get a chance to catch up on some reading after all.

CHAPTER 2

Cochise

The train blew a long whistle blast as it slowed at the Cochise station. After his car lurched to a stop, Carleton tugged his new bowler onto his head, a tingle of excitement tightening his chest. After nine days of riding the rails, he was ready for an extended time on solid ground. When he stepped off the train, he would begin the first day of his new life in the West.

He was well rested for a change, having been fortunate enough to get first-class accommodations aboard a sleeper car for the final leg of his trip. Sleeping on the fold-down bed had been a welcome change from the neck-cramping naps he'd suffered on the bench seats of the less expensive coaches. The sleeper cars had an attendant as well as food-and-beverage service, so the extra expense was a fair trade against the cost of a hotel and a poor meal at a track-side grub house. Staying at a hotel also didn't allow him to cover more miles while he slept.

The sleeper was divided into a galley and two passenger seating areas. The parlor room at the rear of the car included large observation windows and four tiny round tables with two chairs each. Carleton had enjoyed more luxurious seating at a built-in berth in the car's Pullman section. His view was more restricted than it would have been in the parlor, but the booth seating was more comfortable.

The young doctor who occupied the seat across from Carleton stood and collected his things. "It was nice talking with you, Carleton. Best of luck on your new job."

"Thank you. At the risk of wishing harm to my new neighbors, good luck with your practice."

The doctor laughed and waved farewell as he headed toward the exit at the back of the car.

Reaching under his seat, Carleton tugged on the handle of his equipment case. It barely fit in the narrow space, and it jammed a couple of times before finally sliding out. He wasn't looking forward to carrying the heavy black leather case around town. His white shirt and navy blue vest were already wet with sweat from the surprisingly warm October afternoon. Draping his cloak over his arm, he lined up behind the other passengers waiting to disembark.

Carleton gripped the handle of the case with both hands before descending from the platform at the rear of the car. He was careful to take one step at a time, placing one foot down and then the other, but even so, he nearly toppled forward when he misjudged the transition from the car's metal step to the short wooden stairs that had been placed below it. After stumbling forward, he rebalanced himself and set the case down with a thump. Taking off his hat and wiping his forehead with a handkerchief, he looked up at the sound of a throaty chuckle.

Two delvans in hooded, light-gray linen smocks looked him over as they approached. Like most of their kind, they were short of stature and stout of build. Carleton could barely see the delvans' eyes through the darkened glass of their leather goggles. The poor men were sweating worse than he was, partly because of the clothing that protected their sensitive albino skin from the unforgiving sun.

The lead delvan stopped and adjusted the duffel bag he carried over his shoulder. "A wizard," he observed. The shorter second man stayed behind his companion. Because of their dark goggles and bushy white beards, Carleton was unable to read their expressions.

The delvan's gaze was on Carleton's cloak. The man had apparently noticed the embroidered badge on the front. Carleton was mildly surprised that a delvan miner way out in the Arizona Territory would so quickly recognize the seal of the Wizard Guild of the United States. The delvan's eyes rose to meet his, and the fellow's mustache parted from his white beard in a lopsided grin that looked distinctly like a sneer.

"We don't see many of yer kind."

Carleton wasn't sure how to respond, so he settled for polite agreement. "I'm sure that's true."

The delvan chuckled as if Carleton had made a joke.

"Ye travel heavy," said the delvan, setting down his duffel bag.

"Hazard of the trade," Carleton replied as he stuffed his handkerchief back into his pocket and replaced his hat.

A pale eyebrow lifted from behind the goggles. "And what trade might that be?"

A moment of doubt flashed across Carleton's mind. The delvan seemed more than casually interested in his affairs. Carleton knew little about the politics and allegiances of the Western Frontier, so it would probably be wise to keep his business to himself until he had a better feel for the place. Still, the delvan had asked a simple enough question and it would be rude not to answer.

Carleton reached into a chest pocket and withdrew a calling card. Handing it to the delvan, he introduced himself. "Carleton Kazimer, Wizard of Geomancy."

The delvan looked at the card and nodded with pursed lips. "Welcome to the Territory, Wizard Kazimer. I be Jasper Underlight, supervisor at the Commonwealth Mine." He pointed his thumb over his shoulder toward the man accompanying him. "This here be Cragg Steel, one of me crew." Tucking the calling card into his frayed hip pocket, he wiped his hand on his smock and held it out.

Carleton accepted the handshake, bracing himself for the bone-crushing grip he was accustomed to receiving from a delvan. The mine supervisor wasn't quite as tall as Carleton's shoulder, but the delvan probably outweighed him by twenty pounds, with little of it fat. Surprisingly, Jasper Underlight closed his thick fingers around Carleton's hand with firm but considerate pressure.

When the delvan's introduction sank in, Carleton said. "Did you say the Commonwealth Mine, Supervisor Underlight?"

"Aye."

"Then we may be seeing quite a bit of each other," Carleton said. "I've been contracted to help out at the Commonwealth."

The supervisor released Carleton's hand. "Is that so? The manager said nothing to me about hiring an earth wizard."

"It's my understanding that the Wizard Guild had some difficulty filling the position. He might not have wanted to get your hopes up in case the Guild couldn't fill the contract."

The delvan chuckled again. "Get me hopes up?" He glanced over his shoulder and grinned toward his companion, who remained stiffly silent. "I suppose that's one way to look at it."

Carleton had the impression that other ways were more likely. Did the delvans see him as some kind of threat? "I'm sure my skills will prove valuable to you, Supervisor Underlight."

Underlight tilted his head back to give Carleton a considering look. "We'll see about that." Hefting his duffel bag back onto his shoulder, he added, "We'd best be going. Good day to ye, Wizard Kazimer."

"Same to you, sir."

The delvans turned and walked away. The second man gave Carleton another unreadable glance over his shoulder as they left. For no reason Carleton could name, the look made him shudder.

Carleton thought back over the conversation, wondering what he might have said to offend them. He didn't want to alienate someone of influence before he'd even started his new job. Perhaps Underlight had worked with a geomancer in the past and it hadn't gone well. Or maybe delvans didn't like "earth wizards" on general principle. Either way, it appeared that his new job might have unexpected challenges.

~

Carleton looked toward the end of the train. The baggage cars were positioned between the passenger cars and the caboose. Men were already unloading the contents, and Carleton spotted his trunk as it was being lowered to the ground.

Picking up his equipment case, he headed toward the men unloading the train.

"Mr. Kazimer? Carleton Kazimer, sir?"

The question came from a piping voice behind him. He stopped and turned around to find a scraggly looking boy in his early teens. "Yes, I'm Carleton Kazimer." Carleton was entitled to the honorific of "Wizard," but after his encounter with the delvans, he decided not to correct the young man. He would probably be better off accepting the title "mister" for a while.

"The engineer is asking for you, sir."

"The engineer of this train? Why would he want to speak to me?"

"There's a problem, sir. He thinks you might be able to help."

Carleton set his equipment case down and draped his cloak over his arm. He rummaged in his trouser pocket and came up with a few coins. He held up a dime and watched the urchin's eyes go wide. "I'll give you this if you'll carry my case to the front of the train for me."

The freckle-faced boy nodded eagerly, making the cowlick in his sandy hair bob up and down.

"It's heavy," Carleton warned. "Are you sure you can handle it?"

The boy bent down and picked up the case with both hands wrapped around the handle. He held it high with his skinny elbows sticking straight out and his face turning red from the effort. The boy put it down with a triumphant grin and held out his hand.

Carleton was concerned that the boy might hurt himself, but a deal was a deal. He handed the kid the coin and walked toward the steaming engine.

He hadn't gone five steps when the boy shot past him at a full run.

"Hey!" Carleton shouted, but the child ignored him and disappeared around the corner of a warehouse building. Shaking his head and cursing his gullibility, Carleton turned around to retrieve his case.

He was about to lift it when a noise made him look up. The boy came back around the corner of the warehouse pushing a hand truck that was as big as he was.

The youngster rolled up to the case and carefully put it onto the nose plate. "Go ahead, sir. I'll be right behind you."

Carleton smiled at the boy's ingenuity. "What's your name?"

"Davey, sir. Davey Arliss."

"I appreciate your help, Davey. I might have a few other tasks for you if you'd be interested in earning a little more money."

"Yes sir! Long as I can get home by supper."

Carleton gave the boy a quick nod. "I'm sure that won't be a problem. Now, let's go see what the engineer wants."

The train engineer, wearing the traditional striped overalls and cap, jumped down from the cab of the engine and pulled off his gloves. The man looked him up and down and then smiled. "I'm Roy Oriol, engineer of this contraption. You must be the wizard."

Carleton looked down at himself, but the badge on his cloak was hidden in folds of cloth. His attire was otherwise perfectly normal. "Is it that obvious?" he asked with concern.

The engineer laughed. "Don't mind me. I just knew I was looking for an Easterner, and no one wears duds like yours out here unless they're trying to impress someone."

During the journey west, Carleton had noticed a change in dress and a general decrease in formality among the locals. If he planned to blend in better, he'd have to find new clothing as soon as possible.

Carleton tipped his bowler. "Carleton Kazimer, Wizard of Geomancy, at your service."

The engineer walked around the front of the train, waving toward Carleton with his gloves. "Come on over here if you would, Wizard Kazimer. I'd like you to take a look at something."

Carleton followed Roy to the other side of the engine. The engineer stopped next to a tall windmill where a man in a dirty jumpsuit waited. A pipe ran from the windmill to a big tank on stilts. From the bottom of the tank, a long adjustable spout extended to the top of the engine's tender. A third man guided the spout over the opening of the tender's water tank.

The engineer pointed toward the tank. "We've enough water to top off, but Jed here says the pump stopped working. He thinks the well might have run dry. Being as you're an earth wizard, I thought maybe you could check it out for us."

Jed nodded but said nothing in response to the engineer's explanation. He was wringing a dirty old rag between his hands and his eyes were wide. As Carleton stepped forward, Jed took a nervous step back.

Carleton suppressed the urge to roll his eyes at Jed's reaction. He'd run into other people who feared magic, and every attempt he'd made to convince them that they had nothing to worry about had failed. If he were to point his finger at Jed and shout a few nonsense words, the man would probably run screaming.

Carleton looked up at the wooden windmill blades. He knew a little about how the new windmill pumps operated, but if something was broken, he probably wouldn't be able to do anything about it. "I can certainly check the water table for you."

A clang announced Davey's success at dragging the hand truck across the tracks in front of the engine. When the wheels landed on the near side of the second rail, the equipment case nearly bounced off the nose plate, but Davey reached forward and grabbed it before it fell. With an apologetic glance toward Carleton, the boy wiped sweat from his forehead and rolled the case over to the wizard. Fortunately, the contents were well-padded against rough handling.

Carleton folded his cloak and draped it over the handle of the hand truck. He kneeled and unlocked the battered case. He opened the lid, revealing a tray filled with small glass bottles snuggled into padded cells that were lined with red velvet. Carleton selected two of the stoppered bottles and set them aside. Lifting up the tray, he reached into the compartment below and extracted his brass casting ring. The ring was about three inches in diameter, an eighth of an inch thick, and a half-inch tall. Davey had moved alongside him and was watching with interest, so Carleton replaced the tray and closed the lid to discourage curious rummaging.

Carrying his items to the base of the windmill, Carleton kneeled and used his hand to sweep the loose dirt away from a spot on the ground. He set the ring in the cleared area and removed the stopper from one of the bottles. Gently tapping, he coaxed a stiff piece of what looked like dark brown string into his palm. Davey and the engineer had followed him to watch, but Jed hung back, still wringing his rag.

"What's that?" Davey asked.

"It's a worm."

"It's all dried up," the boy observed.

"They keep better that way," Carleton explained.

He dropped the worm inside the ring and stoppered the bottle. Opening the second bottle, he carefully rolled out one of the several tiny round objects in the jar.

Davey leaned in close to get a better look at the tiny sphere in Carleton's palm. "Is that an eyeball?"

A sigh followed by a thud turned everyone's head. Jed had passed out in a heap.

Roy shook his head in bemusement. "Don't worry about him. I'll take care of it." The engineer dragged poor Jed by the armpits and propped him up against a water tower leg that was in the shade.

Carleton turned back to Davey. "It's a fish eye," he said, lifting his hand toward the boy's face. Davey leaned back in alarm, and then grinned when he realized Carleton was teasing him.

Carleton put the fish eye into the circle and tucked the bottles into the breast pocket of his vest. He sprinkled some dirt over the worm and fish eye and then looked at Davey. "I have a special job for you. I need you to be quiet for a couple of minutes and make sure no one disturbs me."

Davey gave him a solemn look and nodded. "Yes, sir. Are you gonna do magic?"

"I am. Does that scare you?"

The boy gulped but held his ground. "No, sir. I trust you."

Carleton smiled. "Thanks, Davey. That means a lot to me. Okay, I'm going to close my eyes and talk to myself for a minute. You'll know I'm done when I open my eyes again."

The boy folded his arms and glared toward the people moving near the train station. "Yes, sir. I'll stand guard." He gave the engineer a stern look and the older man held up both hands in mock surrender.

"Good man," Carleton said.

The wizard placed his palm over the metal ring and closed his eyes. Clearing his mind, he concentrated on the ring. He spoke the incantation for the earth-vision spell flawlessly, having cast it many times before.

As he uttered the incantation's final words, Carleton pressed the brass ring into the ground. A solid thud sounded from beneath his hand as if he had struck the ground with a sledgehammer. Davey gasped and the engineer's boots shuffled back a step.

Letting his awareness flow into the ground, Carleton followed the textures of the earth beneath him. His mind's eye slipped around solid rocks and filtered through gravel. A few feet down, he encountered an odd soil structure that seemed to spread in every direction. Curious, he tested its consistency and found it to be some sort of hard clay. Pushing through, he emerged on the other side after descending through about a foot of the unusual material.

Carleton adjusted his underground course until he found the outside of the well casing. He followed the casing down into the earth until he began to wonder just how deep the well went. Stopping his progression for a moment, he evaluated his position relative to his body on the surface and estimated that he had descended at least two-hundred feet.

He continued another hundred feet or so before he finally reached the aquifer that fed the well. His spell would not allow him to push his awareness into the water, but the fish eye allowed him to sense a fair amount of detail if he concentrated on a small area.

The well casing continued into the water chamber for several feet before ending in a conical screen that kept debris from the aquifer out of the pump. The screen was torn. Inspecting the path of the casing, Carleton could see where it had pushed past an outcropping. A sharp projection of rock had broken free, but not before it had torn the screen.

Carleton couldn't use the water for a closer look, but he could follow the metal well casing and investigate further. As soon as he peered inside the casing through the hole in the screen, the problem was obvious. The bottom valve of the well pump had sucked in a small rock, which had jammed the valve in the open position.

There was nothing more he could do, and he was growing tired from the effort of maintaining such a long distance casting, so Carleton withdrew his awareness as swiftly as possible. He swayed when he returned to his body and would have tipped over if he hadn't been bracing himself against the ground with his hand over the ring.

"I believe I found the source of your problem," he announced. He explained about the torn screen and the valve blockage. "It looks like whatever damaged the screen was knocked clear, so if you replace it and remove the blockage, you shouldn't have the problem again. You might be able to get the pump working temporarily if you disconnect the plunger from the windmill and give it a hard upward pull. The rock that's holding the bottom valve open could come free, but it will continue to rattle around down there."

The engineer grinned and shook Carleton's hand. "Thank you, Wizard Kazimer. From what Jed told me, fixing the pump won't be easy, but it sure beats drilling a whole new well."

"Glad I could help," Carleton replied.

The engineer went over to check on Jed, who was starting to come around. Carleton turned his attention back to Davey while the engineer relayed what they'd learned.

Davey was using the tip of a finger to stir the dirt where Carleton had cast his spell. The boy looked up with a puzzled expression. "Where'd they go?"

Carleton presumed he was referring to the worm and the eyeball. "The magic consumes them in a process called transmutation. They go back to the earth."

The boy stood and brushed off his hands. "Wow. Wait until my pa hears about this! A real wizard right here in Cochise."

So much for lying low. He couldn't swear the boy to secrecy because that would make him seem even more mysterious and gossip-worthy. All he could do is try not to attract too much more attention.

"Come on, Davey. Let's get my luggage over to the hotel."

CHAPTER 3

Hotel Rath

As he had anticipated, it was nice to walk around on solid ground with no immediate plans to re-board the train. Carleton had taken advantage of hotels when possible, but he spent most of the trip either in his seat or snoozing in the bunk of a sleeper car, swaying to the rhythm of the train's rocking.

The Hotel Rath was right across the road from the train station. After Carleton checked in with Lucy Rath, the front desk clerk, her husband Don helped him carry his steamer trunk over from the freight car. Back in the lobby, Carleton settled up with Davey.

The boy closed his hand over the coin Carleton had placed in his palm. "Thanks, Wizard Kazimer. Let me know if you want help with anything else. I work with my pa at the warehouse when I'm not in school."

Lucy gave Carleton a quick glance when Davey used the word "wizard," and Carleton thought maybe he liked it better when the boy had called him *mister*. He leaned forward and held out his hand. "I'll tell you what. Now that we're friends, you can call me Carleton. How does that sound?"

The boy grinned and shook the offered hand. "Yes, sir, Wizard Carleton!"

"Just Carleton will do, Davey. I don't want people making a fuss about me being a wizard."

The boy looked puzzled, but gave Carleton a serious nod. "Okay. If that's what you want. I can keep a secret."

"You're a good man. Thanks again for your help."

"'Bye, Carleton," the boy said with a wave as he charged out the door. Running across the street toward the warehouse, he skidded to a stop when he remembered the hand truck sitting on the front porch of the hotel. He sprinted back, grabbed it, and ran off again with it bouncing and rattling along behind him.

"Looks like you have an admirer," Lucy observed with a pleasant smile.

"He was very helpful," Carleton replied. Changing the subject, he asked, "Can you recommend a place where I can get something to eat?"

"We serve supper here at the hotel at dusk if that interests you. If you prefer not to wait, the general store across the way sells fruit, cheese, and bread."

"Thanks. Your supper here sounds fine. I think I'll settle into my room and then take a look around."

Carleton's simple room had a bed and a small table with a washbasin. Don had managed to drag in the trunk and place it at the foot of the bed. The mattress seemed comfortable enough and the linens looked clean. He looked forward to getting a good night's rest. Pulling the curtain back from the window, he looked out upon a gated side yard enclosed by a picket fence. The space was cozy and would do nicely for the one night he would be there.

After tucking his equipment case under the bed, Carleton took advantage of the washbasin to freshen up. It amazed him how quickly things dried in the West. He wet his hair while washing his face, but it had dried by the time he walked out the front door of the hotel to go for a walk.

The sun was only an hour or so above the horizon, but the temperature was still quite warm for October. However, it wasn't anything like the cloying heat he was used to experiencing during Maryland summers.

The local architecture, such as it was, reflected the different materials, population density, and weather conditions in the West. Unlike at home, the residents weren't crammed together in row houses. No stately brick or stone buildings loomed over the streets, and the roof lines weren't adorned with dormers or finials.

Instead, the buildings in Cochise ranged from simple wooden shacks to adobe-walled structures that looked like they'd grown right up from the ground. A squared-off facade fronted most of the businesses, and deep overhanging porches shaded both the shop windows and the patrons.

Carleton's walk around town didn't take long. He reached one end of the dusty main road and stopped to absorb the scenery. It was all so alien, compared to the abundant water and lush trees of home. Surrounded mostly by low desert scrub, he could see for miles.

During his journey west, Carleton had learned that the wide vistas distorted his perception of distance. Mountain ranges that looked small and insignificant from far away grew to towering, miles-long obstacles with craggy peaks as the train drew closer. Mountains lay in every direction around the tiny town of Cochise although most were miles off. He recognized the telltale color gradation that tinted the slopes. It went from desert beige or reddish-brown at the base to dark green at the top, indicating the presence of juniper and pine forests at the higher elevations.

Earlier in Carleton's trip, the wide open spaces had made him uncomfortable. The first time he'd exited the train to stand in the desert under the endless blue sky, it had seemed like nothing was holding him to the earth. He'd envisioned himself lifting off the surface and tumbling into the void. His pulse racing, he'd fled back to the safety of the enclosed rail car with relief. But the panoramic view had begun to grow on him.

Carleton turned to walk back toward the hotel when a sparkle caught his eye. He kneeled and plucked a plum-sized chunk of white quartz from a dry creek bed next to the road. Rubbing off the dirt that covered part of it, he turned it over in his hand. The specimen seemed reasonably pure.

The wizard closed his eyes and spoke an incantation. He fed swi into the stone and mentally observed how the flow of energy scattered through the milky crystal. After a moment, images started to flash against the back of his eyelids as his magic triggered the crystal's innate powers of divination.

It was like stepping into a room filled with mirrors. No matter which direction he turned his attention, the images were all of Carleton looking back at himself. He waited patiently for a moment and was rewarded when several of the mirrors shimmered and showed something different.

In one of them, a delvan appeared. It might have been Jasper Underlight, but the image wasn't clear enough for him to be sure.

Another showed birds flying in the distance. While he watched, the creatures flew closer until he could discern that they were enormous, and that each creature was being directed by a rider. The lead rider pointed a long spear in his direction and the group descended toward him. The image shimmered again and went back to a reflection of himself.

Carleton cut the flow of swi to the stone and the images quickly faded. He opened his eyes and smiled in satisfaction. The quartz had performed remarkably well. He pocketed the stone so he could add it to his collection.

While walking back to the hotel, Carleton considered the visions the stone had given him. He didn't have much faith in the practice of divination, particularly when *he* was the practitioner. A few friends in college had been genuinely talented at foreseeing events, but Carleton's visions were invariably tied to whatever was weighing on his mind at the time. His images came from the past as often as from the future, and the connections between them were rarely clear.

The encounter with Jasper Underlight and his companion had probably inspired the delvan image, although he was sure he would meet more delvans in the days to come. The Arizona Territory was mining country, and where there were mines, delvans were sure to be found.

The flying creatures in his vision had to be the wyverns he'd read about before coming out West. The wyvern riders were avens, the tiny natives of the area's local mountains, who supposedly flew the beasts on occasional raids. How would the images from his vision compare to reality? Given how dangerous the wyverns were reputed to be, it was probably best if he never had the chance to find out.

As Carleton passed the warehouse next to the train station, Davey waved to him through the open freight door. Carleton smiled and returned the greeting.

Entering the hotel through a door that opened into the main hall, Carleton inhaled the aroma of cooking food. His stomach growled in anticipation of a good, hot meal. Even though it was still a bit early, he went directly to the dining area so he could get a good seat.

~

Carleton entered the dining room and chose a secluded table in the corner even though less private seats with a better view of the garden area were available. The surly delvans and the fainting workman had spoiled his interest in casual conversation. It wasn't unusual to encounter people who feared magic or were otherwise biased against wizards, but that didn't make the experiences any less bothersome.

As a concession to the warmth of the room, he rolled up the sleeves of his shirt, revealing his gemstone-studded leather wristband. Mindful of his desire to keep a low profile, he unbuckled the strap and tucked it into his inside vest pocket.

Other diners wandered in over the next fifteen minutes until every table in the room was occupied. Carleton estimated that the room could accommodate more patrons than the hotel's rooms could hold, so he guessed the kitchen served customers from the entire community.

A few folks did a double take upon entering the room, noticing Carleton's attire. Others spotted the new bowler on the hat rack and searched the room until their gaze landed on him. Most of the people were dressed in well-worn work clothes that had missed out on the benefit of a wash tub for some time. Carleton's clothing was hardly fresh after his long trip, but he'd never felt more conspicuous.

Lucy came in and announced the evening meal, giving the diners a choice between two dishes. She took a tally of everyone's selections and nearly bumped into a late arrival on her way out. She waved away the man's apology and took his order before going on her way.

The newcomer stepped into the room and looked around. He was average in height—a bit shorter than Carleton's six feet. His shoulder-length, sandy brown hair framed a pleasant face with a closely trimmed beard and mustache. He was dressed like many of the other people in the room, wearing loose-fitting pants and a lightweight, waist-length jacket over a shirt. Noticing the empty holsters at his hips, Carleton remembered seeing a sign in the lobby requesting that visitors check their weapons at the front desk.

The man spotted the empty seat opposite Carleton and threaded his way among the tables, passing up a couple of arguably better options along the way. He nodded once as his green eyes met Carleton's brown ones. "Mind if I join you?"

So much for having a private meal. Carleton masked his annoyance at the intrusion and gestured toward the chair. "Not at all."

As he sat down, the man pushed his hat off his head and let it hang down his back by the chin strap. Holding out his hand, he introduced himself. "I'm Peregrine Maine, but everyone calls me Perry."

Annoyance forgotten, Carleton grinned and eagerly returned the handshake. Perry had found him as easily as Marshal Keenan promised he would. "Pleasure to meet you. I'm Carleton Kazimer, but you probably knew that already."

Perry nodded in acknowledgment. "I figured." He casually scanned the room. "Most of these folks are regulars." The other diners were busy with conversations at their own tables, but one hard-looking character seemed to have a steady interest in watching Perry while his table partner stole glances their way over his shoulder.

Perry rested an arm on the table and sat back in his chair. "Is this your first visit to Cochise, Mr. Kazimer?"

"Please, call me Carleton. And yes, this is my first time in Arizona."

"What brings you to the Territory?"

Even though the occupants at the nearby tables *seemed* to be minding their own business, their conversations quieted noticeably following Perry's question. Carleton darted his eyes around the room. No one was looking their way except the two surly men who were too far away to hear their conversation. Still, he had the impression that everyone was waiting for his answer.

Carleton glanced at Perry, and a sly smile ticked at the corner of the other man's mouth. Carleton took the hint to remain circumspect. "I've taken work at the Commonwealth Mine."

The normal buzz of conversation resumed almost immediately. That answer was apparently common enough to deflect the interest of the other folks nearby. To distract them further, Lucy and a young female helper came in right then to deliver the first meals. As attentions turned elsewhere, a tenuous sense of privacy descended around Carleton's corner table.

Perry had sat up eagerly when the servers came in. He used the movement to place his arms on the table and lean toward Carleton. In a low voice, he said, "Everyone will know about your *work* soon enough, but it would be best for you to get to the mine safely first."

Carleton blinked and sat up straight. "Is there cause for alarm?"

Perry frowned and glanced toward the two men who had been watching them. "This is a wild land. There's always cause for alarm. Settlers with your talents are rare, and folks develop strange notions about things they don't understand."

Carleton shook his head in bewilderment. "Why do you stay?"

Perry's eyes took on a distant look. "This is a special place, and it won't always be wild. Civilization and law are slowly getting here. I intend to help usher them in."

Carleton nodded in understanding. Perry's words appealed to the sense of justice he'd developed while working with the marshals, and he grabbed onto the familiar attitude like a lifeline. "Perhaps I can be of assistance."

Perry smiled and leaned back as Lucy and her helper set plates before them. "I sure hope so." Still speaking to Carleton, he looked up and gave Lucy a wink. "In the meantime, eat up. You're about to taste the best vittles for miles around."

Lucy gave Perry a playful back-handed slap on his shoulder as she headed back to the kitchen. Carleton was left with the impression that these were the *only* "vittles" to be had for miles around.

Carleton picked up his spoon and dug into the stew that he'd ordered. After the food he'd had to endure during his journey west, the simple heartiness of the stew was satisfying in spite of its bland flavor. Flicking his eyes up to the far corner of the room, he caught their watcher staring at him before the man quickly looked down at his plate.

Perry had said that the West was a wild land. Carleton understood that the dangerous wildlife and the surrounding wilderness weren't all he was talking about. The locals, largely left to govern themselves on the frontier, could choose to help build a productive society or they could choose to prey on the builders. It seemed the West had more than its fair share of the latter. Fortunately, after Carleton's time with the marshals, he was used to dealing with predators.

CHAPTER 4

Diamondback Morning

Carleton woke from a dreamless sleep. Faint light glowing through the curtained window told him it was nearly sunrise. He had made it to Arizona and was about to begin his new assignment. But something was off.

The rough cotton sheets and dry, dusty odor of his room were unfamiliar, but they weren't the source of his unease.

He rubbed sleep from his eyes and yawned, stretching his whole body. An unexpected weight shifted between his knees and an odd rasping noise filled the room.

Carleton quickly levered himself up, sliding his legs away from the weight. "Hey!" he exclaimed in alarm.

The unnerving sound increased sharply, and he froze. The dim light of dawn illuminated a sinuous form between his ankles. Less than three feet away from Carleton's face, the snake flicked out its forked black tongue. Its shivering tail rose straight up from thick coils and seemed to be the source of the strange noise. The sharp-angled dark pattern along its back shifted dizzily as the snake coiled itself tighter. With a gasp, Carleton recognized that the sound would be more accurately described as *rattling*, not rasping.

His hands were at his sides, pressing into the mattress. Could he move fast enough to throw the sheet over the snake? He experimentally moved his hands forward to grip the edge of the fabric. The creature lifted its head into a poised arc while the rattling sound rose in intensity again. Carleton froze and gulped with relief when the snake's rattle slowed.

The rattler's tongue darted out while Carleton considered his options. If he moved his legs to slip out of the bed, it would probably strike. Could he lift the edge of the sheet fast enough to protect himself and envelop the creature? How quickly could a snake react?

The reptile's fixed slit-eyed glare and continuous rattle were wearing on Carleton's nerves. Convinced it would strike no matter what he did, he snapped into motion and lifted the sheet as high as he could, hoping the snake wouldn't target his hands.

The sheet punched toward his face as the creature hit the other side. In a frenzy of revulsion, Carleton threw the sheet over the snake while folding his legs back and under him. Scooping his hands under the nearest fat bulge of fabric, he heaved the bundle off the end of the bed. It bounced off his trunk and slipped to the floor.

Out of immediate danger, Carleton's rationality returned to warn him that he'd missed an important detail. He should have flopped the sides of the sheet over the center to trap the snake inside. It was only a matter of time before the thrashing snake would slip out one of the open ends.

Carleton scrambled off the bed and moved toward the end. The snake still writhed inside the sheet. Maybe he should tuck the loose ends underneath. Could the snake bite him through the fabric? Where was the business end of that thing?

His next step forward connected with the leg of the bed frame. The shock and pain unbalanced him, and he toppled to the floor, reflexively clutching his abused toes. The stream of curses that followed his scream of agony was cut short when the sheet wriggled aggressively near his head. He had fallen onto one end of the sheet.

He let go of his foot and put his hand down to raise himself up. A thick mass writhed under his palm and he jerked back, his chest and chin hitting the floor.

With an aching jaw and stars swimming in his vision, Carleton turned his head toward the other end of the sheet. The snake's wedge-shaped head had emerged. He watched in helpless dismay as the creature exited its temporary prison, a tunnel of fabric collapsing behind the slithering form.

Crap.

The snake turned and headed toward the door, which brought it closer to Carleton as well. By the time Carleton had gathered his arms under his chest and started lifting himself up, the diamondback had spotted him and instantly swirled back into a defensive coil. Rattle held high, it was once again about three feet from his face.

"Carleton?" called a muffled voice at the door. "You okay in there?"

"Been better," Carleton responded in a low voice. The snake weaved its head as he spoke, as if in agreement.

The door opened slowly and Peregrine Maine peered into the room. Carleton specifically remembered locking that door the prior evening after the attention he'd received from the unsavory characters in the dining room. Maybe the snake hadn't come into his room on its own.

"Don't move," Perry whispered. The snake swiveled its head and shifted position in response to the new threat.

Not planning on it. Carleton didn't say the words out loud for fear of aggravating the snake.

"That's a big one," Perry commented in a soft voice. The barrel of a gun slowly edged past the door. "This is gonna be loud," he warned.

Carleton would have covered his ears if not for the severely agitated poisonous reptile. As it was, all he could do was cringe in anticipation.

As Perry aimed, the snake arched its body in preparation to strike. Could the snake reach him if Perry missed? The blast of the gun made Carleton jump and put his hands over his ears in reflex. Something thumped to the floor, and he scrabbled backward on hands and knees until he bumped into the wall.

Carleton stared toward the doorway as the black gunpowder smoke cleared. Perry hadn't missed. The body of the snake writhed, leaving a messy trail of ichor across the sheet. The head had simply disappeared in a spray of flesh and blood that stained the wall and floor.

"You okay?" Perry asked as shouts and footsteps thundered in the hallway.

Carleton nodded and got to his feet so he could straighten his nightshirt. A second later, the door to his room swung open and Don Rath stepped into the room, a shotgun held ready.

He took in Carleton's undressed state and the twitching snake on the floor. "What happened here?" he demanded. He covered Perry with the shotgun, and Perry raised his empty hands in surrender, having already holstered his gun.

At Perry's subtle nod to go ahead, Carleton pointed at the rattlesnake corpse. "That snake was on my bed when I woke up this morning. Mr. Maine heard the commotion and came to investigate. He shot it before it could strike."

Rath lowered his shotgun and inspected the snake. He glanced over at Perry's holstered six-guns. "You shot it with a pistol?"

Perry lowered his hands and nodded. "These are all I had handy."

Rath shook his head. "That's some fine shooting."

Perry shrugged. "It was pretty close range. Still, I wish I'd had my coach gun."

Rath kneeled next to the bed and inspected the bullet hole in the floor.

"I'll pay for the damage, Mr. Rath," Carleton offered.

Rath shrugged. "Seen worse. Along with your story, it'll give the room extra character." He frowned at the blood sprayed around the room. "It'll take some work to clean up this mess, though."

The hotelier looked at the remains of the rattler. Pinching off the headless end that still dripped blood, he stood and held the body aloft. The snake stretched from the floor to just above Rath's head. He grinned at Carleton. "Six-footer. Tell you what. You let me have this, and we'll call it even."

Carleton lifted his hands in a gifting gesture. "By all means. It's yours."

Rath walked toward the door with the snake in hand. "Lucy will be thrilled. We'll be serving rattlesnake chili for dinner tonight!" At the doorway, he ran into others who had gathered. The snake corpse resulted in a variety of exclamations from appreciation to revulsion. Perry closed the door as Rath started to inform the other guests.

The look in Perry's eyes as he turned to Carleton was speculative. "What are you thinking?" Carleton asked.

Perry stared at the bloody sheet. "I'm thinking that snake didn't get in here by itself." He looked down at the bottom of the door. "Not much of a gap there. I don't think it could have slithered under."

Carleton nodded. "I had the same thought. I'm sure I locked that door last night. But why would someone do this?" He was pretty sure that if the Munseys found him, they wouldn't bother trying to make his demise look like an accident.

Perry stepped closer to Carleton and lowered his voice. "Until you figure that out, I suggest we get you out of here and on the road to the Commonwealth. Sorry, but you'll have to miss out on Lucy's rattlesnake chili."

Carleton shuddered. "I think I can make that sacrifice."

~

Carleton gathered his things and prepared to leave before Rath could change his mind about the mess in the room. The metallic stench of burnt gunpowder hung in the air and the meaty odors of the snake's fluids made it even less appetizing. Perry left to get his wagon and team from the livery while Carleton packed.

By the time Carleton had checked out and moved his luggage to the front porch of the hotel, Perry was pulling up with his buckboard. Behind Perry's perch on the high driver's seat, the wagon's cargo bed was filled to the top of the side boards and covered with a brown canvas tarp.

Perry's rig was unremarkable except for one detail: the draft team. Carleton could hardly believe his eyes, and he noticed that he wasn't the only person in town who was staring. Perry grinned hugely and gestured toward the animals. "Pig power!" he exclaimed.

The term seemed apt, for the wagon was being pulled by a team of four large creatures that looked a lot like pigs, except that they were much leaner and covered with light-gray wiry hair. Dark-gray leopard-like spots dotted their torsos, standing out sharpest along their backs and fading toward their bellies. The largest animal, presumably a boar, stood nearly three feet at the shoulder with an inch of sharp tusk poking out from under its upper lip. The boar eyed Carleton and grunted.

The three other beasts were smaller, but not by much. The smallest of them was positioned behind the boar and had the look of a juvenile. It fidgeted in its harness, looking distressed and ready to run off. Perry jiggled the traces leading to the agitated creature and made soothing noises at it.

Carleton was at a loss for words. "That's … remarkable," he stammered.

Perry set the brake and tied the leads to the footboard of the wagon before jumping down. He went around to the back of the wagon and untied the tarp, gesturing toward Carleton's trunk as he lowered the rear gate. "That all your luggage?"

Carleton tore his gaze away from the unusual draft team. "Yes, just the trunk and this," he answered, pointing down at his equipment case. The surprisingly chilly morning air prompted him to reluctantly tie on his Guild cloak over his suit jacket. After the reception he'd received from the delvan miners the prior day, he had hoped to avoid wearing the cloak and its prominent emblem.

Perry and Carleton loaded the trunk into the back of the wagon along with the equipment case. Perry tied the tarp down over the load again. He was pulling the final knot tight when they were interrupted by a deep voice.

"Hey, there. You the wizard?"

Perry and Carleton turned in unison. Carleton looked up into the eyes of a big man who had dark, unfriendly eyes and thick shoulders filling out his shirt. He was one of the men who had been staring at them during dinner the prior evening.

The big man's wiry partner stepped up onto the hotel porch, flanking them from a higher vantage point. He leaned against a post and slipped his thumb under his belt, his hand a short distance from the gun tucked into his waistband. Perry's hands drifted toward his pistols.

Carleton tried to ignore the sudden tension in the air. "What can I do for you?" he asked the big man.

"I'm Willie and this is Jacob. We're supposed to escort you to the mine. There's a seat reserved for you on the stage." He tipped his thumb toward the warehouse across the street where a few passengers were loading into the stagecoach. Jasper Underlight, the delvan mine supervisor, was climbing in while the driver shifted luggage around in the rack on top.

"That's a kind offer, but Mr. Maine here has generously offered to give me a ride, and we've already loaded up my luggage."

Jacob was chewing tobacco and chose that moment to spit toward Perry's team. The stream landed next to the smallest animal, which squealed and danced in its harness. Perry directed a dark look at the man, who returned an ugly tobacco-stained smile.

Willie leaned to the side, looking pointedly around Perry toward the front of the wagon. He made a disapproving face. "The stage will get you there in half the time, and you'll have shade. We can take care of your luggage for you."

Carleton's initial impression of the man was not improving with conversation, but he tried to keep his voice light and conversational. "I do appreciate your consideration, Willie, but I'm looking forward to continuing my conversation with Mr. Maine, and a little extra travel time doesn't bother me."

The big man shared a glance with his partner. "We're supposed to make sure you get to the mine safely. I suppose we'll have to follow along with you and Mr. Maine."

"That really won't be necessary ..." Carleton started to say, but Perry interrupted him.

"That wouldn't be a good idea. I need to go by my place on the way to the mine, and I'm taking High Lonesome Road to shorten the trip."

Willie frowned and shook his head. "High Lonesome goes through little demon territory. It wouldn't be right to put Wizard Kazimer in danger like that."

Perry reached up and patted the tarped load. "The avens know me, and they know my rig. I have permission to pass through, but I don't know what they'll do if they see strangers riding alongside."

Given the incident in his room that morning, Carleton might have been happy for the extra protection unless it was Willie or Jacob who put the snake in his room. But nothing in his communications with Bart McLaury, his new employer, had said anything about an escort. The most recent telegram said he should have no trouble getting transportation from Cochise to Pearce. It was possible that Willie and Jacob were looking for another opportunity to attack him.

Watching Willie carefully, Carleton asked, "How much do you know about rattlesnake wrangling?"

The big man's brow wrinkled in confusion at the change of subject. "I don't wrangle 'em, I shoot 'em. Why?"

Carleton glanced at Jacob, but the man's face gave away little. He folded his arms across his chest and kept chewing. Carleton didn't detect anything that would indicate guilt. If anything, he seemed bored.

"I found a rattlesnake in my bed this morning. Mr. Maine was kind enough to shoot it for me."

Willie's eyes narrowed on Carleton and his voice dropped to a low growl. "Are you suggesting I had something to do with it? If I wanted you dead, Wizard Kazimer, I wouldn't use no rattlesnake. How do you know Mr. Maine didn't plant the snake and then kill it to gain your trust?"

That thought had briefly crossed Carleton's mind after the excitement of the snake encounter had passed and Perry left him alone to pack. Carleton was inclined to take Perry at face value because he had learned to trust his instincts about people. He trusted Perry a lot more than he trusted Willie or Jacob even if Perry had not been a former marshal and the brother-in-law of his former boss.

Carleton glanced at Perry, who seemed to be amused by Willie's question. Perry raised an eyebrow, inviting Carleton to answer.

"Mr. Maine has been nothing but friendly and helpful. I have no reason *not* to trust him. If he wanted something from me, it wouldn't make sense for him to put my life at risk."

Willie seemed to be losing patience with the conversation. He shook his head and huffed. "Whatever you say, Wizard Kazimer. The rattlesnake only proves that you could use our help."

Perry nodded. "Actually, I think you're right. How about we do it this way. You escort us to High Lonesome Road and then go around to meet up with us again at my place. No one would dare follow us onto aveni land, so we'll be safe until we get through to my ranch on the other side. By the time you catch up, I should be ready to head out again. From the ranch, we'll all ride down to the mine together. Your boss will see you ride in with us as if we'd been together all along."

Willie glared at Carleton, looking ready to argue again, but then he took a deep breath and glanced at Jacob.

Jacob shrugged in indifference and said, "If he won't cooperate, there ain't much we can do about it. The boss said to escort him, not to abduct him."

"Fine. We'll do it your way," Willie said. He turned on his heel and walked away. Jacob tipped his hat mockingly at

Carleton and Perry before stepping down off the porch and following his partner.

Perry climbed up into the bench seat of the wagon and waved Carleton to get up on the other side. As Carleton climbed aboard, Perry reached behind the seat and took a short-barreled shotgun out from under the tarp. He handed the weapon to Carleton. "You're the official shotgun messenger for this ride."

Perry gave him a sidelong glance as Carleton reluctantly accepted the gun. "You know how to use a coach gun?"

Carleton broke the gun open and verified that shells were loaded into the barrels. He snapped it shut. "I'm competent with firearms, but prefer not to use them." Carleton slipped the shotgun into a leather scabbard attached to the outside of the seat.

Perry chuckled and flipped the reins to get his team moving. "Must be nice to have alternatives." The boar grunted several times and started pulling, which seemed to encourage the sows and the nervous youngster to do the same.

Once the pigs were moving, Carleton understood what Willie had meant about the trip taking longer. The animals eventually settled into a trotting gait, but their short legs moved the wagon forward at about half the speed of a fast-walking horse.

"What kind of pigs are they?" Carleton asked. "I've never seen their like."

"They aren't truly pigs; they're peccaries. The avens domesticated them ages ago for pulling carts, although a few wild bands still roam this region."

"Are these the javelina I read about? They're much bigger than I expected."

"No, javelina are collared peccaries. These here are spotted peccaries. They're bigger, smarter, stronger, and don't smell as bad. Certain predators think they're tastier too, so outside the domestic herds, you won't find many around."

Carleton couldn't help noticing that the townspeople were staring at the unconventional team. "I get the impression that peccary-drawn conveyance isn't common here?"

Perry shook his head once and grinned. "Not yet! But I aim to change that. This team is hopefully the first of many. I've been raising and training peccaries ever since the avens gave me a starter herd last year and showed me how to work them. They may not be fast, but they're strong and easy to feed."

Willie and Jacob had caught up to them by then. Willie had overheard Perry's claim and scoffed loudly. "You don't really believe people are going to trade in their horses for bunch of slow pigs, do you?"

Perry cast a dark look toward Willie, but shrugged in concession to the man's doubts. "Maybe not. But they might work out well for other things. Your boss has agreed to try a couple of them for mine work. Their size will be an advantage for hauling carts out of the mine."

"Haulin' carts is what delvans are for," Willie said.

Perry's lips pressed into a thin line. "Your boss disagrees. He wants the delvans doing what they do best … digging ore."

Willie looked like he was going to argue some more, but Jacob spat and interrupted. "Aw, leave him alone, Willie. You won't change his mind. Besides, if all else fails, he can hold a big pig roast."

Perry's face went red while Willie and Jacob chuckled, but he didn't say anything in response.

They mostly rode in silence for the next several miles. Carleton didn't want to carry on a conversation with Perry while the other two men were listening, and the escorts seemed content to watch the road ahead. When they ran across a rise or turn in the road that might conceal an ambush, Jacob would ride ahead to check things out, but Willie always stayed back with the wagon.

As the sun rose in the sky, the landscape heated quickly. Carleton removed his cloak and tucked it under the seat, where he discovered a box of shotgun shells. He grabbed a handful of shells and tucked them into his vest pocket.

Perry took notice of his precaution. "I have a bandolier if you want."

Carleton looked down at his pinstriped trousers and matching vest over a white buttoned shirt. He also had on his bowler, but at least he wasn't wearing his bow tie. Either way, a bandolier draped across his chest would look utterly ridiculous. "I think I'll pass on that," he said. Perry laughed and patted him on the back.

By the time they reached High Lonesome Road, everyone was ready to part ways. Willie and Jacob were losing patience with the slow progress of the wagon, and Carleton was sick of hearing their muttered insults about it.

Perry stopped the wagon at the turn. "Well, this is it. We'll meet you at my place in a couple of hours."

Willie looked down High Lonesome with a considering expression. Carleton hoped he wasn't going to insist on accompanying them after all. Finally, he said, "Don't keep us waiting. I want to reach the mine before sundown."

Perry looked up toward the sun, which hadn't quite reached mid-sky. "That shouldn't be a problem."

Jacob had already started riding away when Willie turned his horse to join him. No one bothered waving or saying goodbye.

Perry twitched the reins to get the peccaries moving again. Once they were well out of earshot, he mumbled, "Glad to be quit o' *them*."

Chapter 5

Aveni Hunting Party

High Lonesome Road took the wagon up out of the valley and meandered toward the base of the mountains. The vegetation changed from yucca, low shrubs, and thin grassland to ocotillo with tall, leafy stems and an occasional viciously thorned mesquite tree. Perry was happy to share the names of the plants he knew about, and he warned Carleton that almost all of them were armed with some kind of spine, thorn, or sticker. Sturdy clothes and tall boots were a necessity for moving around the desert countryside.

Carleton had come to Arizona expecting a bland desert of dunes and a few tufts of grass, but the vista surrounding him was nothing like that. The flora and fauna were different from what he was accustomed to, but plenty of both were in evidence. He was shocked to learn that the elevation of Cochise was over 4,200 feet, higher than the tallest peak he knew of in his home state of Maryland. The high desert had turned out to be a diverse and vibrant habitat.

A coyote appeared on the road ahead, stopping to stare at the oncoming wagon. It sniffed at the air once before slinking off into the brush. The lead boar barked once and clacked his teeth a few times, but the team didn't slow down.

"Are coyotes a problem for your peccary herd?" Carleton asked.

"Not really," Perry answered. "A coyote is no match for an adult, and the adults do a good job of protecting the young." He nodded toward the team. "Peccaries don't see too good, so the boar probably reacted to the coyote's movement and size without knowing exactly what it was."

Half a mile later, a huge hare leaped away from the road, its long ears appearing and disappearing as it bounced a zig-zag path through the shrubs. Carleton exclaimed, "That's the biggest rabbit I've ever seen!"

Perry chuckled. "Jackrabbit. They can get pretty big."

To the right ahead of them, a cluster of low hills merged and grew in size until they became tall peaks crowned by rocky cliffs. Dark green vegetation clothed the top third of the mountain range. As they approached the first hill, Carleton saw that two marker posts had been driven into the ground on either side of the road. A symbol was carved into the wood near the top of each post. It was an eye centered above a pair of outspread wings.

As the wagon rolled between the markers, Perry confirmed Carleton's guess. "We're entering aveni territory now," he said. "They don't normally bother with me, but if we run across any of them, let me do the talking."

"If they are so protective of their land, why do they let you cut across?"

Perry glanced over at Carleton with raised eyebrows. "Marcus didn't tell you? I left my position as a deputy marshal so I could become the aven agent for the tribes here in the Sulphur Springs Valley. It took a while, but the elders mostly trust me now to represent their interests. My property shares a border with the Siri Tan tribe here in the Dragon Mountains, so I've gotten to know them well."

Since they'd entered aveni land, Carleton had been watching the sky, expecting the vision he'd had of flying riders descending upon him to come true. Knowing that Perry had a good relationship with the tribe was comforting, but Carleton would be just as happy to reach Perry's ranch without meeting any avens. The nervousness that Willie had displayed regarding the avens was contagious.

"Why did Willie call the avens 'little demons'?"

Perry frowned and shook his head. "A lot of the settlers around here call them that. The avens are much smaller than us and their ears are pointed. Between that and their darker skin, I guess some people think they look like demons. Aveni shamans can speak to the elements, and the more religious folks attribute that ability to some kind of infernal power."

Nothing in Carleton's reading had indicated magical abilities among the avens. "How do they 'speak to the elements'?"

Perry shrugged. "You'd probably call it magic, but from what little I understand about the subject, I don't think it's the same as what wizards like you can do. The shamans can supposedly convince the spirits of earth, wind, fire, and water to do their bidding."

Carleton went silent, musing over the new information. The elemental spirits the shamans could control sounded a lot like elementals from the old legends and myths. Myths often began as a way to explain incomprehensible phenomena. The shamans might even believe that spirits were the source of their powers. Merging their magical abilities with some sort of tribal religion would transform their frightening skills into miracles.

It was a savvy strategy. Historically, whenever magic and religion came into conflict, the outcome was usually fatal for the magic-user.

Carleton was thinking he'd like to learn more about the shamans' magic, when a series of shadows strobed the sunlight. He and Perry both looked up, shading their eyes. The vision he'd had with the crystal had come to life. Five wyverns, each one directed by an aveni rider, flew a course parallel to the road. When the lead rider pointed a spear toward them, the entire flight banked and descended.

Perry pulled on the reins and drew his team to a halt. He glanced at Carleton and spoke quietly. "Like I said, just relax. They're probably just checking up on us. They may not even land."

The riders leveled off about a hundred feet above the ground and circled once above the wagon. One of the wyverns let out a cry that sounded like the screech of a hawk—if the hawk had a megaphone. The sound caused the hair on the back of Carleton's neck to prickle.

Perry raised a hand in greeting, but none of the riders returned the gesture. When the lead rider brought his mount into a sharp turn and angled toward the ground in front of the wagon, Perry said, "Damn," under his breath.

Carleton was too fascinated by the arrival of the wyverns to ask Perry what he might be thinking. With a few strong wing flaps, the creatures smoothly touched down in a semi-circle that blocked the wagon. It wasn't until they were arrayed in front of him that Carleton appreciated their true size.

The wyverns easily stood as tall as a man. They had a prehistoric appearance that reminded Carleton of pterodactyl drawings he'd seen when he was in college, except that they had the shape of a normal bird. Their wings and tails were fleshy and bat-like, but they were coated with a fine layer of feathers. The chest and under-wing feathers were a plain, dove gray, while on top they were glitteringly colorful. All of the wyverns had tan along their backs that darkened to a deep crimson at their wingtips, although the pattern varied a little on each animal. Above their eyes, long outwardly curving black feathers quivered as the creatures darted their raptor gaze from the wagon to the surrounding desert.

The avens were as unexpectedly small as the wyverns were large. They were a little more than half the size of a man and almost skeletally thin. The corded muscle visible along their arms as they pulled on the reins to keep their mounts in check hinted at a wiry strength.

When the leader's dark eyes met Perry's, it was easy to understand how the avens had acquired their local nickname. With his dusky-brown skin and pointed ears, the aven resembled the classic depiction of a demon. All he lacked to complete the image was a barbed tail and pointed teeth.

The avens did not dismount, seeming content to remain strapped into their deeply cupped saddles. Perhaps they wanted the option of flying off as quickly as they had arrived.

Or perhaps their mounts were their best weapons. The wickedly curved talons on each of the bird-like creatures' four-toed feet had to be at least eight inches long, and their heavy, raven-like beaks looked like they could chop a human arm in half. One of the beasts returned his stare and tilted its head, as if sizing him up for a meal. Carleton shuddered.

An odd crunching sound distracted Carleton from his observations. He homed in on the source and discovered it was the boar, which seemed to be grinding its tusks together and grumbling. The rest of the team had frozen in place. When one of the birds lowered its neck and took a step closer to the team, the boar and the peccary to its right both squared off against it. They let out a loud, throaty bark and opened their mouths wider than Carleton would have thought possible, exposing every inch of their long sharp tusks. Carleton was glad not to be the object of their fearsome display.

The rider of the advancing wyvern pulled back hard on his leads. The beast let out a low squawk of protest and hopped backward with a flap of its wings. The peccaries closed their mouths, but shuffled in their harnesses uncertainly, going back to grinding their tusks and grumbling. Perry kept constant pressure on his reins and spoke softly to his team, trying to calm them.

The leader of the aveni party slipped the butt of his spear into a pocket of his saddle and raised a hand in greeting. He spoke in a child's tenor, but his voice was modulated with maturity and strength. "Agent Peregrine Maine. You bring trade?"

"No, Chiefson Cearul Sulc," Perry answered. "We travel to my home."

After a moment of thought, the aven shook his head. "You travel here, you trade."

To Carleton, it sounded suspiciously like the aven was demanding some kind of toll, but Perry didn't look concerned. In fact, he smiled as if he had expected the aven's demand. Perry set the wagon brake and handed the reins to Carleton, saying, "Pull back gently with steady pressure."

Perry got up and bent over the back of the seat, rummaging around under the tarp. When he straightened, he held a wooden box in one hand. He climbed down from the wagon and walked slowly toward the chiefson. As he passed the nearest peccaries, he rubbed his hand along their backs and made soothing noises. The young peccary behind the boar jumped when Perry's hand initially made contact.

The chiefson's wyvern didn't seem to care much for the approaching human. It partially unfolded its wings and thrust its head forward with an ear-splitting shriek that made Carleton's heart stop for a moment. The smallest peccary let out a distressed squeal and Carleton could feel it tremble through the reins. Wisely, Perry stopped walking forward. The chiefson sighed and patted his wyvern's wing. He tugged at the laces that crossed his legs and held him in his saddle, slipping smoothly to the ground as soon as the bindings dropped free. He walked toward Perry with a slightly bow-legged swagger in his step.

When the chiefson reached him, Perry opened the box and held it forward. Carleton couldn't see what was inside from his position on the wagon, but the aven nodded appreciatively. "Good trade," he declared. Perry closed the box and handed it to the chiefson, who smiled for the first time and bowed slightly to the human.

Returning to his wyvern with the box cradled under one arm, the chiefson nimbly leaped back into his saddle. He gave his wyvern a couple of sharp raps and the creature stooped forward, making the line of its back nearly parallel to the ground. The aven strapped the box onto a leather platform that was attached to the front of his saddle and appeared to be designed for carrying small cargo.

Perry returned to the wagon and took the reins from Carleton. By the time Perry had settled back into his seat, the chiefson was ready to leave.

The aven raised his hand with his with his palm forward and said, "May your wheels never break, Agent Peregrine Maine,"

Perry returned the gesture. "May the wind favor you, Chiefson Cearul Sulc."

The avens turned their wyverns away from the wagon. With a few running hops and several wing flaps, the beasts and their riders rose into the air, leaving dust swirling up from the roadbed behind them.

As the aveni hunting party gained altitude and shrank into the distance, Perry released the brake and flipped his reins, encouraging the peccaries to continue.

Carleton didn't realize how much his chest and shoulders had tightened until his muscles slowly unclenched with the departure of the aveni hunting party. He took a deep breath and turned to Perry. "What was the price of our passage?" he asked.

"Brass buckles. Avens don't work metal, so they are eager to trade for practical items like buckles and knives. But it wasn't a gift. The chiefson will find something of equal or higher value to trade back to me the next time we meet."

"It's lucky you had that box of buckles."

Perry glanced at Carleton with a wry smile. "It wasn't luck. I know better than to pass through their land without having something to trade. They don't often stop me like that, but when they do, I'm ready."

Carleton thought back to the encounter. In the end, it was merely a trading transaction, but it had seemed like an ambush at the start. "I got the impression that the chiefson and you aren't close friends. Do you trust him to give you a fair trade?"

Perry paused before replying, his expression thoughtful. "Avens don't trade the way humans do, and it's one of the reasons they avoid dealing with us. Human trade often involves deceit and guile. Aveni trade is based on trust and respect. The chiefson did me an honor by accepting a forward trade. He has to give me back something of equal or greater value to keep his reputation as a good trader. The longer I have to wait for his return trade, the higher its value will be. But you're right. He doesn't like humans in general and barely tolerates me. I get along much better with his father, the chief."

Carleton nodded his head and went silent with thought. The avens and their mounts were every bit as intimidating as he'd anticipated, although he thought the nickname "little demons" was undeserved. Then again, none of the riders had demonstrated any of the magical abilities avens supposedly possessed. He was relieved that the riders had mostly ignored him. He didn't know how they would react to a human wizard, but his reception since he'd arrived made him feel cautious about revealing his skills.

As the wagon bounced and bumped down the road, relief swept through Carleton. For the second time that day, he felt like he had escaped a potential trap. He began to suspect that snakes and avens were only the first of many challenges he'd have to face in the West.

Chapter 6

Sunrise Ranch

The blazing sun was high in the sky when Perry pointed toward a branch of the mountain range ahead and to the right. The stubby cactus-covered hills angled away from the base of the taller mountains and toward the valley. "We're almost there. The ranch is set up against the last of those hills."

As the sun drove away the last bit of morning chill, Carleton's dark clothing collected heat and made him drowsy. He slipped off his jacket, sighing when the breeze cooled the sweat on his neck and back.

As the wagon bumped along the dusty road, Carleton kept his eyes on the entrance of a wide canyon that disappeared into the mountains on their right. They were passing uncomfortably close to the foot of the range and the heart of aveni territory. Enormous boulders of rounded stone walled the canyon and reached for the sky. Marching up the mountainside, they formed a magnificent rocky saddle between the peaks. The pinkish-tan monuments were like giant teeth, waiting to grind up anyone foolish enough to trespass into the hills.

Noticing Carleton's nervous vigil, Perry nodded toward the canyon and said, "That's the entrance to the chief's stronghold. It's an amazing place."

"You've been there?"

A note of pride entered Perry's voice. "I have. Being agent to the aveni tribes has its advantages. I've met with the chief several times, although I wouldn't go up there without an invitation."

The road curved away from the mountains, and a few minutes later they passed between another pair of boundary markers. Carleton let out a sigh of relief as they left the aveni lands behind.

Perry slowed the wagon and turned onto a narrow, two-track road while High Lonesome continued east toward the valley. Ahead of them, the primitive road went up the widely flared base of a hill, zigzagging between rocky prominences and prickly pear patches before disappearing over the top. The peccaries picked up their pace, in spite of the uphill grade and the rougher terrain.

Perry chuckled. "They know we're getting close to home."

Sure enough, cresting the hill revealed Perry's home, Sunrise Ranch.

The ranch occupied a flat area that seemed to have been chopped out of the apex of the hill. The remnants of the rounded peak ended in a low cliff that backed the property. A fence enclosed the left half of the grounds, encompassing an old shack that was slumped next to a dark hole in the cliff. A cluster of peccaries milled around by the shack near a feeding trough and a circular stock tank.

The ranch house itself was a simple, single-story building with a few small windows and a covered front porch. The exterior was well weathered, but appeared to be sound.

Two horses in a corral to the right of the house watched their approach, nickering as the wagon rolled to a stop. One was a bay and the other a white appaloosa with gray spots. Perry nodded toward the horses. "The welcoming committee are Peppy and Remington. Remington's the appaloosa." Sweeping his eyes across the property with pride, he added, "It ain't much, but it's home."

Perry jumped down and started unhitching the team. Carleton got down as well and watched Perry work for a moment. "Can I do anything to help?" he asked.

Perry stood and considered the question. "Well, if you don't mind getting those fancy duds a little dirty, you could start moving crates from the wagon to the porch. I'll sort them out later. Anything in a sack can go inside."

While Perry moved his team to the larger paddock with the other peccaries, Carleton untied the tarp and made a couple of trips to the house carrying crates, which he set down on the porch as instructed. On his next trip, he grabbed a sack filled with rounded shapes he guessed were potatoes. He stood at the front door, unsure of the protocol. Was the door locked? Should he wait for Perry?

Perry walked up right then and noticed Carleton's quandary. "Go right on in," he said, waving his hand toward the door.

Carleton lifted the latch and pushed the door open. "You don't keep it locked?"

"Not much point. There's nobody around this place for miles. If someone had a mind to break in, they could make all the racket they wanted. A lock wouldn't hardly slow 'em down. Besides, I don't have much worth stealing."

Carleton entered a tidy and cozy home that belied its rough exterior. The atmosphere was a little stale from the house being closed up, but it was soothingly cool after the warm wagon ride. Lacy curtains trimmed the windows, suggesting a woman's touch at some point in the home's history.

Perry took a deep, satisfied breath as he walked in. Carleton was about to ask where he should set the sack he was carrying when Perry held up a finger as if to say, *wait*. With his other hand, he drew one of his pistols.

Cocking his pistol, Perry checked behind the front door and then stalked across the room to a wall that had two doors in it. He stopped at the door on the left and listened. Pointing his pistol into the room, he pushed the door open slowly with his free hand. The hinges didn't squeak until just before the door bumped against the wall. Perry stepped into the room and out of sight.

Carleton set the sack down and pushed his shirt sleeve back, revealing his stone-studded bracer. He touched a black agate and fed a stream of swi into it. When the gem accepted the flow, he softly spoke a trigger word. A faint gray shimmer arced around him in a half-circle about two feet away. It did not quite reach the floor, but it rose to several inches above his head. He moved slowly to his right toward the kitchen, hoping to change the angle of his view and see what Perry was doing.

His new vantage let him see that Perry was closing the doors of a free-standing closet in what appeared to be a bedroom. When he exited the room, he looked at Carleton and shook his head. He'd found nothing so far.

Giving the second room the same treatment, he emerged a moment later and shrugged his shoulders. He holstered his six-shooter and, speaking in his normal voice, he said, "I didn't think anyone was still here, but you can't be too careful."

Carlton mentally pinched off the magical essence he was feeding the shield and it flickered out. "How did you know someone had been here? Is something missing?"

Perry picked up the bag of potatoes and set it on the kitchen table. Looking around the room, he shook his head. "Nothing's missing so far as I can tell, but the place felt off when we came in. Someone's been in here poking around, but they tried to hide it."

"Could Willie and Jacob have beat us here?"

"Naw. They'd have had to run their horses hard to get here first, even if we account for our little delay with the chiefson. And they'd still be here, considering how het-up Willie is about escorting us into Pearce."

Perry went back outside and walked slowly around the front of the house, staring at the ground. Assuming that Perry was searching for evidence of strange boot or horse prints, Carleton stayed up on the porch to avoid adding any more of his own tracks.

After wandering around for a minute, Perry made a sound of disgust and said, "I'm no tracker and this gravel don't hold a print too well. Let's finish unloading before the dastardly duo gets here."

Ten minutes later, they had moved everything except Carleton's luggage to the inside of the house or onto the porch. Perry went to fetch a fresh team of peccaries while Carleton washed his hands and tried to brush the dirt off his clothes. His "duds" were already looking a bit worse for wear. After cleaning up, he went out onto the porch and took a moment to admire the view from the hilltop ranch.

Perry's hill was a bump in a wide, alluvial plain at the base of the Dragon Mountains. The plain descended into a long valley that stretched from north to south as far as the eye could see. Directly across the valley to the east, the plain ascended again to meet the base of another range of tall, darkly forested mountains.

The sparsely populated valley Carleton beheld was probably the size of the entire state of Rhode Island. Although the clear desert air made the mountain range on the opposite side of the valley seem close, he would be willing to bet that it was a full day's ride away.

Distant movement caught his eye, and Willie and Jacob appeared over the curve of the hill. "Our escorts are here."

Perry was hitching a new team of peccaries to the wagon. "Just in time. We'll be ready to go in a few minutes."

By the time Willie and Jacob arrived, Perry had the team harnessed and hitched to the wagon. He led two more peccaries around to the back of the wagon and tethered them to it. Both had fur that had been rumpled by harness straps.

"Were those two part of the team that brought us here from Cochise?" Carleton asked.

Perry nodded and gestured at Carleton to get onto the wagon. "Yep. That was their final test run. They're good and tired and won't put up too much of a fuss when I leave them with their new wrangler in Pearce."

Willie shook his head in disgust. "I still can't believe you talked the boss into paying good money for pigs we can't eat."

"That's because you don't work inside the mine," Perry responded. "The delvans are going to love them."

Willie didn't look convinced. "We'll see about that. So far, they don't seem too impressed by the idea."

"They'll come around," Perry said in a confident tone. Whipping the reins, he started the wagon rolling.

Carleton enjoyed the views during their descent to Pearce. A breeze had come up, but the sun on his back kept him warm and relaxed. The West was turning out to be full of interesting surprises. Some of the surprises were worrisome and others were wonderful, and he hadn't even arrived at the mine where he'd be working yet. He could hardly wait to see what it would be like.

Chapter 7

Commonwealth Mine

Rolling out of the foothills toward the valley, the topography allowed Carleton several glimpses of Pearce before they arrived. The main street was flanked by classic western buildings with tall front facades. The sound of hammers carried up the rise for miles as carpenters expanded the growing town that had arisen to serve the Commonwealth mine and other claims being worked in the area.

Driving through Pearce, people gave them the same curious and confused stares they'd received from the folks in Cochise. One fellow shook his head in disgust at the peccary team as they trotted past him.

Business seemed to be thriving. Carleton counted three saloons and a general store. "How many saloons does one town need?" he asked Perry.

"The more miners and teamsters, the more saloons. Most of the workers around here don't get too far with their pay. It vanishes pretty quick at the poker tables, into the hands of a bartender, or nestled in the bosom of a dove."

"Dove?"

"Soiled dove. Lady of the evening."

"Ah."

A tall cowboy stood leaning on a post in front of the Prickly Pear Saloon. "Hey, Perry," he shouted with a wave. "I see you brought lunch!" His joke elicited several snickers and laughter from the townspeople within earshot.

Perry waved a hand at the fellow dismissively. "Smart-ass," he muttered.

About halfway down the main street of Pearce, Perry turned right at an intersection between the hotel and the post office. The buildings thinned out quickly as Perry drove toward a lumpy peak etched with a zig-zag of road switchbacks.

"There it is," said Perry. "The Commonwealth Mine."

The mine wasn't much to look at from a distance because the real action was underground. In addition to the vertical shafts and horizontal drifts that followed the ore, delvans housed their miners in underground villages known as subtowns.

As they drew closer, Carleton spotted the first buildings littering the base of the hill. While he watched, a wagon rolled down the last switchback of the access road, the driver leaning hard on the brake. The rear of his wagon was heaped with ore.

"Where do they take the ore?" Carleton asked.

"Cochise. From there, they load it into a rail car and haul it to the mill in Benson. The railroad is talking about putting in a spur line to Pearce next year if the mine keeps producing. The investors are even thinking about putting in a stamp mill to process the ore on site."

Perry angled the wagon toward a nice home that stood out in sharp contrast to the ramshackle outbuildings that stood around it.

A tall man standing on the covered porch waved Perry over. At his left was a pretty red-haired woman in a light-blue dress, twirling a parasol against her shoulder. On the man's right was a delvan like none Carleton had ever seen.

The sturdy miner was dressed in the hooded cloak and tinted goggles that were typical delvan attire for above-ground work, except that he wasn't wearing gloves, and Carleton was astonished to note that his short beard was blond, not the snow white of most delvans.

Carlton had heard of pigmented delvans, but had never met one. Delvans were mostly an albino species, but a small percentage of their population was born with blue eyes, flaxen hair, and enough skin pigment to freckle or tan. Among their own people, such delvans were sometimes called topsiders, although the term was considered an insult.

Perry pulled back on the reins, bringing his team to a halt. Setting the brake, he jumped down and met the tall man, who had stepped down from the porch to meet them. The young woman and the miner followed close behind.

"Good day to you, Mr. McLaury," Perry greeted. He tipped his hat to the lady. "Miss Penelope." He then spoke to the delvan, tilting his head toward the wagon. "Hey, Flint. I brought down the new cart team. They're all yours."

Flint nodded and thanked Perry before lumbering toward the wagon.

Carleton dropped down from the wagon seat and loosened the tarp so he could retrieve his belongings. He noticed Flint keeping an eye on him while the delvan untied the two peccaries at the back of the wagon. Because of the hood and the goggles, it was difficult to read Flint's expression, but when their eyes met, the stocky little man nodded in acknowledgment and then led the two peccaries away.

Carleton turned at the sound of approaching footsteps. Perry came around the wagon with the tall man and the woman close behind.

"I'll give you a hand with that in a second, Carleton. But first, let me introduce you to Bart McLaury, the general manager of the mine, and his facilitator, Miss Penelope Cartwright."

Carleton extended his hand to the man who was going to be his boss for the foreseeable future. "Pleasure to meet you, Mr. McLaury. Wizard Carleton Kazimer, at your service."

"Damn straight, you're at my service!" McLaury said with a smile while he shook Carleton's hand. "I paid the Guild a good sum of money to get you out here. I expect to get a good return on my investment." The joking tone he used did little to soften the edge in his voice.

The young woman gave Carleton a once-over with her striking blue eyes and pushed her braid of bright red hair to her back. She twirled her parasol and said, "Go easy on the man, Bart. He just got here and isn't used to your unique sense of humor."

Bart glanced over his shoulder at the girl. "Thanks for the advice, Penny. Next time, wait until I ask for it."

She gave him a disapproving frown, but remained silent.

Bart caught sight of Willie and Jacob talking to a third man at a long building across the street. "Willie! Get over here and help Wizard Kazimer take his things to the bunkhouse."

He turned around and headed back toward the house. Over his shoulder, he called to Perry. "Come on inside, and I'll take care of the bill for them pigs." Perry shrugged and waved goodbye to Carleton as he turned to follow the mine manager.

Penelope stayed behind for a moment. She smiled at Carleton and said, "It was a pleasure to meet you, Wizard Kazimer. I hope you enjoy your stay here."

Carleton dipped to a shallow bow and tipped his hat. "Thank you, Miss Cartwright." He raised an eyebrow at the retreating back of Bart McLaury and added, "I hope so too."

Glancing over her shoulder, she lowered her voice and said, "Don't worry about Bart. He takes some getting used to, but he's mostly a fair man. Well, I have things to attend to as well. I hope to see you around."

"It would give me great pleasure, ma'am."

She bestowed another sweet smile upon him before turning to go back to the house. Carleton's gaze lingered on her as she departed, thinking she could probably get almost anything she wanted with that smile.

"Don't even think about it," said Willie from right behind him. "The boss will feed you to the rattlesnakes if he catches you makin' eyes at Miss Penelope."

Carleton turned his attention to helping Willie with his trunk. "Sounds like the voice of experience," he said.

Willie shook his head as he grunted, lifting the trunk out of the wagon bed. "Not me. The key to getting along with Mr. McLaury is learning to follow orders. Besides, Miss Penelope is a bit delicate for my taste."

Carleton didn't want to hazard a guess at what Willie's taste in women might be like. And while Miss Penelope might be delicate, he suspected she was anything but fragile.

He decided to take Willie's advice at face value. "Thanks for the tip." Willie grunted in reply. "Perry said she was a facilitator. What does that mean?"

"Far as I can tell, it's a fancy word for a bookkeeper," Willie answered, his tone growing impatient. "You'd best keep your mind on your job and off Miss Penelope."

Carleton went silent, thinking Willie's suggestion was probably wise.

Since Willie knew where they were going, he led the way, waddling backward with his end of the heavy trunk. When they entered the bunkhouse, it took a moment for Carleton's eyes to adjust to the gloom. The bunkhouse was equipped with a couple of high windows at each end. The long room was dirty and had the musky odor of infrequently washed blankets. Rough bunk beds lined the walls on both sides with a narrow walkway down the center.

Willie stopped just inside the door. "This is your bunk," he said as he dropped his end of the trunk alongside the first bed. The bottom bed had been slept in recently, judging from the indentation on the pillow and the thrown-aside blanket. A folded blanket had been haphazardly tossed onto the top bunk along with a relatively clean pillow.

"I'm on top?" Carleton guessed.

"Yep. When you get settled in, report at the house."

Carleton peered around the room, searching for evidence of a better option. Being right near the door was going to be unpleasant. "Do you have anything else available?"

"Nope. We're full up."

Jacob spoke from the doorway. "You should be thankful for what you got. Most mining camps are a bunch of tents or leaky shacks, and you sleep on the floor. These here are top-shelf accommodations."

Willie nodded. "He's right, but don't worry about it. Fellers are always coming and going around here. Something else will open up soon enough."

Jacob spat and grinned. "Yeah, but then you have to negotiate for it. There's a peckin' order around here."

Willie glared at Jacob. "Don't you have something else to do?"

"I'm waiting on you, big man. You're the one who told me that the boss wants us to make a run back to Cochise before the end of the day."

"Well, go get the wagon ready, and I'll be along in a minute."

Jacob spat and nodded before clearing the doorway.

After Jacob left, Willie lowered his voice and took a step closer to Carleton, glancing around the bunkhouse to make sure no one would overhear. A couple of men had slept through the racket of Carleton's arrival, or at least they were pretending to. "Listen, this can be a rough crowd. The boss told me to make sure you stay out of trouble. Anybody leans on you, tell me about it quick. The boss don't tolerate stealing, fighting, or drinking on the job. Best keep that in mind."

"I understand," Carleton said. As Willie left to follow Jacob toward the livery, Carleton mulled over Willie's unexpected offer of protection. He knew better than to take the man up on it. In a group of hard cases, he was sure that tattletales ran into all kinds of anonymous grief and "accidents." He would have to take care of any misunderstandings on his own.

~

The word "Commonwealth" was etched into the stone archway over the mine entrance. Steel rails exited the mine and ended at a dump ledge. A wagon waited on a landing below for the next load of ore.

"Watch your head in there," Bart McLaury warned Carleton. "Delvans build for their own convenience, not ours." Carleton nodded his understanding.

Penelope stood with them. Once again, Carleton wondered what role she truly played. She had changed into pants and a long-sleeved shirt. The shirt looked borrowed, as it was several sizes too big for her, and she had rolled up the sleeves to right below her elbows. She was prepared to get dirty, it seemed.

Carleton still wore the clothes he'd arrived in. They weren't suited to spelunking, but they were nearly ruined already, and he didn't have anything more appropriate.

The trio stepped under the archway and walked into the passageway beyond, which made a sharp turn to the right, quickly choking off the light from outside. After several more paces, Bart raised his hand and brought them to a stop. "We'll wait here for our eyes to adjust. The delvans ain't much for light. They run a few candle lanterns along the passages, but that's about it."

Carleton had assumed the mine would be dark. Delvan eyes had evolved to accommodate low-light conditions, which was why they wore dark goggles whenever they visited the surface during the day.

After their eyes had adjusted to the gloom, Bart led the group forward. Following Bart's example, Carleton ducked under an arched roof support made of closely fit block. The keystone was etched with delvan symbols and the English word "Main."

Not long after virtually all of the sunlight had faded behind them, they came upon an intersection with a passageway to the left. Block walls and arches supported the entire intersection. A candle lantern gave Carleton enough light to see the word "Subtown" etched into the arch above the left passage. "Main" was repeated above the forward passage and the tracks disappeared into the dark in that direction. He jumped when a delvan miner suddenly appeared under the archway to the subtown.

Bart angled his head toward the delvan. "I understand you've already met Jasper Underlight, our mine supervisor. He'll take you down to the face so you can see what you're dealing with."

"You aren't coming with us?" Carleton asked.

"I got no reason to stumble around down there in the dark. I'm here to see the subtown head-woman." He looked down at the delvan. "I want you to look after Wizard Kazimer while he's down here. Make sure he gets what he needs, within reason." Underlight acknowledged the orders with a nod. The way Bart had instructed the delvan to look after him hinted at something more dangerous than a bump of the head on an archway, but maybe his nerves were making him paranoid.

Orders delivered, Bart moved past the delvan and started down the subtown passage. Penelope followed in his wake.

Jasper handed Carleton a hard leather padded cap with a narrow brim and chin straps, identical to the one he was wearing. "Strap that on yer noggin. The head-wall has some low spots."

Carleton put on the cap and adjusted its straps. "Thanks."

"Let's get a move on, Wizard Kazimer." The stout miner started down the forward passage. Carleton ducked under the tunnel support and followed.

"Please call me Carleton, Supervisor Underlight. It seems we may be working together for a while."

"Fine. Jasper will do for me."

A few yards beyond the subtown intersection, the passage began to slope downward. They had gone another thirty feet or so when a squeaking noise came from ahead. Jasper halted at a widened part of the passage and waved Carleton toward an alcove set into the wall.

"The cart's coming. Wait here for it to pass."

Carleton followed Jasper's example and backed into the alcove, careful not to bump into the candle lantern that was affixed to the wall. The squeak of wheels grew louder and was accompanied by deep huffing sounds. A moment later, one of Perry's peccaries plodded into view, straining at a harness attached to the front of an ore cart.

Flint walked alongside the cart, one hand resting on the front edge near the hand brake. The hood of his cloak was down and he had shifted his goggles up onto his forehead. He acknowledged Jasper and Carleton with a nod.

"Stop the cart," Jasper ordered.

Flint shook his head. "We need to keep moving. It'll be hell to get going again if we stop."

Jasper's voice took on a sharp edge. "Stop the cart, Flint."

Flint let out a raspy sigh of frustration. "Aye, Uncle." He called, "Whoa," to the peccary, and as the cart slowed to a stop, he set the brake. The peccary coughed once and stood still, taking snorting breaths through its nose.

The protective clothing delvans wore on the surface normally made it impossible to compare features, but down in the mine with no hoods or goggles, Carleton could see the family resemblance between Jasper and Flint in the shape of their faces.

"What's happening below?" Jasper asked.

Flint scratched his head. "Same as always. Tully's crew is working the face and I'm working the cart. Maybe two more loads waiting to come up."

Jasper nodded toward the panting peccary. "That one of the new pigs? Looks played out."

"He'll be fine after I work him a few days," Flint answered. "Just needs to toughen up a bit."

Jasper peered into the cart and reached in, riffling through chunks of ore. He lifted a few pieces and sniffed at them. Legend had it that delvans could smell the presence of precious metal. "The run be holding strong," he declared.

"Aye," Flint confirmed. "So far, anyway."

Jasper stepped back from the cart. When he spoke, his voice had a mocking tone. "Maybe the wizard here can tell us how much farther it'll go."

Flint gave Carleton an appraising look with his uncommon blue eyes. "That would be useful," he said.

"Bah," Jasper scoffed. "We've kept ye long enough. Best get that cart topside."

Flint placed his hand on the brake handle and whistled at the peccary. "Git 'em up," he called. He didn't release the brake until the peccary started pulling on the leads, and even then, the cart didn't move forward. It rolled back a couple of inches while the peccary's legs shook with strain.

Flint went quickly to the rear of the cart and started pushing, but to no avail. The cart rolled back another couple of inches.

Carleton looked over at Jasper to see if he was going to help his nephew, but the older miner folded his arms. "They can handle it," he said confidently.

Carleton wasn't convinced. He left the alcove and positioned himself at the back of the cart next to Flint.

"Come away from there, wizard," Jasper protested. "Ye'll get yerself hurt, and I'll never hear the end of it."

As if to prove his point, the cart suddenly grew heavier and pushed Carleton and Flint back a couple of inches farther. Flint grunted with the increased strain. "Pig's more tuckered than I thought," he said through clenched teeth.

Carleton risked moving his right hand from the cart to the gemstone band on his left arm. Careful to touch the amber only, he cycled a bit of swi through the polished stone and triggered it with a word. Flint watched without comment.

As strength rushed into his muscles, Carleton put both hands back on the cart and pushed. It started to roll slowly forward. Flint grinned at Carleton and called to the peccary, "Ha! Git 'em up, Stomper."

The cart rolled faster as Stomper took more of the weight. They quickly reached the apex of the tracks where the incline flattened.

"Thanks, we got it from here," Flint said with an appreciative nod. Carleton stopped and watched the cart roll away toward the mine entrance.

Pinching off the flow of swi, the excess strength drained from his muscles, leaving them tired and shaking. It had been a while since he'd used that spell. He turned and walked back to where Jasper was waiting at the alcove.

The mine supervisor still had his arms crossed and was frowning. "We need to get something straight right now, wizard. Inside Commonwealth, you answer to me. When I say 'come away,' you do it. Is that clear?"

"But they needed help," Carleton argued.

"If I thought they needed help, I'd have stepped in meself. Flint's stronger than he looks, and the pig was being stubborn. Flint needed to sort that out for himself."

Although Carleton wasn't convinced that Flint could have gotten the cart up the incline without help, he saw the sense in following Jasper's orders. He was in delvan domain, and his life was in the mine supervisor's hands. For the moment, anyway.

Carleton straightened up and brushed his hands across the front of his vest. The effort applied more dirt than it removed. "I understand, and I apologize."

Jasper gazed at him for a moment and then nodded once, seemingly satisfied with Carleton's sincerity. "Good. Let's get moving. The candles ain't getting any taller."

A couple of minutes later, the passage split. The left branch curved away into inky darkness, its floor littered with chunks of rock. The cart rails in that direction were dusty from disuse. Jasper followed the branch that curved to the right, much to Carleton's relief. Flickering lights illuminated the passage in that direction.

As they rounded the corner, a faint noise that had been teasing at the edge of Carleton's hearing became more distinct. The unmistakable percussive clang of metal on rock echoed toward them from ahead. Peering around Jasper to look beyond him, Carleton's head connected with a rock protruding from the ceiling, knocking him back a step. "Ouch," Carleton exclaimed, although he was more startled than injured. He reflexively put his hand to his head, thankful for the helmet padding that had absorbed most of the impact.

"Ye hurt?" Jasper asked.

Embarrassed, Carleton shook his head. "Sorry, I'm not used to walking in tunnels." He motioned for Jasper to continue.

The miner pointed toward another protrusion. "Keep yer eyes on the head-wall. The closer we get to the face where me crews are working, the rougher it gets. And this ain't a tunnel, it's an adit. Tunnels be open to air at both ends and an adit only one. We'll reach the stope soon, and ye'll have plenty of room."

Seeing that the passage did indeed continue to narrow in width and height, Carleton gave up on walking upright and crouched down to Jasper's height. He made an effort to follow in Jasper's footsteps from that point on.

The passage opened up again after a few dozen yards. As they moved forward, the walls retreated and the ceiling rose until it seemed safe to stand straight again. They'd entered a small cavern, or stope, as Jasper had termed it, and the racket of three delvan miners working at the far wall was nearly unbearable. Jasper whistled a few times to get their attention, and one by one they left off their work to lean huffing on the wooden handles of their implements.

The cavern was slightly better-lit than the passageway, having several candle lanterns positioned along the walls. Rock dust filled the space, floating and sparkling in eddies stirred by the miners' movements. A large pile of ore filled one side of the cavern, next to where the cart rails ended. Smaller piles of discarded gangue, the useless material that surrounded the ore, were set aside around the stope.

"Listen up, muckers," Jasper shouted. "This here be Carleton Kazimer. He'll be working down here on occasion, and I want ye to give him space when he needs it."

The middle miner pulled some kind of plug from his ear and shifted his clear goggles to his forehead. His expression was a mix of incredulity and confusion. "A human miner?"

His disbelief was understandable. Mining was almost entirely a delvan occupation and most humans were happy to let the delvans take care of the underground work. Once the ore reached the surface, the delvans were equally willing to let humans take over the transportation and processing of the ore. It was a partnership that had been established centuries before.

Jasper chuckled. "Nay, he's no miner. He's a rock mage, here to sniff out what the boss thinks we can't."

The frowns and grimaces in response to Jasper's announcement warned Carleton that he'd have to watch himself while he worked inside the mine. He wasn't sure what the term "rock mage" meant to the delvans, but it apparently wasn't a compliment.

"I'll try to stay out of your way," Carleton promised.

"Aye, ye do that," said the one who had expressed surprise that a human would be working in the mine.

Jasper pointed a thumb toward the man who'd spoken. "That's Tully Ironfoot, the crew foreman." He threw a serious look at the miner and raised his voice. "If he knows what's good for him, he'll make sure you get what you need and keep you out of trouble while you're working down here." He then addressed Tully directly. "Don't give me reason to push ye topside, Tully. Mr. McLaury has taken a personal interest in Wizard Kazimer's success."

The muscles of Tully's jaw worked for a moment before he answered. "No need to get testy, Jasper. I'll do me job."

Jasper's voice lost some of its edge. "I know ye will. I just want to make sure ye understand the cost of getting careless."

Tully glanced at Carleton. "Appreciate the warning."

A rumbling and the squeal of brakes presaged the arrival of the ore cart. Flint sat inside the cart, slowing its descent with the brake lever. The peccary was tethered to the back, jogging to keep up. The cart came to a stop with a soft bump against the timber bumper that capped the end of the line. Flint leaped out of the cart and put in earplugs like Tully's.

"Ye need to see anything else right now?" Jasper asked Carleton.

"No, sir. Now that I know what I'm dealing with, I can prepare for my next visit."

"All right, let's let these men get back to work."

Waving toward the foreman to carry on, Jasper went around the cart and started back up the passage. Conversation was impossible over the ensuing din of Flint shoveling ore into the empty cart and the other miners breaking up the chunks that had been freed from the wall.

On the return trip up the passage, Carleton started a mental list of things to gather. He needed some work clothes and a set of earplugs like the miners wore, and he'd have to ask Jasper if he could keep the padded helmet for a while.

He had never cast a spell in such a noisy environment. An incantation usually had to be spoken aloud, but would it work if the words were drowned out by other noise? He would find out soon enough.

If necessary, he could probably ask Tully to stop the crew for a few minutes, but he'd use that option as a last resort. He'd try to make his unwanted presence as unobtrusive as possible.

Back home, Carleton's skills were respected and sought after, but out West, the opposite seemed true. He was disappointed by the wariness reflected in the eyes of the delvan miners and Bart's callous attitude toward him. If he were going to make the contract work, he would have to find a way to win over all of them.

Chapter 8

Starlight

That evening, Carleton sat around a campfire near the mess tent. The food was uninspired but satisfying. He picked at his plate of beef and beans while the teamsters talked and joked among themselves. Other than a few surreptitious glances, they pretty much ignored him.

After the meal, Carleton didn't feel like hanging around the campfire or retiring to the bunkhouse. The night had turned chilly, so he grabbed his jacket and went for a walk. The full moon drew him out to commune with the desert in solitude.

Mindful of snakes, Carleton wandered away from the buildings. He followed a shallow wash around to the base of the mountain that embraced the mine. He didn't carry a lantern, but the moonlight gave him enough illumination to avoid toe-stubbing rocks and needle-sharp cactus spines. Clambering up the hillside, he found an outcropping of rock that gave him a view of the manager's house and the campfire below.

The stars overhead were dimmed by the light of the moon, but even so, the clear sky revealed details he'd never observed in the city. The Milky Way was a cloudy strip of smoke arcing across the sky. Stars sparkled like he'd never seen before. In the city, the tiny pinpoints of light had always seemed like monochromatic white jewels, but above the open desert, many of them shimmered with a red or blue hue. He looked forward to the next new moon when he'd be able to observe the firmament in its full glory.

Carleton wondered if anyone back home was looking up at the same stars he was seeing that evening. Most likely they were all settled inside, enjoying a quiet conversation over tea. He would miss his weekly visits to his parents' house and his mother's comforting smile. Even his father's gruff teasing would be an improvement over the suspicion and skepticism it appeared he would face at Commonwealth.

Laughter and the clanking of tin plates carried up to him from below, adding to his feeling of isolation and loneliness. It was definitely not his crowd. When he'd set out for Arizona, he had no idea what to expect. He knew he'd be leaving behind everything that was familiar, but he hadn't suspected how truly different things would be.

That Perry fellow seemed okay, but he had his ranch and peccary business to attend to. All of the people he'd met at the mine either ignored him or were outright hostile. Except for Flint. He seemed to be all right. But he was delvan, and human-delvan friendships were rare due to the logistics of above-ground versus below-ground living. Delvans were usually insular to the point of rudeness.

Penelope was nice too, but Willie had warned him about trying to cultivate *that* friendship.

So far, the women he'd met on his journey into the West were like Penelope: a curious mixture of strength and femininity. The desert seemed to instantly recognize weakness and pounce upon it, and delicate flowers were short-lived. Of all the things a man might expect to find by adventuring into the West, a wife was probably not among them. Not that Carleton was looking for a bride. Still, one never knew when or where one might find the right person.

Carleton was distracted from his ruminative stargazing by a figure moving up the wash toward his overlook. He couldn't tell who it was, and he had no interest in engaging in conversation with one of the teamsters right then.

Searching his memory for a spell he hadn't used in months, he placed his hands on the rock that served as his perch. He practiced the incantation in his mind a couple of times before speaking it aloud in a low voice. He flowed swi into the rock and completed the incantation while the figure started the short climb toward him. With a secret smile of satisfaction, Carleton was confident that the interloper would see nothing more than a desert rock formation.

The person continued to climb and stopped at the rocky overhang, hands on hips. Then, with careful steps, the slight figure came over and sat down next to Carleton. It wasn't a teamster. It was Penelope.

Carleton sat as still as possible, moving only his eyes to watch what she was doing. She removed her hat and shook out her tresses, their red color barely discernible in the moonlight.

"Well, are you going to just sit there, Carleton, or are you going to say hello?" she asked.

Carleton dropped his spell, as much from shock as intent. Apparently, his illusion skills were rusty. "Sorry. I wasn't in the mood for company. How did you know I was here?"

"You aren't the only one who likes this spot. I come up here when I need some time to think. It didn't take much imagination to connect the arrival of a geomancer with the new boulder perched at my favorite viewpoint. But I can leave if you want to be alone."

Carleton's desire for isolation had drained away the moment she sat down. "No, I welcome the company of anyone who doesn't look like they want to cut my throat."

Penelope turned toward him, the moonlight glittering in her eyes and lighting the soft oval of her pale face. "Is it really that bad? The drivers can be rough, but a lot of it is false bravado. If you stand your ground, you'll probably find a friend among them."

Carleton thought her prediction was unlikely. "Maybe."

They sat together quietly for a moment, enjoying the peaceful and isolated viewpoint while they looked out over the silhouettes of the desert landscape.

"Is it safe for you to come out here alone?" he asked.

"As safe as anywhere else," she answered. "You'll want to be careful in the summer, though. Rattlesnakes love to lie on sunbaked rocks and on the sand of the washes in the evening."

Carleton shuddered. "I've had my fill of rattlesnakes."

"Sounds like there's a story behind that statement."

Encouraged by her interest, Carleton told her the story of his morning encounter with the rattlesnake and Perry's timely intercession.

When he finished his tale, she sat silently for a minute before commenting. "I can see why you think everyone's out to kill you. But snakes do come inside sometimes."

"True, but Perry seemed to think the snake had been placed there intentionally. He insisted on helping me get to the mine safely. That's why I rode in with him this morning."

"I wondered about that." Penelope said. "Bart sent Willie and Jacob to make sure you got onto the stage, so I was surprised to see you arrive on Perry's buckboard."

"Yeah, Willie wasn't too happy about Perry getting involved, but we didn't give him much choice in the matter."

"Well, good," she said. "You're standing up to them already." She shivered under her light shawl and folded her hands under her arms. "It's colder out here than I thought."

Carleton stood and removed his jacket. The dry evening air was cool against his skin, but he was used to much colder and wetter weather. He draped the jacket over Penelope's shoulders.

The gesture of kindness seemed to surprise her. "I'm fine," she protested, but she pulled the jacket closed and shook off another chill. "Thank you."

They sat silently for a few moments, and then she spoke again. "Once the sun goes down, the desert cools fast. I'm not sure what it's like where you come from, but it's common here to have a forty-degree difference between the daytime and nighttime."

Where I come from, a lady wouldn't be surprised when a gentleman offered her his jacket.

He answered her oblique question. "Baltimore. I'm from Baltimore, Maryland."

"What did you do in Baltimore?" she asked.

"I ..." Carleton started to answer, but then checked himself. He wanted a friend at Commonwealth, and he wanted to trust Penelope, but he knew nothing about her. Marshal Keenan had warned him to keep his involvement with the U.S. Marshals and the Munseys to himself. They couldn't know for sure if the Munseys had connections in the West.

Nevertheless, he was so tempted to blurt out the truth that he had to restrain himself from saying anything, just so he wouldn't do so. He struggled to collect his thoughts about his feeble cover story of working for a Baltimore excavation company.

After the long silence, Penelope leaned away and looked at him closely. "Is something wrong?"

"I'd rather not talk about it," he finally managed to answer. He mentally kicked himself for making his past sound so mysterious. His former boss had warned him to stick to his cover story and keep it simple. Simple and direct answers deflected curiosity.

"I think I understand," she said with a sigh. "The frontier is filled with people who are trying to start a new life and leave a past life behind."

Her words sounded like they related to personal experience. Carleton thought maybe he could distract her with a few questions of his own. "What about you? Are you here to leave a past life behind?"

She tensed and there was another moment of silence before she answered. "Perhaps I'll tell you about it some day when we are ready to trust each other."

As much as he wanted to get to know her better, building trust between them would take time.

Penelope stood and removed his jacket, holding it out for him. "Well, Wizard Kazimer, it was nice to share the view with you. Bart will be wondering where I've gone by now, so I shall bid you goodnight."

Carleton stood as well. She had addressed him formally, so he did the same. "Goodnight, Miss Cartwright. Thank you for making my evening much nicer than I expected it to be. Would you care for an escort back to the house?"

She waved him away and started down the hillside. "No, thank you; I can manage. It would probably be better for both of us if we aren't seen together."

Carleton watched her pick her way down the hillside, aching to go hold her hand to steady her, and berating himself for having such thoughts. Willie was probably right about keeping a distance from her. Given her relationship to Bart McLaury, Penelope Cartwright could be a great help or cause him a lot of trouble, and the last thing he needed was more trouble.

Chapter 9

Invasion of Privacy

By the time Carleton made his way down from the viewpoint, the campfire had died down to smoldering coals and everyone had gone inside.

With reluctance, he entered the bunkhouse, hoping to get some rest for what promised to be a busy next day.

He sensed tension in the air the moment he walked through the door. Two men were playing cards at the far end of the room under one of the lanterns. Both glanced his way when he entered. With smirks, they returned to their game.

Carleton stopped short when he noticed that his trunk and case were both open and half of his things were strewn over the bunk below his. "What the hell!" he exclaimed.

He clenched his jaw and fought down a flush of anger. All of the other men in the room were watching him, waiting for his reaction. He shook his head and started collecting his items, concentrating on the most important geomancy tools and putting each back into its proper location in his case. He quickly realized that something significant was missing.

"Where is my brass ring?" he asked in a loud voice. Standing, he moved to the aisle and looked into the eyes of each man. Most looked away when his eyes met theirs. One man glanced at the youngest of their group, and that one stared back at Carleton with an insolent grin.

"I need that ring to do my work," he announced. "I'm sure Mr. McLaury won't be pleased when I tell him I can't do my job because someone stole my equipment." He turned an accusing gaze at the young teamster. "Give it back now, and that won't be necessary."

The grin left the kid's face and he leaped off his bed. He came into the aisle and stopped a few feet away from Carleton. "I don't like the way you're lookin' at me, mister. You accusing me of stealing your little brass ring?"

Carleton shifted his stance, alert for signs the kid was going to get physical. "I don't know who stole it, but I'm betting you do."

The kid ran his hand through his hair, wiping the stringy locks back from his face. "I don't know nothin' about no brass ring. You probably lost it, and now you're blaming it on us."

"If I search the bunks, I'll bet it will turn up soon enough."

"You ain't searchin' my bunk. That there would be an invasion of privacy."

"What about my privacy? Who dumped all my stuff out and stole an important piece of equipment? It isn't worth much to sell, so give it back and I won't mention the theft to the boss."

The kid rubbed one hand over the other. "It still sounds like you're talkin' like I stole it," he said in a warning tone.

"I think you know exactly who stole it."

The kid looked at him askance. "Maybe. But I ain't a rat."

The young man's shirt shifted in response to his hand motions, revealing that something heavy was in the chest pocket. The bottom of the pocket was stretched into a semi-circle that was exactly the right size for Carleton's brass ring.

The kid looked down, following Carleton's lingering glance. He looked back up, the insolent grin firmly back in place, as if to say, *what are you going to do about it?*

Carleton stepped forward and reached for the pocket, but the kid twisted away. "Hey! Don't you touch me." And then he threw a punch.

Carleton had anticipated the punch and knocked it aside with his forearm. Moving into a defensive crouch, he said, "Give me back the ring. I won't ask again."

"Come get it," the kid growled, stepping in with another punch to Carleton's head.

The kid's over-confidence and unimaginative attack wasn't a challenge for the training Carleton had received while he was working with the marshals. He grabbed the punching arm, stepped into the lad's body, and threw the kid over his shoulder. The young man slammed into the floor on his back, shaking the building. While the thief writhed and groaned, Carleton reached into his pocket and snatched the brass ring.

He stood up and checked the ring, satisfied that it hadn't been damaged. He was about to step around the kid and return to his bunk when something hit him from behind and everything went dark.

~

Carleton awoke to a rough shaking and a splitting headache. He groaned and sat up on one elbow, probing the back of his skull to find a big lump that explained the pounding in his head. He was relieved to find no evidence of blood, dried or wet.

"What happened here?" Willie demanded.

Carleton became aware of lumps on the mattress pressing into his body and gingerly rolled out of the bunk to avoid crushing the sample bottles he'd been laid upon. Investigating the weight in his vest pocket, he found he still had the brass ring he'd retrieved from the thief, and clutched his hand around it in relief.

"What are you doing in my bunk?" asked Jacob.

Willie held up a hand. "Shut up, Jake. Something happened here, and I want to get to the bottom of it."

The bunkhouse lanterns had been extinguished, so the only light came from the lantern in Willie's hand and moonlight through the nearby doorway. A glance around the bunks showed that everyone else was in bed. A couple of the men had turned to observe the commotion, but the rest were either asleep or faking sleep.

"There was a misunderstanding," Carleton said, rubbing the back of his head.

Willie lifted the lantern and peered at the spot Carleton was rubbing. "That misunderstanding come with a free lump?"

Mindful of what Willie had said about stealing and fighting, Carleton chose to play down what had happened. The brass ring in his hand and the fact that he was still alive told him he might have gotten his point across and earned a little respect in the process. It was an inauspicious beginning, but he had to stand on his own because Willie obviously couldn't do much to protect him.

Carleton kneeled next to the bed and started collecting the sample bottles. "It was an accident," he said over his shoulder. "I think we sorted everything out." He put away the last of the bottles and placed the brass ring into its proper spot in his kit.

"Uh-huh," Willie responded doubtfully.

Carleton put the equipment case on top of his trunk and pushed the trunk back into the corner where he'd left it earlier in the day. He hoped the others would leave his stuff alone in the future. His father had lost the key to the trunk lock years before, and anyone with a nail and about five seconds of spare time could have picked the simple lock on his equipment case.

As soon as Carleton was squared away, Willie walked down the aisle, kicking every bunk as he went. "Wake up, you bunch of swine. Wake up!"

The men grumbled and sat up, turning their heads toward where Willie was standing next to the card table at the end of the bunkhouse.

"Listen up. I don't know what happened here tonight, but if there's more trouble, I'll trade every one of you in for a new crew. The boss put a lot of money into getting Mr. Kazimer out here. More than any of your useless hides are worth. You mess with him again, and I'll give you a lump you won't forget."

The young man who had stolen the ring rolled his eyes and huffed.

Willie set the lamp on the table, and after three quick steps, he lifted the kid out of the bunk with his right fist, holding the young man upright by his undershirt only inches from Willie's angry face. "That goes double for you, you little pissant. You've been making trouble since the day you arrived. I've a mind to toss you out right now."

The kid finally managed to get his feet under him, wincing and rubbing at his back as he tried to step backward. Willie released him with a flick of his fingers, and then held up a clenched fist in front of the kid's face. "You got that, Dell?"

Dell looked down at the floor, still rubbing his back. "Yeah, I got it. We didn't mean nothing. We were just joking around with our new buddy Carleton."

Willie huffed out a laugh. "Yeah, right. Next time you're feeling funny, you let me know, and we'll put you on stage down at the saloon. Then we'll see how good your jokes are."

Willie took a couple of steps backward before turning and picking up his lantern. Carleton doubted Dell would have been brave or stupid enough to tackle the man, but Willie was obviously a wary soul. It was probably one of the things that kept him alive and in charge.

"Now get some sleep," he ordered as he walked back toward the bunkhouse entrance.

Dell climbed back into bed, groaning as he lay back. His sudden contact with the floor earlier had apparently done some damage. The other men returned their heads to their pillows.

By the time the confrontation between Willie and Dell was over, Jacob had stripped down to his undergarments and climbed into the lower bunk. Shifting position, he grunted and reached under his backside. Holding up a small glass bottle, he shuddered at the shriveled contents and held it out for Carleton to take.

The moonlight shining through the open doorway gave Carleton enough light to put the sample back into his case. When he arose the next morning, he planned to arrange everything back in its proper place so he could tell if anything else was missing. Stifling a yawn, he started to disrobe.

Willie passed by and stopped at the door, looking like he might say something. Glancing toward the others, he seemed to think better of it and simply walked out, leaving the door open behind him.

Carleton went to close the door, but Jacob spoke up from his bunk. "Leave it. It can get mighty close in here at night, and it's too cold for snakes to be out. You'll sleep better with the fresh air."

Acknowledging Jacob with a nod, Carleton vaulted into the top bunk and gathered the blanket around him. He lay on his back for a while, listening to the crickets and the occasional yipping of the coyotes. He slowly drifted off to sleep to the throbbing of the lump on the back of his head.

CHAPTER 10

Under Pressure

Breakfast the next morning was biscuits and gravy, which sounded and smelled a lot better than it tasted. The thick gravy was so greasy that Carleton was burping acid within minutes of mopping up the last bits from his plate.

Unsure of when Jasper would be down to collect him, he hurried back to the bunkhouse to reorganize the mess he had made of his equipment case the prior evening. The top tray of the kit was a padded honeycomb with a cell for every bottle, and after all the bottles had been put away, one cell remained empty.

Everyone else was still outside, so Carleton searched Jacob's bed for the missing bottle. Jacob had left his blanket in the position it had landed when he got up, so Carleton didn't think he'd notice the intrusion.

Finding nothing in the bunk, Carleton dropped to his hands and knees to look under the bed. The light from the doorway was briefly eclipsed by someone entering, and a familiar mocking voice came from behind him.

"I hope I'm not interrupting some important magical ceremony here," said Dell.

Carleton rose to his feet quickly and turned to face the young teamster. He narrowed his eyes and prepared for another confrontation. The kid's sandy-blond hair was still tousled and his blue eyes were a little bloodshot, probably from a poor night's rest on a sore back.

Dell held up his hands in surrender. "Now, don't get testy. I'm just funnin' with ya." He shook his head and gave

Carleton a look of exasperation. "You need to grow yourself a thicker skin there, Carl."

"It's Carleton. What do you want, Dell?"

"We got off on the wrong foot, and I'm sorry about that." He glanced down at the open case. "We don't get too many wizards around these parts. The boys and me got curious about what you been toting around."

Carleton wasn't buying it, but chose to take Dell's words at face value. "You could have asked, and I'd have been happy to show you."

"Aw, we didn't want to trouble you none. Anyway, no harm done, and no hard feelings, okay?" Dell held out his hand.

Carleton accepted the handshake hesitantly. "Sure. No hard feelings."

Dell grimaced and released Carleton's hand to rub at his back. "You'll have to show me that move someday. I've a feeling it's gonna be a long day on that hard wagon bench."

Still uncertain about the young man's sincerity, Carleton offered an apology anyway. "Sorry about that. You could take your blanket for a seat cushion."

"Naw, it would just get full of dust. But thanks for the suggestion. I might be able to find something else to use."

It was a measure of his distrust that Carleton wondered if he'd return to his bunk that evening to find his own blanket full of road dust.

"What was you looking for, anyway?" Dell asked. "Something missing?"

"One of my sample bottles."

"Well, it's gotta be here somewhere." Dell scratched his head and walked down the center aisle, peering between the bunks.

Surprised by Dell's unsolicited assistance with the search, Carleton stood and stared for a few seconds. Shaking his head, he went back to checking around his bunk and behind the trunk. There was no way he was getting down on all fours again with Dell close by.

Dell was coming back toward the door when he stopped at the other side of Carleton's bunk. Bending with a groan, he asked, "This it?" He held up the missing sample bottle.

"Yes," Carleton answered. "Thanks for finding it."

"No problem," Dell said, tossing the bottle across the bed.

Carleton wasn't expecting the toss, but managed a fumbling catch. He suppressed a spike of anger at the young man's carelessness, but pressed his lips together and said nothing.

"Good reflexes, Carl," Dell said with an innocent grin. "Well, I gotta hit the trail. I hope you have a good day doin' whatever it is you do."

"See you later, Dell," Carleton responded. He waited for the young man to leave before putting the bottle into its proper cell and closing the lid of his equipment case.

The light through the doorway dimmed again and Carleton turned around with a sigh, expecting Dell to have returned to give him more grief. But it wasn't the teamster. It was Flint. The miner flipped his hood back, revealing cornsilk-blond hair pulled back from his face into a tight braid. He moved his tinted goggles up onto his forehead and squinted up at Carleton.

"Morning, Wizard Kazimer. In all the excitement of yer arrival, we've never been officially introduced. I'm Flint Underlight." He held out his hand, and Carleton leaned forward to shake it. The stout miner was only about four-

and-a-half feet tall. "Uncle Jasper had other business today and asked me to escort ye into the mine."

"Thanks, I appreciate that," Carleton said.

Flint glanced at the trunk. "I hope ye don't need all that stuff. We'll have to use the mine cart to get it in and out."

Carleton picked up the equipment case. "No. I only need this one. The trunk has clothes and personal belongings." He was dressed in his most sturdy pants and a heavy linen shirt he'd bought at an exorbitant price from Jacob earlier that morning. Under his arm, he'd tucked the miner's cap that Jasper had loaned him, and he carried a pair of waxed-cloth earplugs in his pocket.

Flint glanced around the bunkhouse before saying, "Ye might want to find another place to keep the trunk. Personal belongings don't stay personal for long around here."

Carleton gave the miner a wry smile. "So I'm learning." He raised a hand to touch his receding bump in memory of the previous night's activities. Hefting the equipment case, he added, "I'm more worried about this, truth be told. It has things I need for my work that can't be easily replaced."

Flint stared at the case, his lips pursed in thought. "We might be able to find a safe place to store it inside the mine," he suggested.

Carleton considered the offer. He preferred to keep the case nearby, as little good as that had done the previous evening. Given enough time to poke around, someone might find the secret compartment in the side that hid his remaining cash. And while Flint might be trustworthy, Carleton wasn't so sure about the other delvans.

"Thanks for the offer," he responded, "but I'll figure something out."

"Suit yerself," Flint said as he adjusted his goggles over his eyes and put up his hood. Motioning toward the door, he said, "The wagon's waiting."

The wagon Flint was referring to turned out to be one of the ore wagons that was heading up the hill to fetch a load. They both climbed into the empty wagon bed for the ride. The teamster flipped the reins and started up the hill as soon as they were on board.

At the entrance to the mine, they hopped out of the wagon, and Flint led the way to the pen where the peccaries were kept. The four spotted animals snorted and grunted when they saw Flint. Two came toward the gate while the other two carried on with rolling in the dust and chewing at bits of prickly pear pads.

"Some of them seem to like you," Carleton observed.

"Aye, they're wary at first, but they come around."

Flint opened the gate to the enclosure barely enough to slip in. He grabbed a rope that was draped over the fence and approached one of the peccaries that had stayed back. "Come on, Porky. Time to earn yer feed."

The peccary snorted and took a couple of steps backward. It let out a coughing bark and flashed a set of sharp tusks. It ground its teeth the way Perry's team had when they met the aveni riders.

Flint didn't seem intimidated. He moved forward and slipped a loop over the peccary's head. "Ye've some nice teeth there pig, but use 'em on me and ye'll be what's for dinner." Whether or not the peccary understood Flint's threat, it seemed resigned and subdued once the rope was tight around its neck.

Exiting the pen with the peccary in tow, Flint shook his head. "They can be pig-headed," he said with a wink at Carleton, "but once ye get them in a harness, they work hard."

"Why not take one of the more cooperative ones?" Carleton asked.

"Oh, they'll get their chance. Porky here be one of the new pigs that Perry brought in yesterday. I'll work her a little extra until she learns to be cooperative too."

Flint led Porky and Carleton to an ore cart that was waiting at the mine entrance. "Hop in," he said over his shoulder.

Carleton clambered into the cart while Flint tied Porky to the back. He released the hand brake and gave the cart a push to start it rolling. Once it was moving at walking speed, he jumped on and climbed in.

Flint used the hand brake to keep the cart rolling slowly enough for the peccary jogging behind them to keep up. They quickly traversed the drift down to where the miners were already hard at work. A substantial pile of ore awaited Flint's arrival.

And so did Tully. "It's about time ye got here. What kept ye?"

Flint let out an angry grunt and jumped out of the cart onto the pile of ore. Carleton climbed out on the opposite side and stepped back as Flint roughly shoveled the first chunks of ore into the bottom of the cart with a crashing bang.

Tully stepped forward, his face red and his eyes glaring. "I asked ye a question, topsider. Where have ye been?" He had shouted loud enough that the other two miners on Tully's crew stopped working and turned to watch the confrontation.

Flint stopped in mid-stroke, about to sink his shovel into the ore pile. He straightened with a narrow look at Tully, holding his shovel sideways with tight fists. Carleton thought he might strike the larger delvan for the insulting reference to his pigmentation. Tully squared his shoulders and casually swung his pickax, as if daring Flint to make an aggressive move.

"Jasper told me to get the wizard," Flint finally growled in answer. He put in his earplugs, clearly indicating his lack of interest in continuing the conversation, and went back to shoveling ore.

"Bah," Tully exclaimed, dismissing Flint with a wave of his thick hand. He turned his attention to Carleton and lifted the pickax toward him. "Keep yerself and yer trinkets out of our way, wizard. We got work to do."

Turning back to his crew, he yelled, "Who said it was time for a break? Get back to work!" Grumbling, he returned to the laborious task of breaking up ore chunks and piling them at the loading area.

Cringing from the sharp, clanging noises that were trapped in the cavern, Carleton followed Flint's example and put in his earplugs. They didn't block all the noise, but they took the edge off and allowed him to concentrate.

Glancing around, Carleton didn't see any good places to set up for a spell; the floor of the cavern was irregular and littered with ore chunks. Shaking his head at the difficult conditions, Carleton cleared a small space against the wall farthest from where Tully and his men were working. Using variable-sized chunks of rock, he created a relatively flat surface for his equipment case. He'd chosen the spot for his makeshift workspace partly because of the candle lantern directly above it, which gave him enough light to get situated.

By the time Carleton finished setting up, Flint had already filled the ore cart, his remarkable productivity no doubt fueled by the anger that still smoldered in his expression. Porky had folded her legs under herself to rest while Flint worked, so he had to urge her to her feet before he could put on her harness.

For the spell he was about to attempt, Carleton needed a small chunk of ore that contained as much of the mineral they were seeking as possible—in other words, silver or gold. He approached Flint as the delvan was attaching Porky's harness to the ore cart.

"Flint," he shouted over the clanging, "I need a good sample of ore about this big." He made a circle of his thumb and forefinger.

Flint's anger seemed to have cooled, but he looked tired from the exertion of working it off. He stood up and considered the ore in the cart. He shook his head. "Better ask Tully. He has a better nose for it."

"Ask Tully what?" said Tully from behind. He was moving chunks of ore onto the stockpile.

Flint caught Carleton's eye and tilted his head toward Tully, choosing not to participate further in the conversation. He released the cart's hand brake and gave Porky a smack on the rear. "Get 'em up, Porky." With Flint pushing hard to help the peccary get going, the two of them rolled the cart out of the cavern and into the passage toward the surface.

Carleton turned to Tully and repeated his request.

The miner sifted through the rock pile, raising selected pieces to his nose for evaluation. He chose one and used a hammer that hung on his belt to break it into smaller chunks. He dropped a piece into Carleton's palm. "Will that do ye?"

"Yes, thank you."

Carleton thought Tully might ask him what he wanted the rock for, but the miner went back to work without further comment.

Turning the rock over in his hand, Carleton couldn't see any difference between the sample Tully had given him and any other piece of rock in the pile. Granted, the lighting was poor, but he was going to have to take the delvan's word for it that he was holding a sample that contained trace amounts of silver or gold.

Back at the space he'd cleared, Carleton lifted the top tray out of his equipment case and took his spell book out of the cavity below the tray. He thumbed through the pages until he found the spell he sought. Standing up for better light, he read through it again, double-checking the catalysts he'd need and silently mouthing the incantation.

While he prepared, he had the uncomfortable feeling of being watched. Every time he glanced at the working miners, one or another of them would be looking his way with a disapproving expression. Apparently, they didn't care for the challenge he represented to their own abilities to literally sniff out good ore.

But delvan abilities worked only with the exposed face of rock. Carleton's spell could go much deeper than that. If it worked, the spell would allow him to follow the vein of ore for several yards, and maybe even farther. After he became more familiar with the geology, he could potentially find parallel veins that might be hidden only a dozen feet from the existing run.

Sitting cross-legged, Carleton put the brass ring directly in front of him and set the catalysts into the center of it. The catalysts for the spell were the chunk of ore and the claw of a gopher. Chanting the incantation, he placed his palm over the ring and concentrated on the purpose of the spell. He was pleased to note that the earplugs not only blocked out the noise of the miners, but it allowed him to hear his own incantation more clearly. As he spoke the final word of the spell, he pressed down hard on the brass ring.

The floor of the cavern was too hard for the ring to go all the way into the soil as it had when he checked the water pump in Cochise, but it dug in far enough. A deep boom emanated from the ground below him and his awareness slipped into the hard rock below where he sat.

Reorienting himself, Carleton moved blindly forward. The body of ore drew him like iron to a magnet until he estimated that he was below where the miners were working. He angled upward and found the vein. To his subterranean awareness, the precious metals in the ore glittered like fireflies in the dark. The glowing blobs of light varied in size, shape, and color. He wasn't sure what they all meant yet, but he was sure he'd figure it out over time.

Testing the limits of his range, Carleton moved deeper until the lights started to fade. The range was disappointingly short. He might be able to do better if he could sit right at the face of the wall, but that would mean asking the miners to stop working.

Focusing on the individual metals that were within range, he memorized the mental impressions they gave him. He might be able to discern the differences among them if he could practice on smaller chunks of ore that could then be analyzed for their content. The delvans should be able to tell him what each trace was, and he could correlate that information with the sensory perceptions the spell had provided. Eventually, he'd be able to tell gold from silver and other metals.

A sense of disquiet distracted him from his task. Tapping back into his physical senses, he realized that the miners had stopped working and had gathered around him. Carleton withdrew his awareness from the earth and ended the spell. Returning to his body, he opened his eyes. The miners were standing in a semi-circle in front of him with angry and disturbed expressions on their faces. Tully had been shouting something at him, but he had missed most of it.

"… get us all killed!" the foreman finished.

Feeling vulnerable in his sitting position, Carleton got to his feet. "What's the problem?" he asked.

Tully waved a rock hammer as he answered. "The problem? The problem is that ye're bringing the mountain down on us!"

"What do you mean? The spell doesn't move anything. It just lets me see into the rock."

"Well, whatever ye detonated sure moved something. Mag here was nearly crushed by that rock ye broke loose." Tully pointed his hammer at a chunk of rock that was as big around as a delvan torso.

"But I didn't detonate anything," Carleton objected. Then it occurred to him. The concussion from activating his spell was probably responsible. It was a side-effect of his magic manifesting in the physical world. Normally, it didn't cause problems, and it was nothing compared to the blasting the delvans were doing to free the ore, but it was apparently enough to cause problems in a recently blasted and unreinforced area. "Wait," he said. "I think I know what happened."

"We can't have ye shaking the mountain while we're working." Tully declared.

"I agree. We'll work something out."

Tully lifted his hammer toward the passage. "Work it out somewhere else. I'll not have ye putting me men in danger."

"I understand," Carleton said. He started collecting his equipment and putting it away.

Tully directed his men to go back to work while he stood over Carleton with his arms folded and a severe expression on his face.

Picking up his case, Carleton turned to Tully. "I'm sorry about the rock. I'll talk with Jasper and see what we can do."

Tully stalked forward until he was only a couple of feet away. Carleton would have stepped backward if his back wasn't already against the wall.

Tully's voice was barely loud enough to carry over the working miners and get through Carleton's earplugs. The menace in his tone was unmistakable. "Listen here, wizard. I think it's best ye go back to wherever ye came from and let us handle the mining. We don't need ye, and ye're a danger to everyone under the mountain. If ye come back, someone's going to get killed."

Carleton returned Tully's glare. He had little doubt that the miner's words were a not-so-veiled threat. He straightened and squared his shoulders. "I'll make sure that doesn't happen," he said. Then he turned on his heel and walked toward the passageway. His indignant exit was somewhat spoiled when he clunked his helmet on the support at the entrance to the cavern.

Striding up the passage, ducking under the low support arches and rock protrusions, Carleton thought about what he was going to tell Jasper. So far, the teamsters didn't want him around and the delvans didn't want him around. As much as he wanted to call it quits and go home, failing so soon wasn't an acceptable option, personally or professionally. He had to figure out a way to move forward. Fortunately, he still had Bart McLaury's tentative support, but would that be enough to keep him alive?

~

Carleton slogged up the passage, thinking about what he could do to satisfy the recalcitrant miners. If he didn't figure out a way to deal with them, fulfilling his contract would be impossible. However, given Bart's impatience, he would only involve the mine manager as a last resort.

Flint raised a hand as he rolled by in the cart with Porky jogging along behind. Maybe he could ask Flint to negotiate for him, but the one friendly miner he'd met seemed to have little influence among his own people.

As Carleton approached the intersection of Main Drift and Subtown Crosscut, the sound of voices came from ahead. With a sinking feeling, Carleton recognized Bart's forceful tones and the respectful but adamant responses from Jasper.

Carleton slowed down as he got closer. Vague forms resolved in the flickering light of the candle lanterns at the intersection. He was barely able to make out what they were saying as he approached.

"We have to increase production if we want that rail line," Bart said. "Put out the word now to bring in more miners so we'll have them when we need them."

"Ye're puttin' too much faith in yer wizard," Jasper responded. "We bring in miners without the work, and they'll not be thanking us. We got ore enough for three crews and that's what we're running."

"We could put the new men down the crosscut."

Jasper responded with exasperation. "That run's gone to gangue. Ye'll be paying them for tailings."

"Hold on," Bart interrupted. "Who's there?"

Carleton started walking forward again so it wouldn't be obvious he had been eavesdropping. "It's me—Carleton." No one spoke as he approached the small group. Penelope stood silently behind Bart and Jasper.

Bart's eyes glittered in the lantern light. "Shouldn't you be down at the face doing something useful?"

Carleton set his case down as he came to a stop. "I was. I made some promising progress. But there was an accident and Tully asked me to leave."

"What kind of accident?" Jasper asked in a harsh tone.

Carleton took a deep breath, and then exhaled, trying to think of how to explain what had happened in a way that wouldn't be too alarming. "A big rock fell when I started my spell. No one was hurt, but Tully was understandably angry with me."

Bart shrugged. "So what? Rocks fall all the time. What made him think it was your fault?"

"Geomantic concussion," Penelope answered. She blinked, seeming surprised she'd spoken aloud.

Carleton was surprised by her insight as well. Not many people would know that particular term. "Exactly. Geomancy generates a seismic concussion commensurate with the amount of swi required to manifest the spell."

Everyone stared at him.

"Try that again in English," Bart growled.

Carleton dipped his head in apology. "What I mean is that starting my spell created a mild shock wave. The rock that fell was probably loose, and the vibration shook it free."

Jasper folded his arms and frowned. "So much for yer wizard. We can't have him bringing the mountain down on us."

Bart ignored the delvan supervisor. "What did you learn?"

"I learned that my range is limited. I was able to follow the vein, but only for a couple of yards. If I could get closer to the face, I could go deeper."

Jasper shook his head. "We'd have to stop digging—"

Bart held up his hand to interrupt Jasper. "How much deeper?"

Carleton shrugged, "A few more yards, maybe."

"That's it?" Bart shouted. "Your range is less than twenty feet?"

"Told ye this would be a waste of time," Jasper said with disgust.

"Shut up, Jasper. I want to hear the wizard explain why I'm paying the Guild all this money for a wizard who doesn't know his job."

Carleton's face grew hot and he ground his teeth. His words came out before he could think about them. "If you're so dissatisfied with my work, perhaps I should get back on the train and go home."

Bart came forward and got in Carleton's face. "You aren't going anywhere until I get my money's worth. You have the cash to pay back my investment right now?"

Carleton was taken aback by Bart's vehemence, and it gave him some much-needed perspective. He had to salvage the situation somehow, and not only for pride's sake. Walking out wasn't an option. "No, sir. And I apologize for speaking hastily. I believe everything will work out to your satisfaction if you can give me some time. Magic depends on many factors. I'm sure I can improve my range and accuracy with some experimentation."

Bart stepped back, giving Carleton an assessing look, as if he were trying to decide if he could trust the wizard's words. "All right, Wizard Kazimer. You can have more time. But I want to see progress. Don't you string me along. You need anything for your *experimentation*, you talk to Jasper, and he'll make sure you get it." He gave Jasper a hard look, and the delvan acknowledged the implied order with a curt wave of acquiescence.

Bart continued. "By tomorrow morning, I want to hear how you two have worked this out. C'mon, Penny. We got things to attend to."

Penelope looked like she wanted to say something to Carleton, but Bart turned her around and pushed her toward the mine entrance. Carleton watched them leave, curious about the dynamic he'd witnessed.

"Ye're givin' me a headache, wizard," Jasper complained, rubbing his forehead to emphasize his words.

"What's the story with those two?" Carleton asked, tilting his head in the direction Bart and Penelope had gone. "Why is Penelope even here?"

Jasper shook his head. "Ye'd best mind yer own problems. Sniffing another man's ore is a good way to get a bloody nose."

Trying to get information from Jasper was a waste of time. The delvan didn't seem to care much for Bart, but at the moment, he cared even less for the wizard he was forced to deal with.

"Is there somewhere we can talk?" Carleton asked. He was tired of standing in the passage, having to watch his head every time he shifted position.

"Aye. Follow me," Jasper said. He turned around and went down the passage toward the subtown. Carleton picked up his case and followed.

It was Carleton's first visit to a delvan subtown, and he was honored by the invitation. The delvans were an insular people, so he doubted human visits were common. They even policed themselves, for the most part. Human authorities got involved only if the matter extended beyond the delvan community.

Carleton had to remain bent over to accommodate the lower head-wall of the side passage. Fortunately, width wasn't a problem because most delvans had wider shoulders than he did.

While he followed Jasper, a few ideas for how to move forward began to form. The pressure of Bart's antagonism helped him put aside the emotions that had been distracting him from his job. It didn't matter what the teamsters or miners thought of him, as long as they stayed out of his way. If he couldn't work with them, he'd find ways to work around them.

The passageway ended at a large circular chamber with a beehive hearth in the center. A big iron cauldron was heating over the flames that burned within the hearth. Most of the smoke went up through a wide flue that rose to the ceiling, although the sweet pungent smell of burning mesquite filled the room.

Two delvan females looked up when Carleton and Jasper entered. A toddler sat in the younger woman's lap, staring at Carleton with his round pink eyes. The older woman nodded toward Jasper and went back to mending a garment with deft fingers. Both women were dressed in grey homespun shifts that were belted at the waist. They wore their long white hair in ponytails. Carleton was used to seeing delvans outside and completely covered, so he felt like a voyeur observing the women in such a relative state of undress.

Five other passages branched off at regular intervals around the room. Two had stairs that went down, two had stairs that went up, and the opposite passageway went straight. Jasper walked around the hearth and entered the straight passage.

Carleton looked around with interest as he passed through the chamber. He'd read about delvan subtowns, so he recognized the arrangement as a typical quad design. Quad referred to the fact that four living quarters were connected to a common area that had an entrance passageway and a shared dining chamber. Jasper was leading him to the dining chamber.

The chamber was spacious and comfortable by delvan standards. Carleton was able to stand up straight with his leather helmet barely grazing the curve of the head-wall.

The room was dominated by a huge stone table that looked as if it had been carved as the room had been built. The sides curved in to allow for leg-room. Around the table were stone benches and individual columnar seats with thick pads on them for comfort. Jasper went to the head of the table and sat down, pointing Carleton toward the bench next to him. Carleton set his case on the floor and took the indicated seat.

"What's on yer mind?" Jasper asked.

Carleton went for the blunt approach. "I know you and your men don't want me here. I'm not too excited about the job myself at the moment, but I made a commitment and I'm going to do my best to honor it. What I don't understand is why all of the delvans are so hostile. Is it just because I'm human?"

For a moment Jasper stared at him. He seemed taken aback by the directness of Carleton's question. Then he leaned forward and his voice took on a hard edge.

"Ye're a human and an earth mage. Humans have the whole topside and got no business underground. This is our domain. Cragg says ye're an affront to Father Earth. Yer being here will make Him angry and cause trouble for all of us."

Carleton's spirits sank. Cragg Steel was the silently disapproving delvan who had accompanied Jasper on the train. Overcoming a religious bias against him would be nearly impossible if most of the delvans felt the same way.

"Is that what you think?" Carleton asked.

"Don't matter what I think. I have me men to consider, and Father or no, they think ye're bad luck. Can't say I disagree with 'em on that."

It sounded like there was still cause for hope. Luck, he might be able to turn around. Doctrine was set in stone, so to speak. "I'd like to find a way to move forward that will work for both of us."

Jasper closed his eyes and gave a subtle shake of his head, as if to say *this is a pointless waste of time.* "I'm listening," came his reluctant reply.

Carleton chose to focus on the practical matters he could do something about rather than worry about changing opinions that would never respond to logic. "The way I see it, we have two main issues: safety and productivity. We need to figure out a way for me to work without endangering your crews and with minimal disruption."

Jasper looked skeptical. "And how do ye intend to do that?"

"I'll need your help for the safety part. I'll try to reduce the concussion I create with my spell casting, but I can't eliminate it entirely, so we'll have to accommodate it somehow. At a minimum, we should move the miners away from the area while I work. Also, it would be good if we could add supports closer to the face where I'll be working. I don't want to get crushed by falling rock any more than your men do."

Jasper nodded. "If ye don't have to be right at the face, the chisel crew can support an area nearby."

"Chisel crew?"

"The crew that builds the archways. We also call 'em the fourth crew. The quad has three crews of muckers who handle the digging and one chisel crew to build supports."

So far, Carleton had seen only muckers. He'd assumed that the digging crews also built the supports. "Why haven't I seen them?"

"They gather a lot of material from the surface, so they work fourth shift while the sun sleeps." Jasper's tone grew impatient as the conversation drifted from the problem at hand. "While I appreciate yer concern for the safety of me men, everything ye've suggested so far is going to create more work and slow things down."

"Right," Carleton agreed. "Productivity is the second issue we need to address. I'll try to interrupt your crews as little as possible, but I need to experiment with different ways of casting the spell so I can improve my range and sensitivity."

Jasper's brows drew together with concern. "I can't have ye shuttin' down me crews for experiments."

"I understand. I'll only work at the face when I'm ready to do some actual prospecting for my report to Mr. McLaury. The rest of the time, I can work somewhere else where I'm not in the way. I was thinking about using the abandoned crosscut. Could we light it for my use?"

Jasper seemed surprised by the suggestion, and then pursed his lips thoughtfully while slowly nodding. "Aye. That we could."

"Excellent. I might even be able to locate another vein of ore."

Jasper turned an intent gaze on Carleton. "Ye do that, and ye'll be worth all the trouble ye're making."

Carleton grinned. It seemed he may have found a way to win over the miners. "I'll do my best. Do you think it will be safe for me to work at the face of the crosscut?"

"I'll have the chisel crew check it out for ye. If it needs shoring, they'll take care of it tonight."

"Thank you," Carleton said. "I'll plan on working there tomorrow morning. Do you have any other concerns we need to address?"

"When I do, ye'll be first to know." He stood and waited for Carleton to do the same.

Carleton followed Jasper to the main passage and took his leave. Pausing at the entrance of the mine to wait for his eyes to adjust to the bright sunlight outside, he wondered if he and Jasper had worked out a plan that would satisfy Bart.

The manager expected instant results, but that wasn't how magic worked. All wizards knew a core set of spells that could be called upon from memory, but most activity in the field had to be customized for the local environment. His training at Harvard had been focused on how to adapt his skills to whatever the situation demanded, but adaptation took time and patience.

The organic catalysts he'd brought with him were serviceable, but spells always worked better with catalysts obtained from the local area. He needed to learn about desert flora and fauna quickly. Then he would have the distasteful chore of hunting down specimens that could contribute to his stock.

Carleton had to talk Bart into trusting him to get the job done at his own pace. As the morning's events had shown, working in the mine was potentially dangerous. Pressuring him to do too much too fast might get someone killed.

Chapter 11

Experimentation

True to his word, Jasper had the chisel crew prepare the crosscut passageway. When Carleton arrived the following morning, candle lanterns flickered in the crosscut and a new stone arch reinforced the passage a few feet back from the face.

Glad to be able to work without the noise and attitudes of the miners, Carleton set up his equipment case directly under the new archway. He selected several bottles containing the new organic catalysts he wanted to try.

The previous afternoon, he had been surprised when Perry showed up to check on the peccaries and see how Carleton was faring. After learning that Carleton was planning to spend the afternoon searching for burrowing creatures, he suggested that they take a ride into Pearce instead. Perry knew a man who ran one of the livery stables and was a part-time taxidermist. The fellow had an extensive collection of "critter parts."

After an unexpectedly enjoyable and productive afternoon in town with Perry, Carleton had returned to the bunkhouse with serviceable work clothes, a portable candle lantern, and a few new organic catalysts to try with his spells. He hoped one of the new catalysts would increase his range so he could give Bart a good progress report.

He held up the bottle tagged "horned lizard claw." He had picked up many other animal and plant bits during his excursion, and acquiring them had been unpleasant. Back home in Baltimore, Carleton would have gone to his favorite wizard supply shop to purchase what he needed. The taxidermist's studio in Pearce had been a much less sanitary shopping experience. The place stank of decaying flesh, and many of the parts were still attached to the original owner.

Having to use organic catalysts for spells was one of the things Carleton liked least about wizardry. He hated killing things himself to get what he needed, but he had no illusion that buying the parts from someone else didn't make the creatures just as dead.

Carleton vowed to himself that he'd create a casting stone as soon as possible. It took a lot of work to transform a spell into a permanent device, but once he did, he'd no longer need an organic catalyst. All he'd have to do is feed swi into the device, the same way he was able to use the casting stones on his wrist band.

But first he had to optimize the spell with the best catalysts possible. Only then would it make sense to begin imprinting a stone.

Carleton still had the ore sample Tully had given him the day before. With the ore, a lizard claw, and his brass casting ring in hand, he evaluated the end of the passage.

Tapping around the face for soft spots, he began to understand why the passage had been abandoned. The solid limestone face showed little ore-bearing quartz like the vein they were following down Main Drift. The crosscut had served its purpose of measuring the vein's width.

Using a casting ring on a vertical surface was tricky at the best of times, and since Carleton couldn't find a soft spot to press it into, he kneeled and put it on the floor instead. He was experimenting, so it wouldn't matter if he lost a few feet of range.

Placing the ore and the lizard claw inside the ring, Carleton put his palm over the ring and chanted the incantation. He had altered the wording so the spell would detect the quartz gangue that surrounded the precious metals in his sample because he had no idea how rich the ore was at the end of the crosscut. If he failed to find gold or silver, he wouldn't be able to tell if his spell wasn't working or if the metals simply weren't present. Quartz was one of the most common minerals in the earth's crust, so he was confident he could use it as a calibration material.

Finishing the incantation, Carleton pressed the ring into the soil and activated the spell. The expected concussion thudded into the ground as his awareness flowed into the stone at his feet.

As he had anticipated, quartz infiltrated the surrounding rock in abundance. The spell made it glow like cloud streamers at sunrise, twisting and dipping until the formations trailed off at the limit of his range. He was about to shift his viewpoint to another section of wall when the spell was suddenly interrupted and he returned to his body.

Dust swirled into his field of vision and a few chunks of rocky debris rolled past him from behind. Startled, Carleton stood and turned around. A large chunk of rock rested on the ground a few feet behind him. He peered at the irregular surface of the ceiling and easily spotted the cavity where the rock had originated. It had fallen from the other side of the support arch.

How could the chisel crew have missed such a dangerous weak spot? It was right next to where they'd been working, and delvans reputedly had a sixth sense when it came to underground dangers. If a rock that size had landed directly on top of him, he might have been killed.

A chill ran down his back. Maybe that was the idea. Carleton shook his head, halting the train of thought. No. If the delvans wanted him dead, he would be dead. The loose rock might have truly been an oversight, or it might have been a warning. A warning that angered him more than frightened him. He had to figure out a way to make them back off until he had the chance to prove himself. He made a mental note to report the incident to Jasper as soon as he was finished for the day.

Carleton gathered his equipment and moved back to the previous archway. He figured he'd be safer at an older support that had already proven its stability, and he didn't really need to be at the face to conduct his experiments anyway.

Disturbed by the close call, Carleton checked out the exposed head-wall on both sides of the wide archway. His inspection revealed nothing illuminating. To him, the passageway ceilings all looked pretty much the same. Shrugging, he set up a new workstation and made notes about the lizard-claw experiment in his journal.

For his next attempt, he tried a sliver of dragon claw. The small vial of dragon-claw slivers had been his most expensive purchase. Dragons were rare and it was illegal to hunt them. All aveni lands were dragon refuges, and Perry said that the avens would immediately execute anyone caught hunting the creatures in their territory. Perry had personally vouched for the three claws that the taxidermist owned. He'd traded with the avens for them himself, knowing the taxidermist would be thrilled with the find.

Carleton finished the incantation of his spell and released swi into the casting ring. To his surprise, the dragon claw absorbed the power, but it didn't transmute. Without the organic catalyst, his spell faltered and failed.

Carleton lifted his hand and verified that the dragon-claw sliver was still inside the ring. It was apparently resistant to transmutation, which was good information to file away for future reference. Unfortunately, even a failed spell consumed some of his limited energy and reduced the number of experiments he'd be able to conduct that day.

On his second try, he gave the dragon claw extra time to absorb enough swi to transmute. What he forgot was that overcoming the claw's resistance resulted in a stronger geomantic concussion when the spell activated. A few small rocks trailing veils of dust fell from the head-wall in both directions, nearly disrupting the spell.

Carleton closed his eyes to block out the distraction and concentrated on pushing his awareness through the casting ring and into the earth.

The dragon claw made a huge difference. He followed the quartz deposits for twice as far as had been possible with the lizard claw, and the formations stood out sharply from the surrounding material. If the spell worked as well when he searched for gold and silver, he'd have great news for Bart.

As much as he wanted to spend more time exploring, Carleton drew back. He was consuming precious power with every moment. Withdrawing his awareness, he terminated the spell.

Standing, he turned in response to more thumps in the passage behind him. While he watched, another rock fell. He could barely see the next candle lantern through the haze of dust that was building. Then another rock fell. The floor had become littered with stones of various sizes.

Carleton glanced at his equipment case and wondered if he had time to get it and escape the crosscut before the ceiling collapsed. He was answered by a rumble and a cascade of rock and dirt between the archway and his only exit.

Quickly grabbing his case and lantern, Carleton turned to move deeper into the crosscut, away from the unstable section of head-wall. His first step landed on a rock that rolled out from under his foot. He fell headlong, letting go of the case and lantern as he tried to break his fall. The items crashed to the ground and the lantern went out.

Rocks bumped against the bottoms of his boots. He had to get farther away from the cave-in or risk being buried alive. Levering himself up in preparation to run, everything went dark when a heavy blow to the base of his neck threw him back to the ground.

~

Carleton regained consciousness, coughing and blinking. Dim light from a wall lantern farther down the crosscut fluctuated through the roiling cloud of gritty dust that enveloped him. He tried to crawl forward, but something pinned his aching legs in place. A glance over his shoulder revealed that his feet and calves were covered with loose debris.

"Wizard Kazimer! Are ye there?" called Flint in a muffled voice.

Hazy half-conscious memory and the frantic tone in the delvan's voice hinted that Flint had called out to him several times already.

"I'm here!" Carleton yelled as he twisted painfully around to move the rocks that trapped his legs. Floating dust invaded his lungs and every cough seemed to draw in more. He quickly covered his mouth with the bandanna he wore around his neck.

"Praise the Father! Are ye hurt?"

After withdrawing his legs from the rubble, Carleton rotated his ankles and massaged the tender spots on his legs and his neck. Nothing seemed broken. "I'm a little bruised, but otherwise okay." He glanced up at the head-wall and added, "At least for now."

His equipment case was on its side but seemed undamaged. The contents were another matter, depending upon how hard the case had landed when he dropped it. Crawling over to his lantern, he pushed the candle back into its base and lit the wick. A small crack marred the glass and the bottom had a new dent, but thanks to its simple design, the lantern still worked fine.

Straining to see through the dust, Carleton inspected the collapse more carefully, wondering how he was able to hear Flint. It appeared that most of the rock had originated from the right side of the passage, leaving a small gap in the upper left corner.

A few bumps and thumps carried though the pile, and a moment later, a hand came through the gap and waved. "Can ye see me hand?" Flint asked.

"Yes! I see it."

"Okay, good. Don't worry, we'll get ye out of there. I'll be right back with some help." After a little more rustling from the other side of the pile, Carleton was left in silence.

While he waited for Flint to return, Carleton checked out the area around the collapse, ready to run if any more rock fell. The stone archway was still intact, which was an encouraging testament to the strength of the supports. Most of the rubble seemed to have fallen from the ceiling on the other side of the support. The cave-in would have been a lot worse if more material had come loose or if the archway had failed.

Carleton grimaced and shook his head. Things weren't looking good for the future of his employment at the mine if the head-wall disintegrated every time he cast a spell. But it didn't seem reasonable that such things kept happening. It wasn't the first time he'd worked underground, and his spell concussions weren't that strong. When the delvans had used dynamite, the tremor from the detonations would have been ten times stronger than what he had caused—maybe a hundred times stronger.

"Ye still there, Carleton?"

Flint was back.

"Yes, I'm here," Carleton answered.

"The crew was on their way to investigate the noise, so we're ready to get started. But we don't want ye to try to help from your side. Go back and wait by the next support until I tell you it be safe to come through."

"Okay. I understand." Before Carleton had finished speaking, the clunk and rumble of rocks being moved was already carrying through the pile. He picked up his case and retreated down the passage toward the new archway as Flint had instructed.

While he waited, Carleton put away the casting ring and ore sample that he'd hastily slipped into his pockets at the time of the collapse. Although the drop had jostled some of the contents out of position, nothing inside the case was broken. He closed the case and sat on it while he waited for word from Flint, pondering how the new disaster was going to play with Bart and Jasper. Both would undoubtedly be furious.

Carleton sighed. He wished he could gather his things and leave Commonwealth Mine behind forever, but that wasn't an option any longer. When he first arrived, he'd had enough money to get back home, but since then he'd spent a good portion of his stake on supplies and clothes, with the expectation that his pay would make up for it. Contract or no contract, he suspected he was going to have trouble getting his money from Bart, considering how little progress he'd made so far.

It wasn't all bad news. His experiments had been instructive. All he needed to do was figure out why the mine was so fragile. Either the delvan chisel crew was incompetent, or something else was going on. Considering the cool reception he'd received so far, sabotage wasn't out of the question, but as far as he knew, none of these delvans had a specific reason to harm him.

He was so lost in his thoughts that he didn't realize the sound of rock movement had died down until footsteps approached. Carleton stood as Flint appeared, his face creased with worry.

"Let's get ye out of here," he said.

Carleton grabbed his equipment case and followed the miner back to the collapsed area. Tully was peering up into the cavity the material had fallen from. When he spotted Carleton, he waved him forward. "Let me see that lantern of yers for a minute."

He took the lantern and scrambled up the pile. After a moment of inspecting the cavity, he hopped down and handed the lantern back to Carleton. He was frowning and his lips were pressed into a thin line.

Flint noticed his distracted expression. "What?"

Tully glanced at Carleton before answering. "We'll talk later. Get the wizard to safety first."

Carleton almost objected. He wanted to know what was on Tully's mind, but the foreman obviously didn't trust him enough to speak in front of him. Flint took his arm and tugged him toward the crawl space the crew had created.

Carleton went through first, pushing his case ahead of him. A pair of thick hands lifted the case out of the way as it came through on the other side. After Carleton clambered down, the case was thrust at him. "Thanks," he mumbled as he took it back. He received a grunt in response.

Flint led him back to Main Drift. The cart and one of the peccaries waited at the intersection.

"I was coming back down for another load when I felt a tremor and heard the collapse," Flint explained. "Did ye cause the tremor?"

"Probably. I cast a spell right before the collapse occurred."

The two men stared at each other for a moment, not sure what to say. Carleton spoke first. "Have there been a lot of stability problems in this mine?"

"No," Flint answered. "Our *stability problems* started after ye arrived." Carleton could have taken the words as an accusation, but Flint's musing tone put a different spin on them.

"I've been wondering about that," Carleton said cautiously. "I'm not normally this accident-prone or oblivious to dangerous conditions underground."

Flint was so preoccupied with his own thoughts that he barely registered Carleton's comment. "This shouldn't have happened. Cragg be one of the best in the business, or so I've heard."

Cragg. Why did that name keep coming up whenever Carleton had trouble? "What does Cragg Steel have to do with this?"

"Cragg is the new foreman of the chisel crew. He came on about when ye did. Don't care much for the way he waves his religion around, but I don't have to deal with him much."

The crews split the day into four overlapping ten-hour shifts starting at midnight, with a new shift coming on every six hours. The chisel crew worked from nine o'clock at night until four in the morning, so it was no wonder Carleton had never interacted with them.

To hear Jasper tell it, Cragg was one of Carleton's most outspoken critics. As foreman of the chisel crew, he was also responsible for reinforcing the crosscut.

Purposeful booted strides advanced down the passageway toward them from the direction of the entrance. Flint tilted his head toward the sound. "That will be Jasper. Tell him all ye can about what happened, and I'll try to find out what

Tully's thinking." Flint hurried down the crosscut without waiting for a response.

Carleton walked up the passage toward Jasper, intercepting the mine supervisor after a few strides.

"What's going on down here?" Jasper demanded.

"The crosscut collapsed near where I was working."

Jasper looked Carleton up and down. "Are ye hurt?"

"Just bruised. I got out of the way in time. It was a small collapse. Your crew was able to open a crawl space for me fairly quickly."

Jasper blew out his breath and shook his head. "I can't decide if ye're very lucky or very unlucky, wizard. Either way, ye're makin' a mountain o' trouble."

Carleton chose his next words carefully. "I suspect my luck or lack thereof is being … influenced."

Jasper frowned and then rubbed his beard. "Let's not jump to conclusions. Mr. McLaury will want to know the full story, and we'll let him sort it out. Come along now and I'll start me report with yer account."

Carleton followed the mine supervisor back to the subtown dining room, which seemed to double as his office. He wasn't looking forward to the eventual conversation with Bart, but he was encouraged that Tully and Flint seemed to be as disturbed as he was by what had happened.

~

Carleton sat in a chair on the covered front porch of the mine manager's residence, watching a small gray lizard crawl past his boots. It turned its head to look up at him before sprinting off the edge of the porch and out of view. A few seconds later, it reappeared on top of a nearby rock and looked back.

Carleton smiled and thought, *I won't hurt you, but it's good to be wary, little lizard.*

Without warning, a small striped hawk swept past, leaving empty space where the lizard had been. The hawk lifted itself back into the sky with powerful wing strokes, the prize dangling from its grasping talons.

Carleton's surprise turned to wry amusement. *Sorry about the distraction, little guy. I guess the trick to survival is applying your wariness to the most dangerous threat of the moment.*

The clop-clop of hooves announced the arrival of a visitor. Remington trotted up with Perry in the saddle. Perry stopped his horse at the hitching rail next to the house. Flipping the reins around the rail, he patted the horse's neck and ambled over to the porch.

"Hey, Carleton. How are things?" he asked with a grin as he stepped up onto the porch and leaned against a support post. "I figured you'd be down in the mine showing the delvans how it's done."

Carleton shook his head. "The delvans aren't impressed with my magical prowess. I've had nothing but bad luck with this job since I started. Between the teamsters and the delvans, I figure I'm lucky to still be alive." He hadn't meant to whine at Perry, but his low state of mind made the words spill from his mouth.

Perry sat down and adopted a serious tone. "The teamsters giving you trouble?"

"I had some trouble when I first arrived. I feel like I need to sleep with one eye open, if you get what I mean."

"If things get too bad, I have an extra room you can use," Perry said.

Carleton considered the offer. A room at Perry's ranch would seem like lavish accommodations compared to the bunkhouse. "How would I get back and forth? Seems like a long walk."

"We'd figure something out. I'm out and about most days, and I could drop you off and pick you up. You could borrow one of my horses or buy one of your own. Hell, if it came to walking, it's only about forty-five minutes using a few trails I could show you."

The proposal sounded like a lot of inconvenience for Perry. "Thanks for the offer. I may take you up on it at some point, but I think I have things worked out for now."

Perry reached over and slapped Carleton on the shoulder. "Let me know if you change your mind. The teamsters can be a prickly bunch, but most of them are all right once they get to know you. Buy them a beer, and all will be forgiven."

Carleton chuckled. "If I ever get paid, that might not be a bad idea. Right now, I'm waiting to see if I still have a job."

"Something to do with the delvan trouble you mentioned?"

"Every time I use magic," Carleton explained, "rock starts falling. This is either the most incompetent bunch of miners in the West, which I doubt, or this mine is pure bad luck for me."

Perry raised an eyebrow. "Maybe it ain't luck that's the problem."

"You're thinking sabotage?" When Perry nodded, Carleton went on. "I've considered that, but Jasper seems willing to give me a chance, and none of the delvans know me well enough to wish me trouble."

"Maybe it isn't about *who* you are so much as *what* you are."

Carleton threw up his hands in frustration. "But the work I do would help them, if the head-wall would quit falling in on us."

Perry shrugged. "Just thinking out loud. People take all kinds of notions into their heads. You never know when one of those notions will turn them against you."

"Can't argue with that," Carleton said with a frown.

The front door of the house opened and Bart came out onto the porch, followed by Jasper. Carleton rose to his feet while Perry remained seated.

With a grim frown, Bart went straight to the point. "I'm not happy about what's been happening, Wizard Kazimer. I should probably cancel your contract right now, but Supervisor Underlight has convinced me that you aren't completely responsible for the collapse."

Carleton's eyes cut over to Jasper, whose expression was unreadable behind his dark goggles. He had trouble hiding his surprise that the mine supervisor had supported him. He dipped his head once in thanks, but the miner didn't respond.

"I'm giving you one more chance," Bart continued. "Tomorrow morning, you are demonstrating whatever good has come out of this experimenting you've been doing. I want results. If I don't get them, I'm letting you go."

"I understand, sir," Carleton replied. "I'll be ready."

Bart looked down at Jasper. "I want that rubble cleaned out by tomorrow. Tell your men they'll be looking for new digs if it happens again." Turning to Perry, he said, "Mr. Maine, come on inside."

With that, Bart went back into the house. Jasper turned to leave, but he stopped when Carleton said, "Thank you for not speaking against me."

Jasper turned and faced Carleton. "I knew ye were trouble the day I met ye, but I won't lie to cover up a problem with me crews. I'll get to the truth of it, but in the meantime, ye'd best watch yer back."

Carleton sighed. "That seems to be the theme of my existence since I arrived here."

Jasper's mouth twisted into a half smile as he left the porch. He strutted away toward the mine road with a determined waddling gait.

"That was interesting," Perry observed.

"And unexpected," Carleton responded. "If this demonstration is my last chance, I'd better get busy preparing for it."

"Anything I can do to help?" Perry asked.

Carleton had everything he needed except for time. "Not that I can think of, but I appreciate the offer. I'm not sure why you've been so generous to me, but I want you to know that your friendship means a lot."

Perry grinned. "Aw, don't get all sentimental on me, now. You're a good man, Carleton. People like you and me will be the ones to carve a civilized existence out of this wild and lawless land. It's gonna take some work, so keep your cinch tight and your guns loose."

Carleton chuckled. Not having either a horse or a gun, he had to take the expression in the spirit it was given.

Perry rose from his chair. "Well, I guess I'd better get inside and see what Bart wants." He stopped with his hand on the doorknob. "If you change your mind about staying at the ranch, let me know, or just come on up."

Carleton shook Perry's hand and thanked him again. As Perry went inside, Carleton walked across the street to the bunkhouse.

Carleton picked through his trunk for his spell encyclopedia. Carrying the book and his equipment case, he went for a walk in search of a shady spot away from the buildings. He had a few ideas for improving his odds of performing a successful demonstration in the morning.

CHAPTER 12

Demonstration

The next morning, Carleton prepared for his demonstration under Bart's watchful eyes. He set up in the stope that the miners had been working the first time he came into the mine. The drift continued on from the stope, but the passageway narrowed, leaving too little room for everyone to observe.

He had quite a crowd. *I should have sold tickets*, he thought. Bart had invited Penelope, Jasper, and the three crew foreman. The six observers filled the cavern, leaving Carleton barely enough room to kneel on the floor a few feet from the opening that led to the face.

Carleton was used to working with an audience, so that didn't bother him. He was also used to observers who were either fascinated by what he was doing or repelled by it. It was usually a combination of both, and that morning was no exception. A backward glance showed Penelope leaning forward, watching with interest. She gave him an encouraging smile. Bart had his arms folded, his face wearing an impatient scowl, as usual. Jasper, Tully, and the other three delvan crew foremen watched, but they stayed behind the others.

For a moment, Carleton wondered if their wariness was due to the expectation of another collapse, but he doubted they would have put themselves and their boss in the chamber without checking it thoroughly for weaknesses. Someone might have it out for him, but would that person risk hurting everyone? He doubted it.

Carleton's gaze lingered on the men who were least familiar to him. Deep in the mine, the delvans didn't need to obscure their faces with goggles or hoods. One man watched the proceedings with detached curiosity; the other stared directly at him with an unflinching intensity that made his skin crawl. He turned back to his preparations, certain that the intense delvan was Cragg Steel, the chisel-crew foreman.

He chose the dragon claw for his demonstration, having determined that it was the best catalyst he had. He set a special piece of it into the brass ring along with the ore sample. The catalyst was special because he'd worked on it the previous day, conditioning it for the spell. His encyclopedia had given him the answer he needed for attenuating geomantic concussion. Conditioning the dragon claw made it less resistant to transmutation. Unfortunately, it would also be slightly less effective, but it still worked better than any other catalyst.

Carleton's portable lamp was next to him, illuminating his efforts. He hoped it would give enough light for his audience to see what he was about to do.

"Once I get started here, please don't interrupt me," Carleton said. "We can talk again once the spell is going."

"Fine. Get on with it," Bart said.

Carleton placed his hand over the brass ring and began his incantation. He'd made a few alterations to the spell. He figured that if Bart wanted a demonstration, he'd give him an impressive one. At the end of his incantation, the concussion from the spell's activation was satisfyingly mild.

Instead of sending his awareness into the surrounding rock, Carleton picked up a vial of crushed pyrite and held it above the space in front of his chest. As he tapped the tiny particles out of the vial in a line away from his body, they floated and sparkled in a thin, irregular cloud, forming a suspended image. When the last tap of pyrite fell to the floor without adding to the image, Carleton put the vial down.

"What you see here is a representation of the ore vein," he said, carefully maintaining a flow of swi to support the spell. "Each inch is roughly ten feet, so I'd say we're looking at about a hundred-and-twenty feet of ore here."

Everyone crowded closer to see the image Carleton had created. Even the delvans leaned in, curiosity overcoming their aversion.

"How do I know you aren't making this up?" Bart asked.

"He isn't," Penelope answered in a barely audible whisper.

Well, Carleton thought, *at least I have one believer.*

Carleton pointed toward a location about a quarter of the way down the floating image. The sparkling pyrite broke and shifted before continuing. "See this? In another thirty feet or so, the vein is going to come to an abrupt end at a fault. The vein continues, but it shifts up and to the left a bit after a gap of a few feet."

Jasper's voice came from behind. "That just saved us a few days of useless digging. When we lose the vein, we usually work the face clockwise until we find it again. If this is right, we wouldn't have picked up the vein until we'd gone almost all the way around."

Tully added, "Aye, and with that big of a gap, we might have given up, thinking we'd lost it entirely."

His demonstration complete, Carleton ended the spell. The pyrite dust fell onto a strip of cloth he'd lain on the floor to catch it. It had taken him quite a while to gather enough pyrite to use for the demonstration, and he didn't want to waste it.

"How long until the crews reach that shift?" Bart asked.

Tully answered, "Two or three days."

After rolling up the cloth, Carleton rose and faced Bart.

The mine manager said, "Wizard, you just earned yourself another three days. If that shift happens the way you say it will, I'll be happy to keep you on." He turned and left with the delvans in his wake.

Penelope remained behind. "That was an impressive demonstration."

Carleton ducked his head and smiled. "Thanks. I'm glad you think so. Bart didn't seem to think much of it."

Penelope dismissed his comment with a wave of her hand. "Bart is a formidable taskmaster, but not a good leader. The closest he can come to a compliment is telling you he won't fire you today."

Carleton chuckled. "So I've noticed."

She pointed toward the rolled-up cloth Carleton had used to catch the pyrite. "Creating a visual representation of the vein was a brilliant approach. Very convincing."

Carleton's face heated at her praise. "I must admit that was mostly showmanship. Using other techniques, I can prospect in much more detail." Did that sound like bragging? He didn't want her to think him immodest.

Her comment regarding his approach implied that she knew he could have done things differently. "You seem to understand a lot more about magic than most people."

"Magic has always been fascinating to me," she said with a smile. "And you aren't the first wizard I've met, you know."

Penelope's tone suggested something more than a casual acquaintance. It occurred to Carleton that he'd never checked her hand for a wedding band. It would be too obvious to do so right then, so he resisted the urge and said, "Ah, your husband, perhaps?"

She surprised him by giggling. "Why Mr. Kazimer, is that your way of expressing interest in my marital status?"

Blushing furiously, Carleton stuttered, "Um, no ma'am. I apologize if the question was impolite."

Penelope stepped forward and put her hand on his face. Her skin was cold against the heat of his embarrassment, but the intimate gesture made his heart pound. "Oh, Carleton," she said. "You're such a dear. You really don't belong in this nest of miscreants."

She seemed to recognize how forward she was being. She stiffened and stepped back, creating a disappointingly wide gap between them. She took a deep breath and let it out. "In answer to your question, no—my late husband was not a wizard." She lifted her left hand and gazed down at the gold band that adorned her ring finger. She went on in a sad tone. "There were many magical things about our marriage, but they weren't enough to save him."

She was a widow who continued to wear her wedding ring.

"I'm sorry for your loss," Carleton said in a soft voice. "And I'm sorry for bringing up painful memories,"

Penelope shrugged. "It's all right. I've had plenty of time to grieve. Survivors must continue to face the challenges of life without the support of the departed."

"Penelope! It's time to leave," Bart called from farther up the passage.

"I'm coming," she answered over her shoulder. Addressing Carleton again, she said, "I must be going now. Congratulations on the success of your demonstration, Wizard Kazimer."

Carleton was both disappointed and relieved by the sudden end to their conversation. He responded to her formal goodbye in kind. "Thank you, Mrs. Cartwright. I hope you have a pleasant day."

"And you," she said before striding out of the chamber. Her baggy pants and loose-fitting shirt couldn't hide her feminine grace or her beauty. Captivated, Carleton watched her depart, lifting a hand in farewell when she glanced back and waved over her shoulder.

Carleton began packing up his equipment. Tully's crew wouldn't delay their return to work for long. He hoped to be gone before they showed up and started complaining about him being in the way.

But the way the delvan foremen had reacted to his demonstration encouraged him. They had walked away in a tight group, conversing with Jasper about how they would act on the new information Carleton had provided. Even Cragg had followed along quietly, perhaps reconsidering his position. Would proving his worth cause the mysterious accidents to cease? Maybe they could all finally get on with their jobs.

CHAPTER 13

Hide and Seek

Carleton was startled awake by the loud crash of someone slamming open the bunkhouse door. Brushing the sleep out of his eyes, he turned his head to see Bart standing in the doorway with a lantern in his hand.

"Get up!" he bellowed. "All of you. Get your asses out front pronto."

The room erupted in groans as men clambered out of bed. Some started to get dressed, but Bart yelled again. "I said now! I don't care if you're dressed or naked. Get a move on."

Carleton's proximity to the door made him one of the first to exit. As he passed Bart, the man's hot breath washed over him. The hand that held the lantern shook hard enough to make the top rattle slightly. The boss was seriously agitated.

The men lined up along the side of the bunkhouse like undisciplined troops for a surprise inspection. Willie was the last man to leave the building, and Bart pulled him aside. "You keep an eye on these curs," he ordered. Then he disappeared into the bunkhouse.

The sun was just below the horizon, dawn tinting the desert with coral pink. The men wrapped their arms around themselves and stood with their legs tight together to ward off the morning chill. Most were dressed in long underwear, but the less fortunate were bare-chested.

"What's this about?" Jacob asked Willie.

"No idea," the foreman responded. "Best keep quiet until we find out."

Thumps and crashes came from inside the bunkhouse. It sounded like Bart was tearing the place apart. The men looked at each other with a mixture of annoyance and fear. Whatever the purpose of Bart's search, it didn't bode well for someone.

After a few minutes, some of the men were starting to shiver and Bart's cursing and riffling grew more violent. Finally, the search ended and Bart strode out of the bunkhouse with a shotgun in his hand.

He handed his lantern to Willie and walked the line of men until he stood in front of Carleton.

"You want to explain this, wizard?"

Carleton wasn't sure what Bart was asking. Explain what? "It looks like a shotgun," he said in confusion. Stars exploded in Carleton's vision as Bart whipped the butt of the weapon around and whacked him in the side of the face.

"Don't get smart with me!" Bart yelled, leaning in close. Carleton could see every vein in his angry red eyes. "You must be stupid to think you could steal it and hide it right under my nose. Did you think I wouldn't come looking?"

Clutching his throbbing cheekbone with his right hand, Carleton narrowed his eyes at Bart. "I didn't take it."

Bart looked like he might hit Carleton again, but then took a deep breath and stepped back a pace. "You're not only a thief, you're a liar. I found it in your trunk. You're lucky it isn't loaded, or I'd let you have it with both barrels right now."

Dell spoke up and said, "You can borrow my gun, if you want, boss."

"Shut up, Dell," Willie and Bart shouted at the same time. As the young man cowered, Bart added, "If I want anything from you, I'll ask for it. And that ain't likely."

Turning back to Carleton, he said, "I've wasted enough time and money on you. Your contract is canceled. And you can count on that Guild of yours hearing in detail about what a stinking mess you made of this job."

Carleton's hands closed into fists at his sides. He dearly wanted to take that gun from Bart's hands and hit him back. Then he'd beat Dell until the smug creep told what he knew about how the shotgun ended up in his trunk. He had a feeling Dell was responsible, and even if he wasn't, the bastard probably knew who was.

But Bart was bigger, stronger, and meaner. He was also in charge. If Carleton made a move, Willie would step in and things would only get worse from there. Bart wasn't listening, and nothing Carleton could say would make any difference to the angry man, although with a little time, he might be able to prove his innocence.

Bart spat at Carleton's feet and walked over to Willie. Taking his lantern from the foreman, he said, "Get him out of here on the first load to Cochise. If I see him again, I'm likely to put a bullet in him." Willie acknowledged the order with a nod.

Bart turned and addressed the rest of the men. "When you join this outfit, you get a clean slate. I don't care what you did before. But if you bring trouble with you, I'll run you out of here faster than a rattlesnake strike." He turned and started back toward the house.

Willie waited until Bart was nearly to the front porch before speaking to the men. "Might as well start the day," he said. "Get dressed and get the first load ready to go. I'll take care of this myself." The men gratefully hurried back into the bunkhouse.

As Carleton moved toward the door, Willie stopped him with a raised hand. "Well, you got yourself into it this time. I warned you the boss wouldn't tolerate no stealing or fighting."

Carleton stared into Willie's eyes. He didn't see the same accusing look Bart had leveled at him. "You know I didn't take that shotgun."

Willie glanced toward the bunkhouse and lowered his voice. "I got my doubts. But the boss wasn't of a mind for a debate. You ain't a good fit for this operation anyways, so I suggest you take advantage of the excuse to be quit of it. Now go get your things together and I'll get you out of here."

Carleton went inside and collected the mess Bart had made of his belongings, studiously ignoring the other men. He felt their eyes on him, but none of the teamsters said anything. His thoughts spiraled as his frustration and anger grew. Commonwealth had been the source of nothing but trouble from the day he'd arrived. He'd faced bullying, thievery, and even threats on his life. Willie was right. He should be glad for the opportunity to get away from the godforsaken place.

But being forced to leave in disgrace for a crime he didn't commit rankled him. What would Penelope think of him? Would the Guild sanction him? A botched contract could set his career back or ruin it altogether. Meanwhile, the real thief was probably right there in the bunkhouse with him, snickering about how easy it had been to set him up.

Where would he go? He couldn't go back to Baltimore. He didn't have enough money to make it that far, even if he did want to give the Munsey gang another shot at him. Maybe he should keep going west. Arizona was full of mining towns. Surely someone would appreciate what he could do for them. It was obvious from his reception that few wizards had chosen to brave the Western Frontier before him.

Carleton finished packing up and dragged his trunk out to the front of the bunkhouse. He sat on the lid, his equipment case by his side. Seething with thoughts of retribution, he almost wished Dell would come out and heckle him. He had nothing to lose at that point, and his muscles ached for a pugilistic workout.

Dell didn't go along with that plan, however. When the young teamster left the bunkhouse, he stayed clear of Carleton and headed straight toward the stable. He spared an insolent smirk in passing, but that was it.

Willie drove up on an ore wagon pulled by a team of four big mules. Jacob rode alongside on a rangy black horse. Willie helped Carleton put the trunk on top of the pile of ore behind the bench seat, working it into a depression to keep it from falling off. Carleton joined Willie on the seat and put his equipment case at his feet. Willie snapped the reins and they rolled away from Commonwealth.

Carleton glanced back only once. Penelope stood on the front porch of the manager's residence, watching the wagon roll away. Carleton hated to think what she must have been thinking of him right then. She was one of the few people to show him some kindness, but the evidence made him out to be a liar and a thief.

He shook his head with disgust. What did it matter? He'd never see her again.

But it did matter, at least a little. What bothered him most was what Penelope, Flint, and Perry would think of him. They were the only three friends he had in the entire West.

Jacob interrupted his thoughts. "Didn't even make it a week, hey Carl? Hell, even I thought you'd last longer than that. Didn't figure you for no thief, though."

Carleton kept his eyes on the road ahead while he answered. "Not that I care what you think, but I didn't steal that shotgun. Someone, maybe even you, put it in my trunk."

Jacob spat on the ground and huffed out a laugh. "Weren't me. This is too sweet a job to risk gettin' caught with my hands on Bart's shotgun. Whoever did it had a powerful reason."

Dammit. Even Jacob seemed willing to accept Carleton's claim of being framed. The only people who seemed to believe him so far were people who wouldn't or couldn't help him. Carleton shook his head and said aloud to himself, "I don't even like guns."

Willie sighed and said, "I noticed that. More than anything, that's what gave me doubts about you stealing the shotgun. But that's an attitude you may want to reconsider. You seem to attract trouble, and you'd best be prepared for it."

"I appreciate the advice," Carleton replied, "but I have other means of protecting myself. I don't own a gun because I've never needed one."

"Suit yourself," Willie said with a shrug.

The wagon rolled through downtown Pearce, which was still pretty quiet that early in the morning. The town sheriff was sitting on a chair outside his office reading a newspaper. He nodded at the trio as they went by and Willie raised a hand in greeting.

Carleton supposed that Bart could have had him arrested and thrown in jail for the theft. At least he had avoided that ignominious turn of events. He breathed a little easier when they had left Pearce behind and were well on their way toward the train depot at Cochise.

"Where will you go?" Willie asked.

Carleton was tempted to respond, *what do you care?* But Willie didn't deserve to be the object of his sour mood. "I'm not sure. Further west, probably. I'm low on cash and thought I might find work in Tucson."

Willie seemed to be deep in thought about something. He spoke in a reluctant tone, as if he wasn't sure about his words. "You might consider staying close for a few days."

The suggestion made no sense. "What for?" Carleton asked.

"The boss has a quick and mean temper, but he's no fool," Willie continued. "Let him cool down for a day or so, and he might start putting some things together. He still wants a wizard. If the real thief comes to light, it will be a lot faster and cheaper to bring you back than to get a new wizard out here."

Carleton wasn't sure what he thought about that. He'd already accepted that he'd never see Commonwealth again, and a big part of him was glad of it. The other part wanted justice and an apology. Would vindication be worth going back to work for a man who had run him out of town without even giving him a chance to defend himself?

In truth, he could use a day to get his own emotions under control. Jumping on the first train out of town was tempting, but it wasn't prudent. "I'll think about it," he said.

They said nothing more until the wagon rolled into Cochise and stopped next to the train station. Jacob hitched his horse in front of the building and walked inside. After Willie helped Carleton unload the trunk, he held out his hand. "Good luck, Carleton."

Carleton shook the big man's hand and nodded. "Thanks. Good luck to you, too."

He watched Willie drive the wagon toward the loading ramp that was just outside of town. By the time the next train arrived, several wagons from Commonwealth would be lined up and ready to dump their ore.

Carleton sat on his trunk to think for a moment. He had plenty of time to go into the station and buy a ticket, and he preferred to wait until Jacob had concluded his business. He had to decide whether he'd get a ticket to leave that day or if he'd take Willie's advice and hold off for a day or two.

"Wizard Carleton! You're back," yelled a familiar young voice. Carleton looked up to see Davey Arliss running toward him. The boy came to a breathless halt. "Are you leaving already? Do you need help with your luggage?"

Carleton smiled at the child's friendly enthusiasm. Make that *four* friends in the West. "Good morning, Davey. Yes, it looks like I'm heading out. I'm a bit strapped for funds at the moment, so I think I'll have to take care of my luggage myself."

A brief look of concern crossed the boy's face. He glanced toward the warehouse and leaned close. "I don't mind helping for free. You paid me plenty last time."

Carleton smiled. His heightened emotional state coupled with the boy's considerate offer choked him up for a second. He blinked a couple of times and took a deep breath before answering. "That's very kind of you. I'd welcome your help."

"Davey!" called a blocky man who was standing in front of the warehouse. "Leave that feller alone and get over here. You got work to do."

"Comin', Pa," Davey yelled back. He shrugged apologetically to Carleton and took a few steps toward the warehouse. "Sorry, I guess I gotta go."

Carleton waved him on. "Don't worry about me. I'll be fine. You should mind your father."

As Davey started running toward the warehouse, he called over his shoulder, "Have a good trip!"

Carleton sighed and stood up. He might as well buy that ticket. There wasn't much point in hanging around Cochise hoping Bart would change his mind. All that would do is waste more of his rapidly dwindling funds. As Willie had said earlier, he wasn't a good fit for Commonwealth anyway.

Jacob came out of the station as Carleton reached the door, and Carleton stepped back to let him pass. The scruffy teamster gave him a nod and said, "See ya, Carl."

Carleton said, "Goodbye, Jacob," and entered the station. Under his breath he added, "And it's Carleton."

Once inside, he consulted with the station agent and bought a ticket to Benson. The smelter there attracted people in the mining business, so he might be able to get a lead on a new job. If not, he could continue on to Tucson and try his luck there.

Exiting the station with ticket in hand, Carleton looked up to find Perry standing next to his luggage. His horse was tied at the rail. "I thought I recognized that trunk," he said. "You taking a trip?"

"I've been let go," Carleton answered. *In a manner of speaking.*

"Job's done already? That was quick. I was under the impression you were expecting to be here awhile."

Carleton sighed. He might as well tell his side of the story. His friend would hear about it eventually, and it wouldn't be a flattering version. "I was fired for stealing Bart's shotgun."

"Somebody set you up?" Perry said in a tense voice.

Thank you. At least somebody gives me the benefit of the doubt.

"Yes. I don't know who. I have my suspicions, but no proof. Bart didn't give me a chance to defend myself."

Perry frowned and nodded. "That Bart's as prickly as a cholla, and just as stubborn when he gets his barbs into a notion. He's a hard man to work for."

The two men stood in silence for a moment, and then Perry asked, "What's your plan?"

Carleton shrugged and waved his ticket. "I'm heading to Benson to see if I can find work there. I don't have enough money to go back home, and that would be a last resort in any case."

Perry rubbed his chin. "Would you consider staying around for a bit?"

Carleton shook his head. "Can't afford it. And Bart said he'd shoot me if he saw me again."

"Coming from Bart, that's not an entirely empty threat, but once he cools down he might start listening to reason."

"Yeah, that's more or less what Willie said. He suggested I stick around for a couple of days in case Bart changes his mind."

Perry seemed taken aback. "You got Willie on your side?"

"I was as surprised as you are," Carleton said. "I think he's mostly concerned that he still has a troublemaker on his crew."

"More than one, I'll wager," Perry said in a droll tone.

Then he waved the subject aside. "The thing is, out here a man's reputation is about all he has. The isolation and lack of lawmen means neighbors have to rely on each other. People are suspicious of strangers from the get-go, and a bad reputation gets around faster than a telegram."

Carleton's shoulders slumped at Perry's words. "What can I do?"

"Well, you can stand up for yourself, and let your friends give you a hand."

Standing up for himself had seemed pointless only minutes ago, but Perry's support changed things. "What did you have in mind?"

"How about staying at the ranch with me for a spell? I got a spare room and could use some help, although I couldn't pay you much more than room and board. It will be worth the delay if we can clear your name with Bart."

Carleton looked down at the train ticket then held it up. "There's just one problem. I spent a big chunk of my savings on this ticket."

Perry scoffed. "Tell Earl you've had a change of plans and get a refund."

It was as easy as that. Earl tore up Carleton's ticket and gave him his money back without even a grumble.

Back out front, Perry was waiting on his horse. Carleton realized a flaw in their plan. How was he going to get out to Sunrise Ranch?

"You wait here," Perry said. "I left the wagon at the livery with a horse that needed shoeing. I'll settle up and be back in a few minutes."

True to his word, Perry returned about twenty minutes later with two horses drawing his wagon. They loaded Carleton's luggage into the back alongside Perry's saddle and a few supplies he'd picked up. A few minutes later, they were bouncing along the road out of town.

Perry rolled past the intersection at High Lonesome without slowing down.

"We aren't taking the shortcut today?" Carleton asked.

"Nope. I'm not prepared to trade with the avens, and the horses will get us to the ranch quickly enough. I avoid High Lonesome unless I'm looking to trade or running peccaries."

The disadvantage of taking the main road was that they had to dodge a couple of ore wagons coming from

Commonwealth. Perry pulled to the side of the road to let them pass. The teamsters thanked him with a wave, but in both cases, the men recognized Carleton and stared with thoughtful expressions.

Word would undoubtedly get back to Bart that Carleton had been seen riding with Perry and probably hadn't left the area. Would Bart make good on his threat to shoot Carleton on sight?

CHAPTER 14

Apologies

After three days of working hard on the ranch with Perry, Carleton was able to let go of the trouble at Commonwealth. Mending fences, mucking out the pens, and helping care for all of the animals was a satisfying if exhausting endeavor.

His room in Perry's cabin seemed like a luxury suite after the conditions he'd faced in the bunkhouse. Between the old but comfortable bed and the privacy of having his own room with a door, he was finally able to get a decent night's rest.

In the late afternoon of his second day on the ranch, Carleton was hanging up a rake in the storage shed attached to the house when Perry showed up.

"Had to repair a bit of silk on the far side of the horse pasture," he explained as he put away his fencing tools and tossed in a roll of barbed wire.

"You should have let me know. I'd have helped," Carleton said.

Perry chuckled to himself. "You know, I'm so used to working this place alone that I didn't even think of it."

Carleton asked, "So, what's next, boss?"

Perry shook his head. "You're a hard worker, I'll give you that. Let's call it a day. I hear a cowboy cocktail calling my name." When he saw Carleton's look of uncertainty, he grinned. "Whiskey."

The two men went into the house and took turns washing up. After cleaning off the sweat and dust, Carleton joined Perry at an old saloon table the rancher kept on the front porch. Perry handed Carleton a shot glass filled with amber liquid as soon as the tired wizard lowered himself into the second chair.

"Here's to love, health, and money. Not necessarily in that order," Perry said, clinking his glass against Carleton's.

"Cheers," Carleton replied. He followed Perry's example and up-ended the glass, downing the entire shot in one swallow.

The whiskey went down smoothly and warmed Carleton's belly. He wasn't much of a drinker, but the relaxing spirits were welcome after a hard day's work. Perry poured a second shot for both of them. That one, they sipped.

"You have a beautiful place," Carleton commented. From the porch, he could see east across the Sulphur Springs Valley all the way to the Chiricahua Mountains, which rose straight up from the valley floor to high peaks blackened with pine. The Pearce Hills filled the view to the south.

"Yep, I got lucky," Perry said with a nod. "Old Brian Lauter, the homesteader I bought it from, had trouble selling because the land is so close to aveni territory. Folks either weren't interested or they didn't offer much. Bart wanted the ranch and said he'd top the highest offer, but Lauter never cared much for Bart."

"I can relate to that," Carleton commented. "So how did you end up with it?"

"This all happened a couple of years ago. I had just given up being a lawman and was at loose ends. I had a stake set aside, but hadn't decided on how to invest it. I met up with Lauter at a saloon in Tombstone, and we got to talking. He sold me the whole kit and caboodle for one dollar more than the last offer Bart had made. Bart wasn't too happy about that, and he's been trying to get me to sell ever since."

Carleton hooked his thumb in the direction of the old mine entrance at the back of the property. "Maybe he's after the mine."

Perry made a doubtful face. "Maybe. Lauter swore it was worthless. The last assay came back too thin to make digging out the ore worthwhile. I poked around in there a bit, but I don't know much about prospecting."

That explained why the peccaries were using the entrance to the cave as a place to get out of the sun. Well, at least the former mine was serving some purpose.

Perry leaned forward, squinting into the distance. "Speak of the devil."

Carleton followed his line of sight and spotted an open carriage approaching. He couldn't make out the faces of the riders, but the pale lavender parasol could belong to only one person: Penelope. Since Bart rarely let the woman out of his site, it was a good bet that he was also on board and that Willie was driving.

Perry went inside and returned with one of his pistols and Carleton's wrist band, which he tossed to the wizard. Carleton strapped on the collection of casting stones and planned what he would do if the visit turned ugly. He wasn't too worried, though. If Bart had mischief in mind, it was unlikely he'd show up in a carriage with Penelope to bear witness.

Carleton touched his cheek, which was still tender from where Bart had struck him. The bruise was at the dark-purple stage, the edges turning to yellow, and it made him do a double take every time he caught a glimpse of his reflection. His jaw clenched at the reminder of how poorly he'd been treated. He'd love an opportunity to return the favor.

The sorrel mule pulling the carriage huffed as it reached the ranch plateau, tired and covered with sweat after the gradual but long uphill pull from Pearce. When the carriage came to a halt in front of the house, Perry and Carleton got to their feet. Perry set his six-shooter on the table, leaving it within easy reach.

Bart and Penelope clambered out. Carleton noted that Willie seemed to be the only one who was armed, which calmed his nerves somewhat.

"Good afternoon, gentlemen," Bart said. He squinted against the sun, which was getting low in the sky behind the ranch house.

Perry answered, "Howdy, Bart. What can I do for you?"

"I came to get my wizard back," Bart declared.

Carleton was momentarily stunned by the announcement. The responses that came to his mind after the initial shock weren't fit for present company.

Penelope stepped forward and spoke firmly. "What Bart means to say is that he owes Wizard Kazimer an apology."

Bart glared at Penelope. "Dammit woman, don't put words in my mouth." She seemed unimpressed by his chastisement. He turned back to Carleton. "Fact is, Dell Patterson confessed to taking my shotgun and putting it in your trunk. The fool got himself corned at the saloon and started bragging about getting rid of you. When he sobered up, he claimed it was a gag gone wrong.

"Willie didn't believe him and gave him a little *encouragement* to tell the truth. Turns out, Dell got the money for his gambling and drinking spree from that new delvan foreman in trade for pulling the shotgun scam. I fired 'em both, and Jasper is personally making sure Cragg Steel goes back where he came from."

If there was an apology hidden in all those words, Carleton had missed it. He folded his arms and stared Bart down. "Seems to me you canceled my contract. The Guild has probably assigned someone else by now."

Bart glanced at Willie, who was watering the mule. "Willie convinced me to hold off on that for a few days, and I'm glad I did. Now that I know the truth, we can put this behind us and get back to work."

Carleton was pretty sure he didn't want to go back to work for Bart. It was probably only a matter of time before the man would blow up about something new. "I was under the impression that you weren't too impressed with my work."

Bart started to respond, but Penelope spoke over him. "Jasper reported this morning that the vein shifted exactly as you said it would. His crews were able to pick it up again without delay. Your work was exceptional, Wizard Kazimer."

As Penelope spoke, Bart's eyes grew wide and his face turned red. Her praise was apparently more than Bart wanted to concede. "Now, no need to make him all uppish, Penny." He wiped a hand over his forehead and calmed himself. "In light of Jasper's report, I'm willing to give you another chance to complete the contract you agreed to."

As much as he loathed the idea, Carleton didn't have much choice. He couldn't stay with Perry indefinitely, earning pennies a day. Technically, he was still under contract with Bart. But that didn't mean he had to make it easy.

"I'll come back under two conditions. I want my full pay for the entire past week and I want an extra day's bonus pay for finding that shift."

Bart narrowed his eyes. "I'm not giving you a bonus every time you find something useful, wizard. That's your job and you get paid handsomely for it."

"Fine. Then let's call it compensation for this," Carleton said, putting a finger to his bruised cheek. He figured that a monetary apology was probably better than a verbal one. It would be more costly for Bart and worth more to himself.

Bart exhaled sharply. "All right. Have it your way. Now, get your things together and we'll take you back to the bunkhouse."

Carleton turned to Perry, who was smiling supportively. "Does that offer of a room still stand?" Carleton asked.

"You bet," Perry said with a wink.

Addressing Bart, Carleton said, "I'll be staying here for now, Mr. McLaury. I'll be at the mine within an hour of sunrise each workday. I'll expect to leave an hour before sunset."

Bart chewed his lip for a moment in consideration and then nodded. "I can live with that. I'll have your pay ready next time you come by the house."

He took a moment to let his gaze wander around the property. His eyes lingered on the peccary pen before shifting to Perry. "You give any more thought to selling this place?"

Perry raised an eyebrow. "You give any more thought to raising your offer?"

Bart shook his head and smiled in a way that said Perry was dreaming to think he'd offer more money. "I think our business is done here." He went to the carriage and waited at the side. "Let's head on back, Penny."

Penelope smiled and gave her parasol a twirl. "I'm glad you decided to continue at Commonwealth, Wizard Kazimer. I look forward to seeing you on Monday."

Carleton dipped his head and said, "Thank you, ma'am. Have a pleasant trip back."

Penelope went to the carriage and accepted Bart's hand to help her climb aboard. Willie had finished his task and was already back in the driver's seat. With a wave, he turned the mule and drove the carriage back toward the mine.

"That Penelope is a whole lot of woman," Perry commented once the carriage was out of earshot. "Makes me wonder what she has on Bart."

Carleton agreed with Perry's assessment of Penelope, but he wasn't sure about the rest. "What do you mean? She's his bookkeeper, right?"

"That's the story. But it seems odd for him to drag his facilitator out here and let her speak up like that. Makes we wonder what that fancy title of hers really means and who she's really working for."

Good point. "Do you have a theory?"

Perry watched the carriage drive off, his brow creased in thought. "Not yet. I was a lawman when Penelope's husband died. Things weren't looking too good for her for a while there. Then I heard she found work but was never clear on what she was doing or who she was doing it for." He pursed his lips and shook his head once. "Something doesn't sit right about those two, and over the years, I've learned to heed my intuition when it comes to things like that."

"Thanks for the warning. I'll try to keep my distance from both of them."

Perry gave him a lopsided grin. "Keeping your distance from that piece of calico might be tougher than you think. She seems to have taken a shine to you."

Carleton didn't quite believe that. "You don't think she's just being friendly?"

"In my experience, women are real careful about being friendly. Fellers tend to read too much into it. Now, the doves in town, they're extra friendly. But it isn't because they like you."

Carleton chuckled and shook his head. "I don't think I'll ever understand women."

Perry poured another shot. "Women are people like you and me, Carleton. The trick to understanding anybody is figuring out what motivates them." He handed a shot to Carleton and then raised his own glass. "Here's to getting your job back," he said.

"Here's to keeping it for more than a week," Carleton replied. He shared a laugh with Perry before settling into his chair.

Carleton sighed deeply, daring to hope that his Guild contract might work out after all. He wouldn't have to go back to that awful bunkhouse, and it seemed they'd finally caught the person behind all of the "accidents" that had befallen him since he'd arrived.

The foreground view darkened with shadow as the sun slipped below the mountains behind them. More than anything, that quick transition from bright to dim signaled the end of the day. They'd still have another hour or so of light as the shadow of the Dragon Mountains raced across the valley floor. The hills on the other side of the valley would darken to gold, then red, and finally purple.

Sipping his whiskey, Carleton thought back on what Perry had said about women. According to Perry, the key to understanding Penelope was figuring out what motivated her. It seemed like reasonable advice, but to learn what motivated her, he'd have to get to know her a lot better. That might be difficult with Bart around all the time, but he was willing to give it a try.

CHAPTER 15

Second Vein

Carleton entered the crosscut on Monday morning with renewed hope and determination. The four ten-dollar gold eagles shifted in his pocket with satisfying weightiness. Three of the coins covered his pay for the prior week, while the fourth was the "apology" he'd managed to extract from Bart.

No one else was around, so he took the opportunity to hide the money in the secret compartment of his equipment case, stuffing the extra space with a patch of cloth to keep the coins from jingling.

Carleton hid the case next to the big rock that had fallen the last time he'd worked at the face of the crosscut. Although the delvan crews had removed the rubble from the big collapse, they hadn't bothered with anything more. He disguised the case with loose rocks and dirt. He could have obscured it with an illusion, but he was coming right back in a few minutes and didn't want to spare the swi.

Carrying his portable lantern, Carleton reached the intersection with Main Drift and headed down the passage to where the miners were working. He had gone about a dozen steps before the telltale rumble of the ore cart and an intermittent screech of brakes came from behind.

Carleton picked up his pace, carefully hunching over to avoid skull-bashers protruding from the head-wall. When he reached a widened part of the passage, he moved away from the tracks and waited for the cart to pass.

The brake screeched steadily as Flint brought the cart to a halt. The peccary tied to the uphill end of the cart grunted a few times. Carleton had no idea if it was expressing a greeting or a complaint.

"Carleton!" Flint greeted. "I heard ye were coming back. I didn't believe it when they told me ye stole Bart's shotgun. It was easy to believe Dell took it, although I'm surprised he had the guts. I guess money can be a powerful motivator, and Cragg really wanted ye gone."

Flint was probably the only delvan Carleton could count on to give him a straight story on what happened. "Do you know why he hated me so much?"

Flint leaned forward, eager to impart the story. "Ye should have seen it! When they faced Cragg down with Dell's confession, he started ranting about humans in the mine angering Father Earth. He claimed yer magic was some kind of sacrilege and that only delvan priests should wield earth magic. I guess he thought it was his duty to be the chastising hand of the Father."

"Some chastisement," Carleton scoffed. "He nearly killed me. Multiple times."

"I hear ye," Flint said. "But ye'll not have to worry about Cragg Steel no more. Jasper says he'll never work in the West again. I don't think anyone was sad to see him go. He made us all uncomfortable, but no one imagined he'd take his beliefs so far."

"I sure didn't see it coming," Carleton said. "But then, everybody here is a mystery to me." Glancing at Flint, he added, "No offense meant."

Flint grinned. "I'll take it as a compliment. My motto is 'always keep 'em guessing.'"

Carleton chuckled and then had an idea. "You might be able to save me a trip. I want to try a new catalyst for my prospecting spell, and ... well ... you can help me with it."

Flint shrugged and said, "Aye. What can I do?"

Carleton took an empty sample bottle out of his pocket and looked at the ground. "This is going to sound like an odd request …"

When the pause grew too long, Flint said, "Well, spit it out. We can't stand here jawing all shift."

Carleton cringed and then looked Flint in the eye. "I need a few nose hairs."

Flint gave Carleton a sidelong squint. "Nose hairs, ye say?"

"Yes," Carleton confirmed. To cover his embarrassment, he quickly tried to explain his thinking. "The best catalysts for magic are closely related to the purpose of the spell. Dragon claw worked well for me because dragons live underground and dig through earth. Your people can smell precious metals in ore, so I was thinking that delvan nose hair might make a good catalyst. It's worth a try, anyway."

Flint blinked at Carleton a few times while he absorbed the idea. "Well, I'm willing, but Tully would be the best choice. I hate to admit it, but Tully has the best sniffer I've ever known."

Carleton closed his eyes and sighed with disappointment. When Flint had happened by, he thought he might be able to avoid talking to Tully. But Flint's reasoning was sound. If he was going to try the experiment, he should use the best catalyst he could find.

"Want a ride?" Flint asked.

Carleton nodded and climbed into the cart. "You're probably right about asking Tully."

Flint let off the brake and the cart started rolling again. He glanced at Carleton with a half-smile and a glint in his eye. "This ought to be good. No offense meant."

Carleton slid to the bottom of the cart with a glum expression. "None taken."

The two men rattled down the tracks to the stope and climbed out. The pile of ore waiting for Flint was considerable, but the delvan mucker seemed undaunted by his Sisyphean task. At least he had peccaries to help him.

Standing at the opening to the drift where the miners were working, Flint called out for Tully.

"What's all this hollerin' about?" Tully griped as he joined them.

"The wizard has something to ask ye," Flint explained, his eyes gleaming with mischief.

Tully looked at Carleton expectantly.

Standing face-to-face with Tully, the request seemed even more silly and personal, but there was no turning back. He gave Tully the same explanation he'd given Flint, with similar results.

Tully gave him virtually the same sidelong glance Flint had. "Ye're wanting what?"

"Nose hairs," Carleton repeated. "I only need a few."

Nonplussed, Tully pointed at Flint, who was openly grinning. "Why not take some of his?"

"Because quality counts," Carleton explained. "Flint claims you have the best nose for metals he's ever known."

"Oh, he does, does he?" Tully said, glaring at Flint. Then he straightened his shoulders and puffed out his chest. "He's right that me nose is the best in the mine."

Carleton held out the sample bottle and some tweezers. Tully considered the offer dubiously. "Just a few, ye say?"

"Just a few," Carleton confirmed with a nod.

Tully took the proffered items and narrowed his eyes at Carleton. "Aye, and if yer experiment is successful? Ye'll be back for more until me nose is plucked clean!"

Carleton rubbed his forehead in exasperation. "I promise to be sparing with them. I only use one at a time, so what you give me today will last awhile. Besides, if you don't mind my saying so, you appear to have plenty to spare."

Tully's lips thinned and his brow furrowed, as if he were deciding whether or not to be insulted. Then he shrugged and said, "Keeps the dust out."

Slipping the tweezers into his nose, Tully gave a yank and let out a squawk of pain before dropping the resulting cluster of hairs into the bottle. Eyes watering from the plucking, he handed the items back to Carleton. "Are we done here? I got work to do." Glancing at Flint, he added, "If ye're done gawking, there's some ore that could use yer attention." With that, Tully strutted back to work.

Carleton stoppered the sample bottle and inspected the harvest. Tully had been generous. Thankfully, he wouldn't need to bother the foreman again for a while. He tucked the bottle and tweezers into his pocket. "I guess I'd better get back to the crosscut," he said to Flint.

Flint clapped him on the back and chuckled. "Thanks, Carleton. That was the best show I've seen in a while."

Leaving an amused Flint to his shoveling, Carleton worked his way back up Main Drift to the crosscut. His equipment case was exactly where he left it, his camouflage undisturbed.

Setting up for the day's work, he thought back over some of the conclusions he'd reached about the job over the weekend. He needed to be wary and take control of his surroundings. The work was still potentially dangerous, even if the people trying to sabotage him had been caught. Besides, he couldn't be certain that everyone who was involved had been caught.

In preparation for returning to work at the mine, Carleton had researched ways to protect himself. The spell book he brought with him, *Geomantic Expressions*, had a section on mining-related spells. In that section, he'd found a structural-integrity spell that could identify weaknesses in passageways. If the delvans knew he was using it, they would probably be insulted by his lack of faith in their skills, but he felt justified, considering the events of the previous week.

The problem was that the spell took time and consumed valuable swi, and given Bart's demand for constant progress, Carleton hated to do anything that would slow things down. But he didn't feel like he had a choice. Trusting his life to the delvans hadn't worked out too well so far.

If he could locate an accessible flow of wild earth magic—a fluvium terra—he'd be able to recharge himself and make up for some of the swi lost to verifying his safety. It was likely that one of the natural flows surfaced somewhere nearby—he just had to find it. That was yet another task to add to his growing list.

For the structural-integrity spell, Carleton used a tiny mud dauber's nest he'd discovered at the ranch. It was shaped like a clay pot, and he'd verified that the larva was no longer in residence. He carefully set it into his casting ring. It would be useless if he broke it.

Next, he took a small piece of polished onyx from his pocket. He didn't need the dark, striped medallion of stone to activate the spell, but it would make things easier for him in the long run. He put it into the ring next to the nest. Every time he cast the integrity spell, the transmutation of the catalyst would imprint the stone. Over time, the stone would help strengthen the spell, and eventually, he'd be able to dispense with the catalyst entirely. All of the casting stones on his wrist band had been imprinted using the same technique.

The process required many castings of the same spell, but if he was going to have to do a structural-integrity check every time he went to work anyway, a casting stone would save him from having to acquire more catalysts.

Carleton placed one hand over the brass ring and chanted the incantation. As he spoke the final words, he placed his free hand against the wall of the crosscut. A soft thud signaled the spell's activation, and a spiderweb of luminous lines spread from his fingertips. The web expanded around the tunnel, its lines following every contour. By shifting the position of his fingers, he was able to direct the webbing so that it covered the face of the crosscut and the surface of the passage for about twenty feet.

The lines were brightest where the surrounding material was strongest, and faded where it was weakest. Not surprisingly, the web faded over the hole from which the big rock had fallen, but not enough to indicate a lingering danger. He was looking for spots where the web went completely dark, which would indicate a dangerously unstable spot. Satisfied that his work zone was safe for the moment, he canceled the spell.

Carleton tucked the onyx back into his pocket. He might imprint a different stone with the prospecting spell he was about to use after he found the catalyst that worked best. First, he needed to find out how the delvan nose hair compared to the dragon claw.

Carleton moved his casting ring as close to the face as he could and sat cross-legged beside it. Carefully extracting one of Tully's nose hairs from the sample bottle, he put it inside the ring. He placed the ore chunk next to it and covered the ring with his palm. When he reached the point in the incantation when the spell would activate, he couldn't help but cringe in anticipation of the geomantic concussion. He was pleasantly surprised when nothing but a mild thump ushered his awareness into the surrounding rock.

He could sense the catalyst's improvement to his spell immediately. The vein of quartz he'd seen before was more sharply defined as a twisting white stream rather than a cloudy mass. Tiny spots of red and blue appeared along the stream, marking locations with trace amounts of gold and silver.

Carleton extended his awareness deeper into the mountain to test his range. His curiosity turned to elation as he easily slipped beyond the maximum distance he'd managed with the dragon claw. About fifty feet farther he hit pay dirt, as the miners would say.

He intersected a new vein that was intermittently stained with blue and red. It wasn't quite as rich as the vein they were already working, and it would take a lot of digging to reach it, but Bart would be pleased. The new vein would certainly justify bringing in another quad of delvans, and it would strengthen Bart's arguments for both a spur line and a stamp mill.

Carleton could feel his swi reserve fading as he neared the end of his magical endurance. He withdrew his awareness and canceled the spell, holding still against a sudden wave of dizziness. Exhausted from depleting himself so thoroughly, he kept his eyes closed and took several deep breaths.

When the vertigo had passed, he opened his eyes and whooped with excitement at his discovery. His experiments were paying off, and the Guild would be pleased with his success. There would be no point in telling them about the rough beginning to the contract, of course. All the Guild cared about was results.

Carleton started gathering his things. He would report his findings to Jasper and spend the rest of the day trying to locate a fluvium. With any luck, he'd be able to recharge himself and return to the mine for a couple more hours of work.

CHAPTER 16
Dragon Fire

Carleton stepped back to admire his handiwork. The prior evening, the chisel crew had installed a new support, and his spell had melded the individual blocks into a seamless arch of stone. Over the past week, he'd mapped out both ore veins in some detail, and he'd started using his skills to help the delvans in other ways.

Tully had become almost civil to him. The three mucking crews were able to focus on digging ore while Carleton guided them along the vein. The crews received bonus pay based on how much ore they removed from the mine, so they were quite pleased with the efficient arrangement.

Bart was finally coming around as well. After Carleton revealed the new vein of ore, Bart put out a call for more delvan miners. New miners were expected within a month, and they would go after the new vein as soon as they finished excavating a new quad. Commonwealth Subtown was about to double in size.

Jasper Underlight had assured Carleton that the chisel crew also appreciated his help. He used his structural-integrity spell to help them identify weak geology that needed extra attention. His new stone-binding spell not only made their arches stronger, but the seamless appearance appealed to the delvans' sense of aesthetics.

Carleton's increased productivity was expensive in terms of swi, but he had finally solved that problem by locating a nearby fluvium terra that allowed him to replenish his reserves.

While exploring the countryside for potential catalysts, he'd discovered dozens of small washes and dry creek beds. Perry told him that water frequently rushed through those channels during the monsoon season in July and August. In many places, the sandy topsoil had been washed away to reveal long stretches of rocks embedded in limestone. Carleton had tested the exposed rivers of natural cement and found that swi flowed along some of them. They appeared to be excellent conduits for earth magic.

The close network of fluvia hinted at the presence of one or more powerful swi vortexes in the area. Vortexes were rare, and when one was found, the Guild usually made sure they were protected. If Carleton were to locate a new one, the Guild might even name it after him.

Kazimer Vortex. I like the sound of that.

Carleton's ruminations were interrupted by a delvan exclamation at the end of the passage. The digging noises ceased and the buzz of conversation lured Carleton forward to see what had transpired.

"Aye, but what's that smell?" Tully asked in a hushed voice as Carleton joined the miners.

The face of the passage wasn't the jagged wall of solid ore that Carleton was used to seeing. The miners had broken through to some kind of underground chamber or passage. Perhaps they'd discovered a natural cave. The hole was about the size of Carleton's head, but he could see nothing in the utter darkness beyond the opening.

A whisper of air flowed out of the hole, indicating that the space beyond eventually connected to the surface. The breeze carried an odd musky odor with it.

Tully sniffed closely at the hole and quickly drew back his head. "Be cautious lads. The air be thick. Clear the hole as best ye can with pry bars, and strike no sparks." He turned to Carleton. "Put out that lantern until we know what we're dealing with." Carleton blew out his lantern as instructed.

Tully supervised while his crewmates Mag Digman and Ledge Quasmin cleared rock from around the opening. Instead of hacking at the stone with their pickaxes, the two worked together with pry bars to enlarge the hole.

When they'd cleared an opening big enough to crawl through, Tully told them to stop. He clambered part-way into the opening and then eased back out, shaking his head. "Can't see a thing. But there be a breeze coming into the chamber beyond."

"Let me go through," Mag volunteered, his eyes gleaming with excitement. Natural cave systems were precious to delvans and getting the chance to explore one for the first time was a kind of spiritual experience for them. "Once I'm in, the light through the opening will be enough."

Tully considered the offer, but then shook his head. "We don't know what lies on the other side. Ye could be crawling into the top of a hundred-foot shaft." Turning to Carleton, he said, "Ye got anything that can help us here, wizard? Can ye make light with no flame?"

Carleton had been so wrapped up in the drama of the moment that the idea of using magic to make light hadn't occurred to him. "Yes … I can do that."

He jogged back to his equipment case and rooted around until he found a rounded and polished piece of milky quartz. Rejoining the miners, he showed them the stone. "I can make this glow, but it will be a lot brighter than the candle lanterns. You might want to shield your eyes and let me do the looking."

All three miners' faces fell at the suggestion. They obviously didn't want to turn the important new discovery over to a human. Glancing down at his lantern, Carleton had an idea. He picked up the lantern and opened the top, turning his back to the delvans to shield them from what he was about to do. Chanting an incantation, he closed his eyes against the brightness to come and fed swi into the quartz. The stone glowed brightly against Carleton's eyelids, and the miners grunted in discomfort. He dropped the stone into the lantern and closed the top.

When he turned around, the miners held up their hands to protect their eyes, but the light was made tolerable by the lantern's directional shielding. He pointed the lantern toward the opening and held it out to Tully, but the foreman motioned for him to give it to Mag. Mag grinned and took the lantern, holding it at arm's length and blinking against the brightness.

Leading with the lantern, Mag peered into the hole. "Looks like a narrow cavern," he said. He climbed through the opening, and Tully moved forward to watch Mag's progress.

Carleton could barely see past Tully's shoulders. The lantern's light flicked around inside the narrow chamber as Mag made his way forward.

"Don't look like much," Mag called back. "Wait … there's an opening up here on the right where the breeze is coming from."

"Watch your step," Tully warned.

"This ain't me first cave," Mag said with irritation in his voice.

Mag and the light disappeared from Carleton's view.

"Father's curse!" Mag yelled.

"What is it?" Tully asked, but Mag had already turned the corner and was running back toward the opening. From deeper in the cave came a scratching sound and the swish of grit.

Mag scrabbled at the other side of the opening. Realizing the lantern was slowing him down, he heaved it toward Tully, who caught it and tossed it to Carleton with the order to put it out.

With no way to extinguish the stone, Carleton quickly removed it from the lantern and tucked it into a pocket where his clothing diminished its glow almost completely.

When Carleton looked up again, Mag was struggling to climb through the opening. A gut-clenching roar from the chamber behind the miner was followed by a searing ring of flame that shot around Mag's body and through the opening. Tully was forced to back away with his arms held up to protect his face. Mag screamed in pain and fear as the fire ignited his clothing and singed his hair.

As soon as the burst of flame subsided, Tully and Ledge ran forward and grabbed Mag's trembling hands. They yanked him through the opening, his clothes still aflame from the waist down. Tully glanced through the crawl space and commanded, "Everybody down!" His tone was such that Carleton and Ledge obeyed without thinking. Another roar was followed by a blast of flame that shot over their heads through the opening.

Tully and Ledge had fallen across Mag's legs, bringing a scream of anguish from the poor delvan, but also extinguishing his burning pants.

Carleton thought he was imagining things when he looked up to find the stones around the opening still burning. Small spots of flame flickered on the floor of the passageway in a swath that led back toward the dark hole. He realized that the flames were fueled by some kind of oil, and that was when he understood the nature of their assailant.

Carleton had just encountered his first dragon.

Tully gestured at Ledge to help him lift Mag. As soon as they'd lifted the groaning miner between them, Tully yelled, "Run!"

Carleton didn't need to be told twice. Tully's command snapped him out of his slack-jawed shock. He turned and bolted from the still-flaming opening as quickly as he could.

A moment later, another roar echoed down the passage and a third blast of oily fire flashed behind them. As Carleton charged past his equipment case, the sound of digging claws and crumbling rock spurred him on. If the dragon made it through to the mine, it would be right on their heels.

Carleton burst into the stope and nearly ran into Flint, who was looking down the passage with his shovel in hand. "What's all the commotion about?" he asked.

Carleton dragged at Flint's sleeve, leading him toward the exit. "Dragon coming! We need to get out of here."

Flint tossed his shovel aside with a clang and patted out a small spot of fire on the back of Carleton's overcoat. Then he ran to untie the peccary. With the peccary's lead in hand, he paused. "Where's Tully's crew?"

"We're here," Tully answered, hustling the unconscious Mag into the stope. "Get moving," he ordered Flint.

Carleton, the peccary, and the four delvan miners hurried up the passage until they reached the subtown intersection. Tully paused to catch his breath. "We have to evacuate Subtown," he said between gasps.

Carleton evaluated the passage into the quad. It was much smaller than Main Drift, but would it be small enough to keep out the dragon? "How big is the dragon?" he asked Tully.

"Not sure. Couldn't see around Mag."

Everyone was silent for a moment, straining to hear the slithering of scales or scratch of claws.

"Do we have *time* to evacuate?" Flint asked.

"We can't leave everyone trapped in the quad." Tully said with a glare.

"I'm not suggesting that," Flint said. "We have dynamite and Jasper's rifle. We can make a stand here."

Tully was stunned. "And risk closing the drift?"

"It beats becoming dragon food," he said with a shrug.

"What's this about closing the drift?" Jasper growled from behind Flint. He rushed forward, pushing Flint roughly aside when he spotted Mag sagging between Tully and Ledge. "What happened? Don't just stand there. Get him to the common room and lay him down."

Tully shook his head. "Flint's right. We don't have time. We dug into a dragon lair, and the beast is coming after us."

Jasper's eyes widened and he glanced down the passage. "A dragon lair? This far into the valley? That can't be right. All the lairs are up in the foothills."

"Try explaining that to the dragon."

Jasper's brow furrowed while he considered the situation. His expression settled into one of determination. "Flint, take the wizard and get a box of blasting sticks."

Flint started running toward the exit with the peccary jogging in tow. As Carleton turned to follow Flint, Jasper said, "Tully, put Mag in the common room. I'll be getting me rifle." He called to Carleton's back, "If ye hear me firing, stay back until I call for ye."

Carleton waved an acknowledgment before going around the daylight curve. He caught up to Flint, who handed the peccary's lead to him. "Put Stomper away while I open the powder shack."

Carleton took the peccary's lead and guided him to the pen. The animal grunted a greeting to the others and went through the gate eagerly. By the time Carleton reached the powder shack, its iron-reinforced door was ajar and Flint was inside rooting around. Flint came out bearing an open box of dynamite, which he handed to Carleton. "Take this to the daylight curve and wait for me there."

Carleton was waiting as instructed when Flint joined him. He carried a tin of blasting caps and a roll of fuse. He kneeled and, with practiced hands, capped three fuses using a crimping tool. "Call out and see if it's clear," he said as he worked.

Tully answered Carleton's shout, saying they hadn't seen or heard the dragon yet. As soon as Flint was ready, both men hustled down the passage to where the others were waiting. Jasper waved them into the side tunnel while he aimed his rifle down the drift. The younger female delvan Carleton had seen on his first visit to the quad was kneeling next to Mag, cutting away what was left of his pant legs and applying a poultice to his bleeding burns. Mag was mercifully unconscious, but his breathing was ragged and Carleton feared he might not survive.

Setting down the box of dynamite, Carleton inched along the wall to stand next to Jasper. "Anything?" he whispered.

Jasper shook his head. A second later, he turned his head to listen as a deep rumble came from below. After the rumble faded, they heard nothing for several minutes.

"Are ye sure it entered the mine?" Jasper asked Tully.

"Nay," Tully answered. "We didn't wait around to see what it would do, but it sure sounded like it was coming through."

After a few more minutes of utter silence, Jasper huffed out a breath of frustration. "Flint, ye got some sticks ready?"

"Three," Flint answered, holding up the primed sticks of dynamite with abnormally short fuses. "That enough?"

"Aye." Jasper patted his fifty-caliber Sharps buffalo rifle. "If the Big Fifty and three blasting sticks don't stop the beastie, we're all dragon fodder anyway."

Carleton shuddered at the thought of being roasted and eaten by a dragon. According to the things he'd read, fatal dragon encounters were quite rare, but the drawings that depicted the giant, armor-plated lizards usually showed them breathing fire or gaping a mouth filled with long sharp teeth.

Jasper addressed the group. "Flint and I will go take a look. Everyone else stay here."

Ledge nodded eagerly, helping the young woman tend to Mag. Tully grunted his agreement and started capping another fuse. He apparently didn't want to be left behind with no weapons, and Carleton couldn't blame him.

"I'm going with you," Carleton declared.

Jasper glanced down at his bracer. "Ye got something that can stop a dragon?"

"No," Carleton answered. "But I think I can shield us all from its fire at least once, if you stand behind me."

Jasper considered the offer and agreed. He quickly put together a plan.

Carleton went first and activated his shield. If the dragon surprised them, they'd be ready for its fiery breath. Keeping the shield going wouldn't use much swi; it was deflecting the dragon fire that would quickly consume Carleton's reserves.

Jasper followed closely behind Carleton. If they saw the dragon before it saw them, Carleton would step aside so Jasper could have a clear shot. Jasper would go down on one knee to fire, giving Flint room to lob a stick of dynamite over his head.

Creeping down the passage, Carleton cringed at every crunch of gravel beneath his boots. The main disadvantage of having him go first was that Jasper's vision was much better in the underground darkness. Carleton kept to the left as much as possible so the delvan supervisor could see past him into the passage ahead. If he spotted the dragon first, he would put his hand on Carleton's shoulder as a signal to stop.

By the time they reached the stope and the abandoned ore cart, Carleton's nerves were tightly strung. His heart leapt into his throat when he accidentally kicked a loose rock and it went rattling across the chamber before it thudded into the wall. He froze, expecting the dragon to slither out of the darkness any second to investigate the noise.

Nothing happened.

All they had left to explore was the passage to the face where Tully's crew had penetrated the dragon's cavern. He started forward slowly, all too aware of how deep they were in the mine and how far they were from any kind of help.

He went past his equipment case which was still sitting exactly where he'd left it. If the dragon had entered the mine, surely it would have smashed the box in passing. He was starting to hope that the dragon hadn't come through after all, but he couldn't see to the end of the tunnel and verify that. The last two candle lanterns near the face had gone out. If the creature were lurking in the darkness it should be able to see them. Why hadn't it attacked?

He came to a stop, unwilling to proceed into the darkness. He needed his lantern, but it was lying on the floor somewhere ahead where he'd dropped it earlier. He suddenly became aware of the glow-stone still weighing down his pocket.

Taking out the stone, he considered the risk of lighting it again. He'd have to drop the shield to do it, and he'd consume some of his remaining swi. Half-turning toward the delvans behind him, he whispered, "Shield your eyes."

Anxiety gripped Carleton as he dropped the shield and redirected his reserves into the glow stone. If the dragon struck right then, it would roast them all. He kept his fingers wrapped around the stone, his hand glowing red when the stone illuminated. Swinging his hand close the ground, he tossed the stone toward the end of the tunnel and raised his shield again as quickly as he could.

Compared to the dim lighting of the candle lanterns, the glow stone was like a light bomb. It bounced and rolled down the tunnel, blasting away the darkness in its path. It bounced against the face and rolled to a stop.

The passage was empty, and there was no sign of the opening to the dragon's chamber except for a few blackened rocks.

"It backfilled the hole," Carleton said with a mixture of relief and surprise. He ran forward and picked up his lantern. Putting the glow stone inside it again, he narrowed the aperture to make the light more tolerable to his delvan companions.

Jasper stepped forward, squinting at the rubble and noting the oily blackened residue left behind by the dragon's fury. "If we keep following this vein," he said, "we're bound to run into the lair again."

Flint nodded his agreement. "In that case, we'd best be ready to do battle with a dragon."

~

Carleton related the story of the dragon encounter as they sat on the front porch of Perry's house that evening.

"I'm sorry to hear about Mag," Perry said. "Is he going to be okay?"

Carleton was still in shock from the stress of the day and was having a tough time unwinding, in spite of the two shots

Perry had poured for him. Perry had brought out the whiskey bottle within seconds of seeing the look on Carleton's face when he had returned home that evening.

"It doesn't look good," Carleton said with a sad shake of his head. "The burns on his legs were pretty bad. The delvan nurse at Commonwealth patched him up as best she could and they took him into town. The last I heard, the doctor said it will take him months to heal, if the pain or an infection doesn't do him in first. They plan to move him to a hospital in Tucson as soon as he's stable enough to travel that far."

Perry considered the news. "He got any family?"

"They're in Kansas somewhere. Jasper said he'd send word."

"What a mess," Perry said, shaking his head. "It's a good thing you found that second vein of ore."

"What do you mean?" Carleton asked.

Perry gave him a surprised look, as if the answer were obvious. "They can't keep working a vein that goes straight through a dragon lair."

"I tend to agree," Carleton said. "But I'm not sure Bart sees things the same way. It sounded to me like he was making contingency plans with Jasper for dealing with the dragon if the miners run into it again."

Perry sat up and leaned forward. "What kind of contingency plans? I hope they aren't planning to attack the dragon."

Carleton caught the shift in Perry's tone and wondered what had him so concerned. "I'm not sure. Bart said he wasn't going to let an 'oversized lizard' keep him from the ore. Why?"

"Because the avens won't tolerate Bart messing with a dragon or its lair."

"Even if lives are in danger and we aren't in aveni territory?"

"It doesn't matter where the dragon is. Our treaty with the avens says we can't mess with them. The beasts are rare and sacred. The terms let us stop dragons from attacking our settlements and chase them away from herds, but we're never supposed to molest them or kill them."

"You should warn Bart," Carleton suggested.

Perry made a sour face. "Bart knows full well about the treaty. Any landowner on the edge of aveni territory knows about it."

Hoping to calm his distressed friend, Carleton said, "The dragon filled in the place where the miners broke through to its cave. It doesn't seem to want an encounter any more than the miners do. Maybe they can follow the vein without running into it again."

Perry sat back with a doubtful look. "Maybe. They'd better hope the avens don't find out about the run-in they've already had."

Carleton shook his head. His contract seemed doomed. Every time he thought things were getting better, some new problem came up. Frustration tinged his voice as he shared his concluding thought aloud. "It's a shame the dragon lair was so near the vein. If the dragons are so rare, you'd have thought the odds of running into one would be slim."

Perry nodded thoughtfully. "Outside aveni territory, the odds *are* slim. Dragons dig deep and take advantage of natural cave systems when they can, but dragon-lair entrances are almost always above five-thousand feet. When the avens established their borders, known dragon lairs were an important consideration."

Perry's musings seemed to spur another concern. "How long is that drift they're working?"

"I'm not sure," Carleton responded. "More than a quarter mile, but less than a half, I'd guess."

Perry's brows drew together in thought. "The Pearce Hills are less than a mile from the aveni border. The avens ceded part of that area because mining operations at Commonwealth had already started, and the hills sit apart from the Dragon Mountains where most of the lairs are. But the miners wouldn't have to go far before they'd be under the border."

Carleton didn't like the idea of starting trouble with the avens. "Do you think the avens will care? The mine will be a couple-hundred feet underground by that point. The law allows the miners to follow a vein even if it goes under other claims."

"Yep, I'm familiar with that law," Perry said in a disapproving tone. "It causes a lot of trouble out here. But I don't think the avens would give it much weight, particularly if they think a dragon is threatened in any way."

Disappointment deepened Carleton's already somber mood. Bart was just starting to learn how useful he could be at the mine, and his relations with the delvans were improving. He didn't like the idea of aiding an operation that might turn out to be illegal, to say nothing of provoking the ire of the avens.

As for the dragon, coming face-to-face with the creature in its own domain had been one of the most exciting and frightening experiences of Carleton's life. But the dragon was only protecting its lair, and it wasn't right for Bart to destroy the beast.

"Dammit," Carleton swore under his breath.

Perry gave him a wry smile. "Sorry, Carleton. You can't seem to catch a break on this job."

It was true. Events at the mine did seem to have spiraled out of control, but he'd managed to avoid total disaster so far. He had to find a way to get out in front of these new problems. It was unlikely that he could convince Bart to stop following the vein at the aveni border, but he should be able to help the miners avoid the dragon.

CHAPTER 17

Onward and Downward

The next morning, Bart called everyone together at the entrance to the mine to discuss how they were going to proceed. The delvans were ready to move on to the second vein Carleton had discovered, having had their fill of dragon fighting. Naturally, Bart argued against that course of action.

Carleton suggested a compromise. He could explore the area around the vein with a spell like the one he had used to inspect the water well in Cochise. He should be able to verify that the dragon had backfilled the chamber where Mag had been attacked. He might even be able to determine if the dragon was still nearby.

"Wait," Ledge interrupted. Carleton was getting better at reading delvan expressions even when their faces were obscured by goggles and a hood, and Ledge looked disturbed. "Are you saying you could have warned us about the dragon?"

"Possibly," Carleton admitted. "But we had no reason to check. Even after your crew found the cavern, none of us expected it to be a dragon lair."

Ledge stared but didn't say anything.

"How long will it take?" Bart asked.

"I think I can do a thorough sweep along the drift in about twenty minutes," Carleton answered.

Bart frowned and turned to Jasper. "How about it?"

"Ye're asking me to trust the lives of me men to the wizard's scrying," Jasper said in a doubtful tone.

"You're in a dangerous line of work." Bart insisted. "If it's not dragons, it'll be something else. The wizard is giving you an advantage for once."

Jasper didn't look convinced, but his silence allowed Bart to push forward. The big man waved Carleton toward the mine entrance. "Go on and get started. Report to Jasper when you're done."

Carleton grabbed his equipment case and lantern and hurried into the mine. As he walked away from the others, he overheard Bart say, "I want that ore, and I'm not leaving it sit because of a damned dragon. Do what you need to protect your men, but I want to see some rock moving within the hour."

Bart's words faded behind him as Carleton turned the daylight corner and descended into the mine. The mine manager clearly saw the dragon as merely another obstacle to be removed. Carleton hoped the creature had abandoned the chamber near the vein and wouldn't come back while the miners were working.

Nothing in the bits of information Carleton had read about dragons gave him a sense of how one would react to sounds and vibrations near its underground lair. Had the miners accidentally attracted the monster with their drilling and detonations? He hoped not. If so, another confrontation with the dragon was inevitable.

Darkness surrounded Carleton and the weak bubble of light cast by his flickering candle lantern. He was the first person to descend into the mine since operations had been suspended. In the meantime, several of the passageway candles had burned out.

Although the dragon had backfilled the cavern opening, many hours had passed since then and the beast could easily have dug its way back into the mine. Feeling suddenly very alone, Carleton slowed his steps.

Unhappy with the limited visibility of candlelight, Carleton stopped and illuminated his glow stone. He extinguished the candle and dropped the glow stone into his lantern. The resulting beam lit the passage ahead for a gratifying distance, but it made him feel more like a target. He brought up his shield.

With a sigh of relief, Carleton finally arrived at the face of the drift and verified that the opening to the dragon's cavern was still sealed. His glow stone was beginning to fade, so he set it aside while he lit the candle in his lantern. He also lit the two closest passageway lanterns so the area would feel less gloomy.

Carleton set up his equipment in preparation for the underground exploration spell. When checking the well at the train station in Cochise, he'd used a fish eye because his destination was filled with water. To adapt the spell for searching caverns, he paired a dried lizard eye with the desiccated worm. Thinking back to the accusing look Ledge had given him, he added a new imprint stone to the ring as well. As long as the digging crews were anywhere near an underground cavern, he intended to use the spell often and watch for dragons.

Thanks to his work at Commonwealth, he was making good progress on creating several new casting stones that would be extremely valuable in his mining work. Even if he left Arizona after the contract was over, he could probably sell the stones through the Wizard's Guild for a decent amount of money.

Satisfied with his preparations, Carleton chanted the incantation and sent his awareness into the earth. He started at the spot where the opening had been. The dragon had packed the small side-chamber that Mag had entered with loose stone. Carleton found the connecting passageway where Mag had reported airflow and followed it a short distance until it opened up into a much larger chamber.

Carleton couldn't see the full scope of the chamber. Using the spell was like looking through a tube that restricted his peripheral vision and let him see only a couple of yards ahead. His viewpoint couldn't leave the surface of the stone, so he had to travel around the perimeter of the chamber and along the floor to verify that the dragon was not currently in residence.

Using the spell was not particularly expensive in terms of swi consumption, but over an extended period of time, the drain added up. By the time he ended the spell, he'd used about half of his capacity.

"What'd ye learn?" Tully asked, startling Carleton as he returned to his normal senses.

"The dragon did fill in the chamber you broke into," Carleton answered as he put away his casting ring and the imprint stone. "But the passage Mag followed connects to a big cavern. I think that's where he first ran into the dragon."

"Is the monster still there?"

"I don't think so."

Tully nodded. "Good. Maybe we scared it off."

"Possibly," Carleton said with doubt in his voice. "But it might be wise to stop every once in a while and listen for unexpected digging sounds until we are well away from its lair."

"I thought ye said it was gone," Ledge objected.

"No, I said I don't think it's there right now. That doesn't mean it won't come back."

Tully frowned. "It will be hard to get any work done if we're half-spooked listening for dragons the whole time."

"I understand," Carleton said. "All the same, I think you should be careful. If the dragon comes through after you've dug past this point, you'll be trapped."

Tully's eyes went wide, raising his bushy eyebrows. "Aye. Good point. How far 'til we're past the lair?"

"The main chamber I found is big, but the wall curves away from us. Another ten feet of digging will put at least ten feet of solid stone between the drift and the lair, and ten feet beyond that should put you past the lair entirely."

Tully pursed his lips, considering the information. "Good job, wizard. Now clear out of here so we can get to work."

Carleton smiled at the gruff compliment. "Aye, sir," he replied, mimicking the typical delvan response. Picking up his belongings, he walked back to where Flint was busily loading ore into the cart.

The delvan had a spooked look and spotted Carleton as soon as the wizard emerged from the passage. He stopped shoveling and pulled out his earplugs.

"Is the dragon truly gone?" he asked.

"For now. I warned Tully that it might come back." He followed Flint's glance to where the miner had propped Jasper's rifle up against the wall. "You know how to use that?"

"I do," Flint replied, although his tone indicated he wasn't looking forward to the possibility. "It's not the best in close quarters, but it packs a hell of a punch."

Carleton shuddered, imagining the circumstances that would lead to Flint needing to use the rifle. The Sharps was a long-range weapon, but in the mine, Flint would probably be less than thirty yards from the oncoming dragon. "Don't miss," Carleton suggested.

Flint give him a wry smile. "I'll do me best."

Leaving the miner to his work, Carleton went back into the drift toward Tully's crew. About halfway to the face, he came to the support he'd been working on when the crew broke through to the dragon's lair. Setting up his equipment, he decided to use what swi he had left to explore the rough dimensions of the cavern system.

The cavity-detecting spell he was going to try was a weak combination of his structural-integrity spell and the prospecting spell. However, what it lacked in strength, it made up for in range. With it, Carleton figured he could check the entire length of the known ore body and make sure the miners wouldn't penetrate other segments of the dragon's cave system. He wouldn't be able to see into the caverns, but he would be able to create a rough map of where they were.

Carleton put in his earplugs to enhance his concentration and positioned himself along the wall of the passage so he wouldn't impede the miners carrying ore from the stope to the loading area.

Carleton cast the spell and sent his awareness into the mountain. He first anchored his point of reference against the existing mine workings. Every underground air space larger than a cubic yard became a black void floating within a three-dimensional landscape of varying clarity. Where the earth was densest, his vision was clearest. At first, the perspective was disorienting because it was the inverse of what he was used to seeing.

His prospecting work had given Carleton a fair idea of where the vein ran, and the relatively hard silicates that made up the bulk of the ore were evident by their clarity. His goal was to find places where the ore body intersected with the dark voids of underground caverns and passages.

He quickly located the space where Mag had found the dragon. From there, he moved forward along the vein, searching for more caverns.

He found several. In fact, he found a surprisingly complex underground network of caverns and passages. Were the caves natural? Or had dragons created them? How many dragons lived there?

Several of the caverns included the ore body as part of a wall, yet none penetrated it. If dragons were responsible for the caverns, one could wonder if they had intentionally sought out the ore. Or they might have stopped excavating because the ore repulsed them for some reason.

With his swi reserves running low, Carleton withdrew from the spell. He got up and stretched after the long session, and then made notes about what he'd learned. He diagrammed his findings while the cavern locations were still fresh in his mind.

Bart wasn't going to be pleased. Carleton had hoped that the miners had been unfortunate enough to happen upon an isolated intersection with the dragon's lair, but that wasn't the case. The cavern system intersected the ore body in so many places that the delvans might as well use the caverns to access the ore instead of driving their own drifts. However, the dragon—or dragons—inhabiting the caves would undoubtedly take exception to that idea.

The miners could continue the drift for another twenty yards or so, but then they'd break into another cavern which was even bigger than the one they'd already discovered.

Exhausted of swi and discouraged about what he'd found, Carleton gathered his things and left the mine to give Bart the bad news. As he passed through Flint's work barea, he gave the mucker a cursory wave but didn't stop to talk. Flint barely looked up from his efforts, nodding an acknowledgment of Carleton's farewell gesture.

The miners would find out soon enough that their dragon troubles were only beginning. There was no point in upsetting them right away. Besides, Bart was going to be the one making decisions based on the new information, and Carleton honestly wasn't sure how the mine manager was going to react.

~

The next day was Saturday, and although the miners were working a regular ten-hour day, Carleton's contract gave him the day off. He was tempted to go down to the mine just to make sure the dragon hadn't returned, but if he bothered to make the trip, he would probably spend the whole day there.

Instead, he stayed at Sunrise Ranch, adding to his collection of catalysts and helping Perry with various tasks.

When they stopped for lunch, Carleton noticed that Perry seemed distracted.

"You have something on your mind?" he asked.

"I'm thinking about the situation at the mine," Perry answered. "The Pearce Hills are actually two separate peaks that rise from the valley floor. When the avens established their territory, the boundary line went between those peaks. The avens were willing to let us keep the eastern hill where Commonwealth had been claimed, but they knew dragons had caverns in the western hill. In fact, I think Pearce is the closest town to a dragon lair of any in the valley. I'm sure the avens didn't realize how extensive the caverns were, or they'd have been more insistent about shutting down the mine to protect them."

Carleton thought about all of the work that had been done on the mine and how much the town of Pearce depended upon it. "It's too late to change that now, isn't it?"

"Yeah, the boundaries have been drawn. But that doesn't change the fact that the treaty prohibits hunting or molesting the dragons. And from what you've told me, I'm fairly certain that the mine is about to extend under the boundary if it hasn't already."

"What will happen if the avens find out about what's going on?"

"I don't rightly know. Up to now, they've defended their borders without compromise. They're worried that any concession they make related to the agreement with our government would open the door to other unfavorable changes. I'd say they have good cause for that attitude."

"Would they attack the mine?"

"It's possible. Even if they don't literally attack the surface installations, they might seal off any part of the mine that enters their territory or invades the caverns."

Carleton wondered how the avens would accomplish the things Perry was suggesting. The warriors he'd seen flew wyverns. Did they fight from the ground as well? And how would the avens move through the caverns without having to fight the dragons themselves?

"You're thinking about the aveni patrol?" Perry asked with a raised eyebrow. When Carleton nodded, he explained, "The miners would be facing a more potent adversary than the aveni warriors. They'd have to deal with the shamans."

Carleton wasn't sure what the shamans would do, but considering they had elemental magic on their side, it probably wouldn't be good. If the avens sealed off parts of the mine, some of the miners could be trapped or injured. Carleton could try to protect the delvans, but he knew little combat magic and had never faced a skilled opponent.

"I guess we'd better hope the avens don't figure out what's happening," Carleton concluded with a shake of his head.

"You're forgetting something." Perry said in an annoyed tone.

"What?"

"I'm the aven agent for this region," he answered pointedly.

Carleton couldn't believe what he was hearing. "You plan to tell them about this?"

"I have to, at some point. Believe me, they'll figure it out for themselves before long. If they suspect I knew about it and didn't say anything, they'll assume I was hiding it from them and they'll lose their trust in me."

Carleton's voice rose in spite of his attempt to keep calm. "But telling them might bring them down on us. People could get hurt."

Perry shook his head stubbornly. "No, I think telling them is the only way to *prevent* people from getting hurt. It's much easier to negotiate *before* a breach of trust."

Carleton had trouble seeing a way around Perry's logic. His friend was probably right, but Carleton guessed Perry was underestimating Bart's determination. He chuckled and muttered, "I think Bart would prefer to ask for forgiveness than permission."

Perry pointed a finger at Carleton. "You say that as a joke, but it would be typical of him. What that saying really means is that it's okay to break the rules as long as you don't get caught. The philosophy is pretty common among criminal minds."

Carleton raised his hands in surrender. "Okay, okay, you've convinced me. But before you inform the avens, I think you should talk to Bart. He's not going to make this easy, and you should know what you're getting yourself into."

Perry pursed his lips and nodded. "Makes sense. You never know. He might surprise both of us." Carleton gave Perry a look that said he didn't believe Bart would surprise them in a good way. Perry patted him on the shoulder. "Have a little faith, Carleton. I got the agent job partly because I'm a great negotiator."

Carleton wanted to believe his friend and hoped they'd find a peaceful resolution to the problem. But how would being a great negotiator help if one or both of the sides were unwilling to compromise?

Chapter 18

Charming Reversal

"I appreciate you letting me borrow Peppy," Carleton commented to Perry as they rode up to the stable behind Bart's house. Over the previous couple of weeks, Carleton had been brushing up on his neglected riding skills. In Baltimore, he'd walked most places or hired a carriage for longer trips.

"My pleasure." Perry got down from his saddle. "I'm sure Peppy will keep you out of trouble, and he can use the exercise. I've been spending so much time with the peccaries, the poor boy was starting to feel neglected."

Peppy wagged his head up and down and nickered as Carleton dismounted. The wizard patted the horse's neck and handed the reins to the young groomsman who had come out to meet them. "I think he agrees with you," he said in an amused tone.

The groomsman reached for Remington's reins, but Perry shook his head. "I'm leaving shortly. I'll tie him to the post out front."

The two men went around to the front of the house, where they found Bart and Penelope stepping down off the front porch.

"Good morning, gentlemen," Bart said. Settling his eyes on Perry, he added, "What can I do for you today, Mr. Maine?"

Given his unusually friendly greeting, it seemed that Bart was in a rare good mood that morning.

It's a shame Perry is about to ruin it.

Penelope was smiling and looking fine as always. She wasn't carrying her parasol that morning, so the few stray hairs that had escaped her bun seemed to flicker about in the sun like delicate flames. Sunlight sparkled on the little glass balls strung along her necklace. She idly fingered one of the spheres, causing a tiny feather within it to float and twirl.

Perry glanced around for other listeners, but the only people within earshot were Carleton, Bart, and Penelope. He stepped closer to Bart and lowered his voice. "I was hoping we could talk about your dragon problem."

Bart and Penelope glanced at each other, and something passed between them. Their posture tensed as they both regarded Perry.

"I suppose you heard about that from the wizard," Bart said.

"Sure, I heard it from Carleton first," Perry confirmed. "But it's big news. The whole town is talking about it."

Bart's grim expression indicated he didn't care much for rumors about the dragon encounter going around. "The dragon isn't a problem anymore, or didn't the wizard tell you that part?"

Perry's mouth dropped open in shock. "You killed it?"

"No," Bart answered, giving Perry an incredulous look. "I didn't kill it. Our friend the geomancer said it plugged the hole we made and it hasn't bothered us since."

Carleton was relieved to hear that the miners hadn't run into any problems over the weekend while he wasn't around. He'd have felt bad if the dragon had returned and hurt anyone, particularly after he'd fought the impulse to come down to the mine on Saturday and check on the state of the caverns.

Perry wiped the back of his hand across his forehead and waved a placating gesture toward Bart. "Sorry, but this dragon situation has me a bit on edge."

Bart huffed out a chuckle. "You and me both." Then his face grew tight. "But you heard what that monster did to Mag. I'd be in my rights to protect my men and destroy the beast."

Perry drew himself up and narrowed his eyes at Bart. "That's where you're wrong. You're walking on quicksand here. You know the Dragon Mountain Treaty forbids you from hunting or harassing the dragons."

"Unless they attack us!" Bart shouted, his face turning red.

So much for his good mood, thought Carleton. He braced himself for the confrontation he could see brewing between his boss and his friend.

"The dragon was only protecting its lair," Perry insisted. "You need to keep the miners away from the caverns."

Bart folded his arms and clenched his jaw. "I can't do that. Some of the caverns intersect the ore, as I'm sure the wizard told you."

Perry shook his head and looked at the ground. In a regretful tone, he said, "The avens aren't going to care about ore. They *will* care if you hurt the dragons in any way."

Carleton shielded his eyes, along with everyone else, as a sudden gust of wind swirled dust up from the road. The eddy circled the group a couple of times and then passed. Dust devils, as the locals called the swirling columns of air, arose frequently and suddenly. Its timing seemed like a confirmation of Perry's remark, and considering that the avens supposedly had access to elemental magic, the idea wasn't ridiculous.

"The avens have no business knowing about this," Bart said in a too-calm voice. "They gave us permission to dig, and that's what we're going to do."

Penelope was the only member of the group who appeared to be completely calm. When the dust devil swept through, she had simply closed her eyes and waited for it to pass, patiently rolling a glass sphere between her fingers. When she opened her eyes, she focused on Perry, who was opening his mouth to speak.

"Perry," she interrupted firmly, getting his attention. He closed his mouth and returned her stare, waiting for her to speak. Her pale, ice-blue eyes drew Carleton in as well.

She took a step forward, leaving Bart a pace behind and commanding all of Perry's attention. "We all understand your concerns for the treaty and the dragons. No one wants to make trouble with the avens." Her voice took on a monotone as she continued, playing with her necklace all the while. "Bart doesn't want trouble. I don't want trouble. The delvans don't want trouble. And you don't want trouble."

Carleton blinked as she paused. Her voice was so much more pleasing to the ear than Bart's. And she was right. No one wanted trouble.

Penelope tilted her head at Perry, who continued to stare into her eyes and didn't move a muscle. She spoke softly, but firmly. "If you talk to the avens, you will only upset them unnecessarily. Wouldn't it be better to resolve this situation quietly, without alarming them?"

When he responded, Perry's voice was almost a whisper. "We don't want to alarm the avens unnecessarily." Carleton found his head bobbing along with the words.

She slowly nodded once. "That's right. This is our problem to solve, not theirs, and we'll do what we can to protect both the miners and the dragons."

Perry echoed her words again. "We'll protect both the miners and the dragons."

The sweet dimples in her cheeks deepened as Penelope's lips curved into a smile. Her perfect oval face made Carleton's pulse pound as he sucked in a breath.

"See?" she said brightly. "You have nothing to worry about. You can go back to your ranch knowing everything is fine at Commonwealth."

Carleton was certainly relieved to know that everything was under control. He looked to his friend to see if he agreed.

A moment of doubt creased Perry's brow briefly, but then he seemed to come around to Penelope's point of view. "All right. As long as everything is fine here, I should be getting back to the ranch. Carleton, I'll see you later."

He tipped his hat to Penelope. "Good day, Miss Cartwright. Bart."

Bart responded with a nod, uncharacteristically silent with his lips pressed closed. Carleton wondered if the dynamic between him and the young woman had changed somehow. Usually, Bart pushed Penelope into the background. It was odd for him to let her dominate a conversation as she'd just done. Carleton mentally shrugged and decided to be thankful for small favors.

While Perry rode off, Bart glanced at Penelope with an odd expression. His narrowed eyes showed a mixture of respect, annoyance, and fear. As usual, Carleton didn't understand what the man's problem was. He always seemed agitated about something.

Penelope ignored Bart's critical look and focused on Carleton, much to his delight. "Thank you for your support, Carleton. It means a lot to me."

Carleton wasn't sure of exactly what he'd done for her, but he smiled and gave her a shallow bow. "My pleasure. Glad to be of service."

Bart stepped forward, ruining the moment. "Don't you have some wizarding to do?"

"Indeed," Carleton agreed. "I'll get to work now. Good day, Miss Cartwright."

After Bart's interruption, Penelope's gaze had become distant and her complexion seemed extra pale. She took a breath and responded with a faint, "Good day, Wizard Kazimer."

Carleton turned away from the pair and walked toward the mine. He whistled a dance-hall tune, feeling more at peace with things than at any time since he'd come to Arizona. Everything was going well at Commonwealth for a change.

Carleton waved down an ore wagon that was heading up to the mine. The driver was kind enough to slow down so he could jump on board for a ride. While the wagon bumped and creaked up the hill, an itchy sensation settled between his shoulder blades. The disturbing feeling made him wonder if he was missing something.

CHAPTER 19

Breakthrough

"Fire in the hole!" Tully shouted from the far end of the passage. A few moments later, he and Ledge hustled into the loading stope and took positions away from the opening to the drift.

Carleton stood well back out of the way, waiting with his heart in his throat. Blasting was his least-favorite part of working in the mine. In the month or so he'd been there, no one had been hurt as a direct result of using dynamite, but it made him uneasy nonetheless.

The miners had progressed far enough down the drift that the blast was anticlimactic when it came. The successive detonations were muffled by the stone they freed, and by the time the cloud of dust made its way to the loading area, it was barely a puff.

Everyone stayed silent for several minutes, listening intently. Bart motioned Ledge out of the way and positioned himself near the tunnel opening. His hands were tightly gripped around Jasper's Big Fifty.

It was unusual for Bart to spend any time down in the mine. He normally delegated all mine operations to Jasper, but it was a special day. Carleton had warned the miners that they were about to breach another cavern and Bart had insisted on being present. He relayed most of his orders through Jasper, but when the blast was eminent, he took possession of the Big Fifty and the bandolier of extra ammunition. "If there's a dragon," he said, "I'll deal with it."

Carleton had used his spell to check for the presence of a dragon and found nothing, but everyone knew he couldn't offer any guarantees. It was possible the explosion itself would attract one from another part of the cavern complex.

Carleton pushed back a feeling of foreboding for the dozenth time that day. Over the past couple of weeks, he'd become more and more uneasy as the delvans dug closer to the next cavern. Tully had also become more snappish than usual, and Ledge was prone to silent brooding.

They had added a third delvan, named Emory, to their crew to replace Mag, but the new man kept mostly to himself. Carleton's attempts to strike up a conversation with Emory received nothing but monosyllabic responses.

Bart nodded at Carleton, giving him the okay to move on to the next phase of their plan for the day. Carleton lit his glow stone and put it into his lantern. He cast his shield and started slowly down the passage. The light from his lantern cut a cube of illumination from the dust that still swirled. He adjusted the bandanna that covered his nose and mouth, giving him the look of a bandit searching for lost treasure. Bart coughed from right behind him.

Unexpectedly, the dust began to clear as they moved forward. When his lantern light fell on the pile of ore at the end of the passage, Carleton understood why. He shifted the light upward, revealing a dark hole that blew clear air into the passage. Carleton dropped his shield so he could climb the rubble and listen intently at the hole. He stayed to the side of the opening, half expecting a blast of flame to shoot through it at any moment.

Carleton shook his head in answer to Bart's questioning look. He winced when Bart's commanding voice shattered their stealthy silence.

"Get this ore cleared away," he said, stepping back from the base of the pile.

The delvans followed the plan they'd made for clearing the ore. They broke it up and hauled it to the loading area as usual, but they stopped every few minutes and listened for sounds of movement from the cavern beyond. Carleton and Bart remained nearby with Jasper, waiting to the side in a previously stoped-out segment of the passage.

Carleton took deep breaths, trying to push back the anxiety that increased as the miners widened the opening into the cavern. Every time he wondered if they were making a huge mistake, the memory of Penelope's voice calmed him.

Over the past couple of weeks, Bart and Penelope had taken to addressing the crews almost daily. Oddly, Penelope had done most of the talking at these brief meetings, reassuring the miners that everything was going well and that they should be proud of their progress. Carleton was amused to think that Bart may have figured out that her style of delivery was more inspirational than his.

In spite of her cheerful message, Penelope herself wasn't looking so well. Dark circles under her eyes and her listless movements indicated that she was under some kind of strain. When Carleton had suggested to Bart that he let the poor woman rest, Bart told him to mind his own business.

Reassurances aside, Carleton swallowed hard when he imagined standing in front of the concentrated heat that had burned Mag so severely. His confidence in his shield waned against the mental image of dragon fire. There would be nothing between him and the beast that spewed such a conflagration.

Flames weren't the only weapons in the dragon's arsenal. Carleton had personally handled the six-inch claws from a *small* specimen. Those same claws that could dig underground caverns would tear him apart with a single swipe. Of course, he would be within range of the dragon's armored head and sharp teeth long before its claws reached him, assuming he survived the dragon's fiery breath.

When the miners had cleared a path large enough to allow a speedy retreat, Bart caught Carleton's eye and tilted his head toward the opening. It was time to investigate the cavern.

Carleton's glow stone had long since expired while the miners had worked, so he recharged it before walking past them. Tully touched his hand to his forehead in the delvan gesture for "watch your head," which was also their sign for "good luck." Carleton gave him a half-smile of thanks.

If a dragon were nearby, surely it would have made its presence known by then, but Carleton thought it would be imprudent to stride into the cavern without having a quick look around first. He stopped at the edge of the cavern and peered into it.

In the light of his lantern, the cavern seemed smaller than when he'd observed it from the even more limited view of his scrying spell. It was roughly diamond-shaped, with the ore body along the wall to their left and a connecting passageway in the opposite corner. As Carleton had anticipated, the cave was empty except for an odd jumble of boulders that had been pushed into one corner. "I think it's clear," he said.

Bart shouldered past him and looked around the cavern. He pointed toward the passageway and spoke to Jasper, who had come up behind them. "Seal that opening so we don't get any unexpected visitors."

Jasper's gaze darted around as he eagerly absorbed the details of the cavern. No delvan was immune to the allure of an unexplored cave system, whether or not its origins were natural. If not for the dragon, he and his men would probably use their day off from work to do some exploring.

Jasper and Tully advanced toward the second passageway slowly, pausing frequently to listen as they drew closer to the dark opening. They inspected the exit carefully, pointing and debating the best way to block it.

Carleton kept his eye on the two delvans, but his attention was mostly drawn to Bart's inspection of the exposed ore vein. Bart seemed to be satisfied with what he found.

Curious about the strange pile of rocks, Carleton was about to investigate them when Jasper and Tully suddenly went silent. The two delvans looked at each other and both ran as fast as their stubby legs could move them away from the far passageway.

"Something big is coming!" hissed Jasper as they ran past Carleton.

Ominous thumps and scratches heralded the dragon's approach. Carleton's heart leaped into his throat, and he brought up his shield as quickly as he could. Glancing back, he saw that Bart had dropped to one knee and was drawing a bead on the opening. He wasn't following the protocol they'd agreed upon.

"Wait until after the first breath!" Carleton reminded him. "And stay behind me so I can shield you."

After a brief look of irritation crossed Bart's face, he frowned and nodded. He got to his feet and moved so Carleton was between him and the opening.

And don't shoot me with that cannon, Carleton added silently.

As Carleton turned his attention back to the passageway, a blunt snout emerged, followed by a wedge-shaped head. Tightly-interlocked scales covered the creature's skull, merging into a frill of curved spikes that protected its neck. As the creature breathed, the air passing through its nostrils sounded like a bellows.

No illustration from a book could have prepared Carleton for the reality of seeing a fifteen-hundred-pound angry lizard with a head the size of a wood stove. His instincts screamed at him to run, but his rubbery legs didn't comply. His breath caught in his throat, and he hoped he wouldn't embarrass himself by creating a warm yellow puddle at his feet.

The dragon peered around the room, its black eyes blinking in reaction to the lantern light. When it spotted Carleton, it froze for a second. Then, with alarming speed, the dragon moved forward and reared back its head. Carleton barely had time to cringe before the dragon thrust its head forward and blew a jet of oily flame toward him.

When the intense heat slammed into Carleton's shield, he felt as if he were stepping into a burning building. The odor of his own singed hair and smoldering clothing reached his nostrils, and every bit of exposed skin was instantly raw with sunburn. Flaming oil splashed off the sides of his shield and flowed to the floor where it continued to burn in a semicircle. As the shield adjusted to the onslaught, it drained power so voraciously that his vision dimmed and his head swam.

Carleton struggled for breath as the dragon fire sucked every bit of available air from the space. When the inferno ceased, he followed the battle plan by necessity more than by choice. He collapsed to his knees as his shield wavered and failed. Reeling and gasping, he blinked up at the dragon through eyes that teared from the residual heat and oily smoke.

The creature took a couple of steps into the room with its head low, sweeping back and forth, assessing the condition of its prey. The Big Fifty boomed from behind Carleton, making his ears ring. The shot hit the dragon right behind its nose, but the angle was bad and the bullet deflected into the cavern wall where it ricocheted with a whining *ping*.

The dragon seemed shocked by the impact of the high-caliber round and it shook its head in reaction. The bullet left a shallow furrow along its nose scales, but the beast didn't seem to be hurt.

Squinting at the dragon from his hands and knees, Carleton knew he was facing his death. He didn't have the power to raise another shield, and if the animal chose to attack with teeth and claws, it would be on him before he could escape.

What might have become Carleton's last moment shifted into slow motion. The sound of Bart cursing and struggling to reload the buffalo gun came from behind him. The dragon stopped shaking its head and settled its eyes upon them. Its head started to rise, and Carleton recognized the prelude to another blast of flame. He was about to be, in a word, toasted.

But then another boom shook the cavern as Bart fired a second round. It hit the dragon below the ridge of its raised chin. The bullet slammed into the creature's softer under-scales near its front shoulder, plowing through flesh and blasting loose a chunk of scale upon exit.

The dragon's roar of pain was nearly as deafening as the report of the Big Fifty. The monster backed out of the cavern more quickly than Carleton would have imagined possible, leaving behind a trail of blood.

A strong hand grabbed Carleton's upper arm, helping him stand. "Told you we could handle the damned lizard," Bart said, but his shaking voice undercut the bravado of his statement.

The boss looked Carleton up and down, his eyes lingering on the frizzled hair below Carleton's helmet. "Looks like you're done for the day." Bart guided him to the narrow passage back into the mine.

More than anything, Carleton wanted to sit down and rest for a minute. He stumbled and coughed, nearly bumping into Jasper, who was coming through from the drift. Jasper's nose wrinkled at the oily smoke that tainted the chamber, and his eyebrows rose when he caught sight of the flickering puddles of dragon breath.

Handing the Big Fifty to Jasper, Bart said, "I doubt the monster will come back any time soon, but keep a watch for it while your men close that passage. I'm going to have Penelope check over the wizard." He lifted the bandolier off his shoulder and passed that to Jasper as well.

"Aye," Jasper acknowledged. "Anything else I should know?"

Bart nodded. "The dragon cocks its head back before it breathes fire, and its scales are tougher than boiled leather. Try to get a straight-on shot at the biggest surface you see. If it raises its head, run."

Eyes wide and swallowing hard, Jasper slung the bandolier across his chest and verified that the rifle was loaded with a live cartridge. Waving his men forward, he yelled, "Get a move on, ye loafers."

As Bart guided him out of the chamber and away from the cloying atmosphere, Carleton's head started to clear. His sense of wrongness came back to the foreground. With sudden clarity, he understood what had been bothering him. Somehow, he'd let Bart and Penelope talk him out of his concerns about continuing the drift.

Carleton's worst fears had been realized. They'd pushed forward until the drift intersected another cavern, and they'd attacked the dragon that came to investigate. Perry would be livid.

His mind wandered back to Perry's meeting with Bart and Penelope. How could he have been so gullible? Bart must have made some pretty convincing arguments to get Perry to back down from his plan to speak to the avens, but Carleton couldn't bring any of those arguments to mind.

He smiled at the memory of staring into Penelope's ice-blue eyes. He took a deep breath, relaxing again as he remembered her reassurances that everything was under control and would work out fine. Then a vision of the dragon's open mouth belching flame burned away the dreamy sense of comfort. He twitched as the cold reality of his near-death experience restored his mental clarity.

"You okay there, Kazimer?" Bart was still walking him out of the mine. The man carried Carleton's equipment case, so they must have stopped to retrieve it along the way, although Carleton had no memory of doing that.

Carleton gently shrugged off Bart's supporting hand. "Yes, I'm feeling a little better now."

"Penny should have a look at you anyway," he said, his tone brooking no argument.

Carleton was certain that seeing Penelope right then was a bad idea. The hairs on his neck tingled when he thought back on the past couple of weeks. He and the delvans had plodded forward, accepting orders without question. In spite of their earlier concerns, he and Perry had hardly discussed the mine in all that time.

It was like we were under some kind of spell.

The realization sent a chill down Carleton's spine. A flash of memory showed Penelope playing with the hollow glass decorations on her necklace. Decorations that held feathers. Just as geomancers imprinted spells on casting stones, wizards who worked with other elements used other kinds of tools.

A feather trapped in a bubble of air? Penelope was an aeromancer.

His mind rejected the conclusion at first. She'd never once hinted at her abilities. Wouldn't she want to commiserate with another of her kind in a place where wizards lived such a lonely existence? He had thought they were becoming friends. Maybe he was wrong.

Carleton knew little about aeromancy. As soon as the Guild determined a wizard's elemental aptitude, all training focused on developing the skills associated with that element. There was no point in Carleton studying aeromancy when he would never be able to use it. Working in the field, he would expect to encounter wizards from other disciplines eventually, but he'd not yet had the opportunity to get to know an aeromancer. Or, maybe he just had without realizing it.

Penelope's actions were illegal. Using a charm on people against their will was assault. He wanted to believe Bart was forcing her to do it, but that thought was probably naive. Why would she do it, then?

Carleton grimaced and shook his head. Talk about naive. He was suddenly quite certain that Penelope was much more than Bart's bookkeeper. Her job was a cover for her real work, the work she had been doing successfully for the past couple of weeks, and maybe even longer. If not for the dragon encounter, Carleton would probably still be under her influence.

"Something on your mind?" Bart asked suspiciously.

Thinking fast, Carleton answered calmly, "It's just nerves. I thought we were goners, but your second shot saved us both."

Bart clapped him on the shoulder. Their shared trauma seemed to have brought a brief moment of camaraderie. "Yeah, you see the way that dragon skedaddled out of there? Nothing like some high-powered lead to take the fight out of the opposition."

Carleton took a few deep breaths and made a show of perking up. "You know, I think I'm fine now. I should probably go back to the ranch and get some rest." What he really wanted to do was find Perry and verify that his friend was under the same charm. And then free him of it somehow.

Bart was silent for a moment. He glanced at Carleton with an assessing look and then shook his head. "We'll let Penelope decide whether or not you're fine."

Carleton started to argue, but couldn't think of a good excuse not to see her. His mind raced for a solution. If he met with Penelope right then, she'd probably recognize that her charm had been broken, and she'd put him back under the spell.

Bart's suspicious glances suggested that she'd warned him that the charm might fail. She must have anticipated that the psychological pressure of fighting the dragon could unravel it.

It pained him to think that she was part of the conspiracy to develop the mine at any cost. By magically pacifying everyone who might expose what they were doing, she was an accessory to the crime of violating the treaty with the avens. Never mind the fact that she was putting all of the miners and Carleton in serious danger. Somehow, Carleton had to reach Perry and warn him before Penelope figured out that her magic had failed.

Chapter 20

Revelation

Carleton thought Bart was taking him to see Penelope at the manager's residence. He expected to have more time to come up with an excuse for not seeing her, but she was waiting for them when they reached the passage to the subtown. Although she was wearing her work pants and shirt, the suspect necklace glinted at her neck.

Her eyes scanned them both, lingering with concern on Carleton. "Are you okay?" she asked, gently putting her hand on his back and guiding him into the passageway toward the quad. "You look a little crispy around the edges. I'm guessing you found a dragon."

"He says he's fine," Bart said. "But I think you'd better check him over anyway."

As they walked into the common room, the delvan woman who had ministered to Mag appeared. The woman left after Penelope's reassurances that none of the miners had been hurt and that she could tend to Carleton herself.

Penelope motioned for Carleton to sit at the table and then asked what had happened. Carleton figured that the less he spoke the less likely it was that she'd detect the broken charm, so he let Bart do the talking while she sat next to him and inspected the red skin on his face and hands.

"It was bigger than I expected," Bart admitted. "I've seen dragons from a distance, but when that monster poked its head into the room and stared at me with them big black eyes, I nearly dropped the rifle."

Bart patted Carleton on the shoulder. "I gotta say, our wizard earned his pay today. When the dragon let loose and filled the room with flame, that shield of his was the only thing between us and a set of angel wings."

I think you mean a new set of devil's horns, Carleton thought.

Penelope had arranged a few first-aid supplies on the tabletop. Apparently, she'd been prepared for trouble. She reached for a small tin and told Carleton to take off his helmet.

"Well, I can't do much about your poor hair," she fussed, "but this salve should make your skin feel better." She wrinkled her nose as she sat closer to gently apply the salve to his cheeks and nose. "You should consider a change of clothes, too. These smell like old frying oil."

Before that morning, Penelope's fingers on his face would have been a welcome intimacy, and the salve certainly relieved his hot, abused skin. But her duplicity made a mockery of her tenderness. He had to restrain himself from pushing her hand away.

Bart sniffed at his own shirt. "Changing clothes ain't a bad idea." He stared at her until she looked up and gave him her attention. "If you have this under control, I'll head back to the house."

The coldness of the assessing glance Penelope turned his way chilled him, but Carleton kept his expression carefully neutral. With Bart there, he had no chance of escaping an unwilling return to ignorant bliss. One-on-one with her, he might be able to talk her out of it.

"Go ahead," she said. "After I finish with Wizard Kazimer, it will take me a few minutes to pack up my things."

With a parting nod, Bart turned and strode out of the quad. His boot steps echoed down the passage until he turned onto Main Drift.

Into the silence that followed, Penelope said to Carleton, "You've been awfully quiet."

"I've been thinking," he said while she put some of the salve on his hand.

She paused for a moment, but didn't look up at him. "Oh? About what?"

"About mines and dragons," he answered. "And treaties," he added in a harsh tone.

That brought her eyes up to his. Under the intense scrutiny of her beautiful blue eyes, he couldn't hide his anger with her. Or his disappointment.

She lowered her hands to her lap, wiping off the excess salve with a rag. "You seem to have something you want to say to me."

For a moment, Carleton regretted letting his emotions get the better of him and reveal that he was no longer charmed. However, her reaction led him to believe that she had already figured it out.

"What is your part in this?" he asked. "Did Bart hire you to keep the crews in line? Or do you have a stake in the mine?"

Penelope took a deep breath and casually raised her hand toward her necklace, but before she could reach it, Carleton's hand closed on hers.

"Please don't," he said. "Talk to me. Help me understand why you are doing this."

Penelope's eyes widened and her hand dropped slowly back to her lap. "How long have you known I'm an aeromancer?"

What should he tell her? If he said he had just figured it out, she'd know he hadn't had time to tell anyone else. On the other hand, she'd know he was lying if he claimed to have known all along. The truth was risky, but he had no better answer. "About fifteen minutes," he said.

Her gaze fell to her lap and her shoulders drooped. "What are you going to do?" she asked, barely above a whisper.

It wasn't the reaction he expected from a rogue wizard. He had been ready to defend himself against whatever magical attack she might try to launch, but her meek posture disarmed him.

He reached out and lifted her chin, making her look him in the eye. "That depends. Tell me why you're doing this."

"I can't." Her voice was pleading, almost desperate.

"Why not?"

She placed a hand on his arm and squeezed gently. "I can't even give you a hint. But you should know that I never wanted to hurt anyone."

"That's easy to say," Carleton responded bitterly, "but you weren't the one standing in front of a dragon a while ago."

"I know, and I'm so sorry," she said. The tears pooling in her eyes inclined Carleton to believe her. She cleared her throat and added, "I can't tell you how glad I am that you weren't seriously hurt."

Carleton lifted his hands, looking over the red skin. "Only a sunburn," he said with a wry smile.

Turning her question back onto her, Carleton asked, "So, what do we do now? Are you going to try to charm me again?"

She started shaking her head before he'd even finished his question. "No. It probably wouldn't work anyway. You've broken the charm and realized what suggestion was made. It would be very difficult for me to restore the charm against your will using the same suggestion."

"That's why you were waiting here," Carleton surmised. "So you could get to me as soon as possible in case the dragon encounter broke the charm."

"Yes," she admitted, lowering her eyes. "Extreme stress or circumstances that reinforce your resistance to the suggestion can break the charm. The dragon attack was both. I warned Bart that he'd need to bring you to me as quickly as possible if something bad happened."

"Are you disappointed that he was too late?"

Penelope brought her eyes up to meet his. When she spoke, he sensed the honesty of her words. "Yes and no. Bart's operations might have continued undetected for a while longer if I'd been able to restore the charm, but it was only a matter of time before the avens would figure out what he's doing."

Carleton nodded his agreement. "A wounded dragon will certainly get their attention."

"My thoughts, exactly. The only way to stop Bart was to let him go too far."

"Even if that meant sacrificing my life and the dragon's?"

"You underestimate your abilities, Wizard Kazimer."

Penelope turned and started putting her supplies away in a small black medical bag. She glanced at him with a frown and said, "The bigger problem for me is that you know I'm an aeromancer. That wasn't supposed to happen, and it puts both of us in danger."

"How so?"

"That's one of the things I can't tell you. Let's just say it would be best if you don't tell anyone else what you know."

Carleton wasn't wired for subterfuge. He would have a tough time keeping her secret unless he understood the stakes. He needed to know more, but he didn't trust her to tell him the truth.

He shook his head. "Not good enough. I can't keep this from Perry on the basis of a vague threat. I think my time is done here anyway, and I'm sorry, but I can't keep your secret because you're afraid Bart will fire you."

"I don't work for Bart." Her hand flew to her mouth the moment the words left her lips, and she stared at Carleton with an expression of horror. That information was apparently one of the things Carleton wasn't supposed to know.

Narrowing his eyes, Carleton started to speak, but Penelope swiftly took her hand from her mouth and covered his. "Please don't ask any more questions. If word gets out about my … talents … I'll have no value to my employer. My father is quite ill. If I'm fired, he'll no longer receive care." She looked down and finished in a bitter tone. "And my only option will be to work in a bordello."

"Aren't you being a bit melodramatic? Why don't you try to get work from the Guild?"

"I'm not a Guild member," she answered quietly.

Carleton stared at her while he considered her story. She truly was a rogue aeromancer. She had lied to him, charmed him and his friends, and conspired to break the treaty. She wasn't only asking him to keep her secret, she was asking him to let her continue her illicit work unobstructed.

She seemed to sense he wasn't convinced. "I don't agree with many of the things I'm told to do," she insisted. "But I'm in a position to take certain liberties with how they happen. Helping Bart put his neck in a noose was the quickest way to stop him." Her eyes grew watery with unshed tears. "Maybe someday, I'll figure out a way to get myself and my family out of this trap we're in."

She was asking for a lot. Before he would consider going along with her, she needed to agree to something that was non-negotiable. "Tell me how I can break the charm on

Perry," he demanded, folding his arms. "And you have to release the delvans. What they are facing is dangerous and they need to have all their wits about them."

Penelope chewed her lip while she considered his demands. Finally, she nodded. "All right, I can agree to that. To break the charm on Perry, all you have to do is ask him why he didn't push the matter on the day he came to speak with Bart and me. Keep repeating his own arguments back to him until the charm stops blocking them."

Armed with that knowledge, Carleton stood to leave. "And the delvans?"

"I'll take care of it," she assured him.

He watched her face for any hint that she wouldn't make good on her promise, then blew out a huff of disgust with himself when he considered how gullible he was when it came to her.

He turned to go, but she stopped him with a light touch on his arm. "To be honest, I don't think the charm works very well on the delvans anyway. They've been willing to pursue the vein because that's their job. They don't seem to care much about human politics."

She didn't have to share that information with him, so her admission made Carleton feel a little better about her. However, when she stood up and moved closer, he was alarmed enough that he had to resist the urge to back away from her.

Her upturned face was less than a foot from his. He'd never noticed the splash of freckles across her nose and cheeks until that moment. And her full lips looked so soft below that adorable button nose …

Stop that! he commanded his traitorous libido. Yes, she was an attractive woman. She was also a criminal.

"Thank you for keeping my secret," she said in a near-whisper.

Her voice was filled with sincerity and relief, and her nearness made him think she might express her gratitude by kissing him. As tempting as that idea was, he eased back and cleared his throat.

"You're welcome," he said. "Please don't give me reason to regret it."

He turned away from Penelope, picking up his toolbox on his way out of the common room. As he left the quad, his heart pounded and his breath came in huffs from the intensity of their exchange. If he was going to keep a clear head, he had to stay away from her. And not only because she was an aeromancer. Her charms were potent enough *without* magical enhancement.

Carleton's next priority was to get back to the ranch and free Perry from the charm. Carleton would keep her secret from his friend as long as he could, but if things became complicated, Perry would need every bit of information that might prove useful.

Chapter 21

Treaty Breaker

As he rode up the final stretch of road toward Sunrise Ranch, Carleton stiffened at the sight of an aveni hunting party near the house. They were talking with Perry, and even from a distance, his body language indicated that the conversation wasn't friendly.

Peppy wanted nothing to do with the aveni wyverns, and Carleton was happy to let him go wide around the group. Remington paced swiftly back and forth along the far side of the corral. Perry glanced once toward Carleton but didn't interrupt his conversation with the chiefson.

Worried about what might be going on, Carleton opened the corral gate and turned Peppy loose inside, saddle and all. Peppy ran over and joined Remington in his agitated pacing.

As Carleton approached Perry and the aveni hunters, all five of the wyverns swiveled their heads and followed his progress with their large yellow eyes. One of the beasts even stepped to the side to keep him in clear view. Although the avens were diminutive, their mounts were anything but; the riderless creature behind the chiefson stood a good head taller than Carleton. At his previous encounter with the hunting party, Carleton's view from the wagon hadn't prepared him for how vulnerable he'd feel standing within range of those sharp talons and long beaks.

"Hey, Carleton," Perry greeted with a tired voice. He did a double take upon seeing Carleton's face, probably noticing the reddened skin and the shine of the salve. "This is Chiefson Cearul Sulc of the *Siri Tan*. Chiefson Sulc, meet Wizard Carleton Kazimer."

The chiefson drew himself up and glared at Carleton. "Wizard? He has magic?" He turned the glare on Perry. "Why you not say this?"

Perry's brow wrinkled in confusion. "I just did. Why does it matter?"

The chiefson narrowed his eyes. "You not speak own words."

Perry shook his head and sighed. "Not that again." He turned to Carleton. "The avens found an injured dragon and believe the miners are responsible. I keep telling them that the miners wouldn't do that. You were there today. Maybe you can convince them."

These were not the circumstances Carleton had expected to be in when he was planning to break Penelope's charm on Perry. It was obvious that the avens had figured out something was wrong, and Perry was operating at a serious disadvantage. How could he break the charm and not reveal Penelope's secret?

He had to try. Perry couldn't negotiate with the avens the way he was.

"Perry, listen. Things are not okay at the mine. Bart lied to us. He lied to everyone."

Perry blinked a couple of times. "But you've been coming back from the mine every day telling me everything is fine."

"I know. He fooled me too. Bart told us he would respect the treaty, but he didn't."

Perry's face reddened and he put his hands on his hips. "Are you telling me he followed the ore under aveni lands?"

Carleton could practically see the charm's influence shredding to confetti as Perry continued to process what he was hearing.

"Yes," Carleton answered. Glancing at the chiefson, he reluctantly added, "Bart shot the dragon this morning."

Perry sucked in a breath and let it out explosively. "What the hell!" He took a closer look at Carleton's face. "You helped, didn't you?" he accused.

The chiefson stepped forward and startled Carleton by grabbing his sleeve and sniffing it. Although the aven was barely taller than Carleton's waist, the stark anger in his dark eyes made Carleton back up a step.

"Breath of Nadi Gaman," the chiefson said, immediately identifying the odor. He drew a slim but lethal-looking blade from a scabbard at his hip and rested the point on Carleton's chest. "You come with us," he said.

Carleton would have slapped the blade away, but the edges looked razor-sharp. "I was tricked," he insisted. "It's not too late to fix this, but we have to act now, before anyone else gets hurt."

Perry frowned at the chiefson's blade. "Now, wait a minute," Perry objected. "You can't take Carleton. There will be an investigation—I'll make sure of it—and if Carleton did anything wrong, he'll be punished by the proper authorities."

The chiefson wasn't having any of it. "Shamans speak for Nadi Gaman. Treaty breaker come with us."

Carleton's alarm was rapidly turning to panic. How could he possibly go with them? The avens were traveling by air. There was no part of departing by wyvern that struck Carleton as good for his well-being. He turned a desperate face toward Perry. "Can't you reason with them?"

Perry gripped Carleton's arm. "I can't let you take him," he declared.

The chiefson made a quick chopping motion. One of the warriors moved his wyvern forward, using the point of his spear to push Perry back and away from Carleton. Perry's hand falling away from Carleton's arm was like a signal that all was lost.

The chiefson motioned Carleton toward his wyvern. Staring at the tall creature with the fierce raptor eyes, Carleton couldn't seem to make his legs move. A sharp poke from the blade unfroze his muscles and he took hesitant steps toward the animal. As he went by the wyvern's head, it started to turn toward him, but the chiefson barked a command and it held still.

Standing next to the saddle, Carleton wasn't sure what was expected of him. He'd watched the chiefson vault into the seat, but all Carleton would have to do was lift his leg over the wyvern's tail. The saddle was designed for a much smaller derriere and would do little more than cradle Carleton's privates. He looked down at the chiefson with an incredulous expression.

The chiefson pushed him toward the bird, and Carleton took the hint to lift one leg over to the other side. The aven then pushed him forward until his body was snuggled right up to the saddle. The wyvern turned its head to the side so it could regard him with one yellow eye. It obviously wasn't looking forward to the coming experience either.

The chiefson put his blade away and held his arms out with his forearms together. He motioned for Carleton to do the same. When Carleton had complied, the chief loosened the laces on the cargo pad above the saddle. Threading Carleton's arms under the laces, he then tightened them down.

"You've got to be kidding me," Carleton said, his terror raising his voice an octave. "I can't move!"

The chiefson gestured toward the laces. "You safe. No fall."

Carleton appealed to Perry. "Do something! They're going to get me killed."

Perry was held back by two warriors, and he raised his arms in a helpless gesture. "You'll be okay," he promised. "I've seen the wyverns carry some pretty big cargo. I'll meet you at their camp and we'll get this sorted out."

Carleton's head dropped in defeat. He was cargo. His first visit to the avens was going to be as a prisoner.

One of the two warriors still keeping an eye on Carleton surrendered his wyvern to the chiefson without being asked. He ran over to the second wyvern and accepted a helping arm up. Hooking his legs in front of his new saddle mate's, he untied a long, thin leather belt from his waist and passed the ends to the other warrior who fastened them around his own waist. The arrangement didn't look safe to Carleton.

"Hey, Carleton," Perry shouted to get his attention. When he looked up, Perry said, "If it makes you feel any better, I've always wanted to ride one of those. Try to enjoy the trip."

The expletives of Carleton's response were drowned out by the rallying cries of the aveni warriors and the answering squawks of their wyverns. After a dozen running steps and several strong flaps of its wings, Carleton's ride lifted into the air. The bobbing of the creature's body as it climbed into the sky, combined with the rapidly diminishing figure of Perry waving up at him, made Carleton's stomach twist and heave. He swallowed hard and closed his eyes, hoping it would all be over soon.

~

A change in the pull of gravity told Carleton that the wyvern was banking. He slowly opened one eye, squinting against the stream of air that flowed across the creature's tan back.

The view was so spectacular that he blinked open both eyes and stared with awe at the desert landscape that stretched from horizon to horizon. The wyvern rested its crimson-edged wings, soaring forward but unable to maintain altitude under the heavy load. Carleton's stomach lurched when the beast resumed its strong wing strokes.

Three of the other wyverns kept pace with his struggling mount. Leaning to the side, he peered around the creature's head to find that the chiefson was leading the formation. The shift in weight caused the wyvern to roll slightly to one side and it had to flap vigorously to level out again. It turned its head toward him and squawked, admonishing him for spoiling their trim. Carleton was careful after that to keep his weight centered over the wyvern's back.

Carleton's amazement quickly turned to confusion when he realized that they weren't heading toward the Dragon Mountains as he'd expected. The chiefson was leading them back toward the mine and was already beginning his descent.

The hunting party lost altitude so quickly that Carleton's stomach seemed to leap into his throat. As they approached a small camp near a cave opening, his wyvern started flapping furiously to control their descent. Carleton stayed as still as possible to help the wyvern land successfully.

On the way down, he'd realized that the camp was on the western slope of the next hill over from the mine. He was probably not much more than a mile from Commonwealth. If he could escape the avens somehow, he could probably get there in less than ten minutes. He'd cross out of aveni territory within five minutes, but that didn't seem to matter much to the chiefson. After all, he'd just abducted Carleton from Perry's ranch.

As they flew closer, he gasped. A dragon had collapsed outside a cave opening and the bloody wound on its shoulder identified it as the one Bart had shot. An aven in a long robe bent over the creature.

The wyvern landed hard and Carleton absorbed some of the force with his dangling legs. The beast let out a grunting squawk as it hit the ground and shook its head. The shake continued down the length of its body, rattling Carleton's teeth. Standing nearly straight up, it spread its wings to full extension and let out a piercing screech. Having expressed its displeasure, it glared at Carleton before stamping its feet and settling back down.

The chiefson came over and patted the wyvern's neck, speaking softly. The creature turned its head away, refusing consolation. *Just get this human off my back*, it seemed to say.

The chiefson gave a low chuckle and loosened the leather straps holding Carleton's arms in place. After sliding his forearms free, Carleton rubbed them to restore circulation and ease the ache where the straps had dug in. At least his wrist band had protected part of his left arm.

Patting the wyvern's back a couple of times, the chiefson gave it a command. It joined the other fliers with a few long hopping steps and partial wing flaps. Its fellows backed away as it approached, wary of its irritability.

At the chiefson's command, two of the aveni warriors slid down from their mounts and approached Carleton with their spears ready. The other two took to the air, presumably to act as lookouts.

The robed aven, who Carleton took to be a shaman, glanced toward them and finished applying a thick salve to the dragon's wound. Carleton was relieved to note that the creature the shaman tended was breathing slowly, merely asleep, not dead. Setting down the tub of salve, the shaman wiped his hands on a cloth and approached the chiefson, his eyes cutting toward Carleton several times.

Carleton's knees were kicked from behind, knocking him to the ground into a kneeling position. The warriors moved alongside Carleton and copied the pose. The chiefson kneeled also, but only on one knee.

As he came forward, the shaman gestured for them to rise, and the avens stood. Carleton looked at one of the warriors questioningly. The two of them were at eye level since he was on his knees. The aven nodded grudgingly, granting him permission to stand.

Carleton's relief at the dragon's survival turned to concern when he considered how close they all were to the resting creature. He stiffened when it sighed in its sleep, the exhalation stirring up a small dust cloud. If the dragon woke up, they would all be within easy range of its flame.

Carleton understood nothing of the conversation between the chiefson and the shaman. The chiefson's gestures toward him, and the shaman's flat glances that followed, suggested the message was not in Carleton's favor. They seemed to think everything was his fault.

Not that he hadn't contributed. He had helped the miners follow the vein and told them where the caverns were. When the dragon attacked, he had shielded Bart from its breath so Bart could fire the shot that wounded it. Carleton's only excuse was that he was under a charm that whole time, but he wasn't supposed to tell anyone about that.

When the chiefson used the word *gishana*, the shaman reacted as if he had been struck across the face. He repeated the word incredulously and moved forward to stand directly in front of Carlton. Looking the human over carefully, he reached out and grabbed Carleton's left arm, inspecting the gem-studded wrist band. He ran his fingers over the stones and released Carleton's arm. He pointed at the wrist band and issued a command. Carleton didn't understand the aveni words, but he got the gist: take it off. When he didn't comply immediately, both warriors prodded him with the sharp tips of their spears.

Carleton removed the wrist band and handed it to the shaman. He sensed that he had recovered some of his magical strength since the ordeal with the dragon, but not enough to do anything useful. Even with his casting stones, he was effectively defenseless.

The chiefson tied Carleton's hands behind his back and guided him to a low-spreading tree with a gnarly trunk and feathery leaves. Recognizing a mesquite, Carleton was careful to duck low under the branches to avoid the thorns he'd painfully discovered upon earlier acquaintance with other trees of its kind.

The chiefson tied the rope that bound Carleton's wrists to the trunk of the tree. At least they had let him wait in the shade.

"What did he say?" Carleton asked.

"Shaman Gafut say, Nadi Gaman choose."

The answer made no sense. "Who is Nadi Gaman?" Carleton asked.

The chiefson gestured toward the sleeping dragon. "Nadi Gaman," he repeated.

Carleton's breath caught. "The dragon will choose what?"

"You treaty breaker, or no treaty breaker."

The dragon was going to decide his fate? That didn't sound promising. Particularly since he'd contributed to the animal's suffering. However, tied to a tree with his hands behind his back and with no access to magic, there wasn't much he could do. His only hope was to somehow escape.

CHAPTER 22

Nadi Gaman

Carleton worked subtly at his bindings, trying not to draw attention to his struggling. The leather, whatever it was made from, had almost no stretch to it and his efforts mostly resulted in chafed wrists.

The warriors guarding Carleton talked quietly to each other and mostly ignored him. With two hunters in the air and two more on the ground nearby, the avens probably weren't worried about the possibility that he would escape. Carleton didn't have much hope either, but if an opportunity arose, he could only take advantage of it if he were free.

Shaman Gafut went back to work on the dragon and quickly lost interest in anything else going on around him. He carefully lifted a damaged scale plate and inspected the exit wound from the fifty-caliber round. He shook his head with an expression of dismay and reached for a clean cloth and his salve.

Having observed the Big Fifty's destructive power first-hand, Carleton thought he understood the shaman's reaction. He doubted the avens had any weapon in their arsenal that could compete. He'd heard that a skilled marksman could take down an enemy soldier from over a thousand yards with the Sharps rifle. It had proven equally deadly in close quarters, particularly when one factored in the risk of ricochet. The next time someone wanted to shoot that portable cannon inside the mine, he'd make sure he was somewhere else.

The dragon stirred and grumbled while the shaman cleaned its wound. Every time it shifted, he paused, and as soon as it settled, he went back to work.

Carleton respected the shaman's bravery. There was no way he'd be willing to get that close to the dragon, even if it was asleep. As for touching it and tending to it? No thanks.

When the shaman started applying the salve, the dragon shifted again and opened one eye. Carleton doubled his efforts at freeing himself. He needed to be ready to run so he could take advantage of whatever disturbance the dragon might create upon waking. What was worse was that he was well within the range of the dragon's fiery breath. All it would have to do was get up and walk forward a dozen steps to enjoy a convenient fried wizard snack.

The shaman noticed that the dragon was waking up. Rather than back away, he rubbed his hand along the bony ridge above the beast's eye and made soothing sounds. The dragon closed its eye and huffed out another sighing breath.

Carleton stared with his mouth open at the amazing exchange. The shaman must have been using some kind of magic to keep the dragon asleep, or perhaps the dragon knew and trusted the shaman. Either possibility was remarkable. Carleton puzzled over what he'd seen while the shaman went back to work with the salve.

Flapping wings and an urgent shout interrupted Carleton's thoughts. The chiefson strode to meet his returning hunter as one of the patrolling wyverns landed. Unlike Carleton's abrupt collision with the earth, the wyvern alighted gracefully, as if stepping from the air to the ground.

The chiefson engaged in a rapid exchange of words and then stood silently for a moment. He glanced at Carleton before dismissing the hunter, who turned his wyvern away from the camp and took off again.

The chiefson barked orders at the two grounded hunters, waving them toward Carleton. They picked up their spears, as did the chiefson. Unsure of their intentions, Carleton tensed as the armed warriors approached with grim faces. He let out the breath he'd been holding when they both turned and adopted a guarding stance nearby.

A minute or so later, pounding hoof beats grew louder as a rider approached on horseback. Carleton's hope surged and he rose to his knees when a glimpse through the mesquite revealed that the rider was Perry.

His friend stopped well outside the camp. Carleton guessed he was picketing his horse where it wouldn't have line of sight to the wyverns. As he walked forward, Carleton noticed the sun glinting off his pair of Colt Frontier six-guns. Perry had come ready for trouble.

The chiefson blocked Perry at the edge of the camp. Perry looked around, returning his attention to the chicfson only after he'd spotted Carleton.

"You bring guns," the chiefson said in an accusing tone. He held his spear upright at his side, not in a threatening position, but ready nonetheless.

"You bring spears," Perry retorted.

The chiefson drew himself up. "We hunt."

Perry narrowed eyes. "I defend my people," he said. His hands rested casually on the front of his gun belt, but Carleton had watched the former lawman practicing and was fairly certain Perry could draw and shoot all four avens before any of them would have time to launch a spear in his direction.

The shaman interrupted Perry and the chiefson with an exclamation and an impatient wave of his hand that silenced them. He peered at the dragon's wounds as he wiped his hands, seeming satisfied with his treatment.

He tossed the rag aside and tenderly patted the dragon's head before walking toward Perry. He stopped a few steps behind the chiefson and spoke a question.

The chiefson interpreted. "You fight or you listen?"

"I'll hear what he has to say," Perry answered.

The shaman launched into a series of short, choppy statements. The chiefson interpreted between pauses. "He say Nadi Gaman hurt, but live." He pointed toward Carleton. "Nadi Gaman speak to Gafut. Choose treaty breaker or no treaty breaker."

Perry had lots of practice with understanding aveni attempts at speaking English, so he seemed to understand what the chiefson was saying. "And what if Nadi Gaman says Carleton is guilty?"

The chiefson repeated the question to the shaman. After throwing a merciless glance toward Carleton, the shaman answered with words that meant nothing to Carleton, but in a tone that said volumes. The chiefson hesitated before translating, "Treaty breaker feed Nadi Gaman."

Feed the dragon?

Carleton was pretty sure they didn't mean he would have to find food and give it to the creature. It was more likely that he would be the main course.

Carleton worked harder at loosening his bindings. He'd rather be killed trying to escape than be eaten alive by the monster snoozing near the cave entrance. How could they let his fate be determined by an overgrown lizard? The creature had indeed seen him in its lair, but it couldn't possibly know he had been under a charm at the time. He wasn't the person who attacked the dragon, but his shield had protected the man who did.

Perry stiffened at the chiefson's words and his hands strayed toward his pistols. The chiefson's hand tightened on his spear and he eased a step back from the rancher. Carleton went absolutely still when one of the guardian avens rested the tip of a spear on his neck. The second crouched with his spear ready. A loud screech from above warned them that two of the airborne avens were circling low, spears at the ready. If Perry chose to fight, Carleton would be dead before his friend's pistols cleared leather.

Perry lifted his hands in in a gesture of surrender and the tension eased. "Let me speak to Carleton," he said. The chiefson nodded his assent.

Perry walked over to where Carleton was sitting and kneeled a few feet away. "Well, my friend, you've fallen into the cholla this time. I've never seen a shaman speak to a dragon before, so I'm not sure what to expect. Just tell me … did you have anything to do with this?"

"I tried to tell you back at the ranch," Carleton answered. "I was there when they found the dragon's lair and I defended myself when it blew fire at us, but I didn't shoot it."

"Why were you there in the first place?" Perry said with a frown. "You had to know they were mining under aveni territory and that they'd find that cavern."

Carleton hung his head. He could blame everything on Bart and Penelope, but he was angry with himself for not figuring out what was going on and putting a stop to it. "All I know for sure is that Bart lied to both of us."

The lie was actually Penelope's, but Carleton was resistant to drawing attention to her role. Was that because of his feelings for her, or had she managed to put another charm on him after all? Either way, Carleton was sure that Bart was the primary force behind all of it. "I believed Bart would respect the treaty right up to the moment when he shot the dragon."

Perry looked into Carleton's eyes, trying to judge the truth for himself. He didn't look entirely convinced, probably detecting Carleton's equivocation regarding Penelope. He finally nodded and said, "Okay. I believe you. Let's hear what the dragon has to say. If necessary, we'll shoot our way out of here."

That plan didn't sound promising. In fact, it sounded like the next-best thing to suicide. Carleton sighed. "Please don't let them feed me to the dragon while I'm still alive."

Perry chuckled. "This ain't over yet, my friend. The avens have their own ideas about justice, but they aren't unfair. If they believe the shaman can get to the truth of the matter, they may surprise you."

A low rumble drew the shaman to the dragon's side. It opened its eyes and raised its head off the ground slightly, sniffing at the air through nostrils the size of five-dollar gold pieces. Letting its head fall to the ground again with a thud, it drew in a long breath and exhaled a stream of oil-tainted air.

Shaman Gafut placed a hand on the dragon's head and one large eye rotated toward him with a slow blink. The shaman spoke to the dragon and closed his eyes for a moment. After communing with the dragon, he turned toward Perry and Carleton and made an announcement.

The chiefson translated, "Nadi Gaman awake. Bring treaty breaker."

～

One of his guards untied Carleton from the mesquite tree and waited while he got to his feet. The chiefson and the other guard kept an eye on Perry while the first guided Carleton toward the shaman.

The dragon's eye swiveled to regard Carleton, making a chill run down the wizard's spine. When he slowed his steps, the shaman waved him forward impatiently while the guard pushed firmly on his back. Carleton winced at the contact, expecting a sharp spear point.

Carleton moved forward until he was standing next to the shaman, who still had one hand resting on the dragon's head. A rumble came from the dragon's throat and it moved its head a few inches toward him. Carleton went still and closed his eyes, expecting to feel the dragon's jaws close around his leg at any second.

Shaman Gafut gave the guard an order, and the warrior removed the bindings from Carleton's wrists. Carleton opened his eyes to find that the shaman was holding a hand out toward him. He hesitantly reached out and let Gafut wrap his fingers over the top of Carleton's much larger hand.

Standing so close to the most-feared predator of the Southwest made Carleton a little nauseous. Its scent was strong and musky overlaid with a bitter oiliness that matched the odor still embedded in his clothes. Right behind the shaman, the dragon's huge front foot flexed long claws, digging furrows into the rocky ground.

Gafut bowed his head and closed his eyes. He started to sing in a soft voice, and the guard backed away. A moment later, a refreshing breeze arose. The breeze grew stronger and started to swirl nearby, on the other side of the recumbent dragon. The swirl tightened until it formed a column of air that picked up loose dirt and bits of vegetation from the ground. It was like a controlled dust devil.

The shaman opened his eyes and addressed the column of air as if it could hear him. The column wavered for a moment and then tipped sideways, enveloping the head and shoulders of the shaman. Squeezing his eyes shut against the detritus floating in the stream of air, the shaman spoke again and the column of air lifted from the ground. Its turbulence washed over the shaman and followed his arms to flow around the dragon and Carleton before subsiding.

At first, Carleton thought he was passing out. His vision grew dim and he couldn't move. A moment later, his shoulder throbbed with a dull pain, and a distorted view of the aveni camp appeared as if through a dirty window. When the perspective fully registered, Carleton realized that he was seeing through the dragon's eyes and feeling the pain of its wound.

Gafut spoke, and Carleton was shocked to realize that he understood the words. No, that wasn't quite right. He understood the *meaning* of the words. The shaman encouraged the dragon to remember its injury.

The dragon responded. It expressed panic and then rage. Images began to form in Carleton's mind. With them came a sense of accusation that he resisted but couldn't refute.

The dragon shuffled down a tunnel to investigate unusual sounds coming from ahead. Light flickered at the end of the tunnel, alarming the creature. It slowed as it approached the cavern. Peering into the cavern, its eyes were drawn immediately to the new passageway that had been blasted into the far corner, and then it spotted Carleton standing his ground. It grew angry when it noticed how close Carleton was to the rocks in the corner of the cavern. Carleton suddenly understood that the rocks were arranged around a pair of dragon eggs. Her eggs.

In the back of his mind, Gafut said something like "show magic." As the dragon moved into the room to attack, a pair of auras formed. A brown flickering glow outlined Carleton's magical shield, and a thin shell of pulsing yellow light enveloped his head. In the next instant, the room was filled with fire as the dragon released its breath.

When the flames died down, the dragon was shocked to see that the invader was still alive. Carleton had fallen to his knees and a second invader stood behind him, pointing something. The shield's brown aura had disappeared, and the yellow shell around Carleton's head was quickly fading.

A horrible bang followed by a hard strike on her nose stunned the dragon, and she shook her head in reaction to a wave of dizziness. A second bang resulted in a heavy jolt that tore through her shoulder with searing pain. The wound made it nearly impossible for her to raise her head and throw flame. She understood that she would die if she remained, so she backed into the tunnel and sped away from the cavern as quickly as she could manage on three legs. The eggs were lost.

While the images of the dragon struggling to escape danger played in the foreground of Carleton mind, the shaman addressed him through their mental connection.

"The shield was yours?"

"Yes," Carleton confirmed. "I did not know about the eggs," he added, hoping the shaman would believe him. He sensed no reaction from the shaman, but the dragon seemed surprised and relieved.

"Your will was not your own," Gafut stated.

"True."

"Who stole your will?"

Carleton hesitated before answering. Did the strange trance allow Gafut to read his mind? The shaman had proof that someone had tampered with his will. How much did Gafut really care about knowing who had done it?

"I don't know," he finally answered. Carleton mentally held his breath while he waited for the shaman to call him a liar. If the shaman insisted, he'd have no choice but to reveal Penelope's involvement.

After a long delay, Gafut moved on. "Who hurt Fire Tongue?" he asked. Thanks to the mind-sharing trance, Carleton realized that Nadi Gaman translated literally as Fire Tongue.

"The mine manager, Bart McLaury."

The dragon's memories played forward while they talked. The creature reached the cave entrance and collapsed in the same position she was in when Carleton encountered her later. The shaman said, "We are finished," and the dragon's viewpoint began to fade.

Carleton was swaying on his feet when he broke free of the trance. He steadied himself and blinked a few times while his normal vision returned.

Gafut released Carleton's hand and stared at him. The lines around the shaman's eyes and mouth seemed more pronounced than they had earlier. The shaman was showing the strain from working what Carleton guessed was a powerful spell.

The dragon closed its eyes and drew in a deep snorting breath. The experience had probably been draining for her as well, and Carleton certainly didn't feel at the top of his form. Images from the dragon's memories kept surging to the foreground of his mind, distracting him.

The shaman grabbed Carleton's forearm and walked him away from the dragon. The message was clear; let Nadi Gaman rest. Carleton was happy to comply with anything that put more distance between himself and the injured she-dragon.

Carleton and Gafut converged with Perry and the other avens. Perry's tense face and tightly folded arms made it appear that he was trying to keep his hands from reaching for his guns. No one said a word, waiting for the shaman to make his pronouncement. Carleton readied himself to break from the shaman's grip and run.

Shaman Gafut chattered an unintelligible string of words at the chiefson, whose eyebrows rose as the message was conveyed. "Nadi Gaman say not treaty breaker. But no go to mine."

Carleton's relief at being exonerated was tempered by confusion. "What does that mean? I'm supposed to stay away from the mine?"

"Yes," the chiefson confirmed. "You stay away."

"But I work there," Carleton objected.

The chiefson shook his head. "No. You work, you treaty breaker."

Technically, the chiefson was right. If Carleton went back to work in the mine under his own free will, he would be helping Bart break the treaty. There went his contract. Bart wouldn't be too pleased when he heard the news, either. Carleton sighed in resignation. "There's going to be trouble."

"Huh," came the chiefson's sour response. "Trouble *now*," he said, pointing a finger toward the ground for emphasis.

Carleton couldn't argue with that. But what bothered him most were the dragon eggs. They needed to be protected. The delvans had no idea the eggs were there, and flying debris from one misplaced blast into the ore body could damage them. He also didn't trust that Bart would move them to safety. He needed to handle it himself, and he needed to do it before the dragon was healed enough to go back and fight for them.

"Can I at least go back and save the dragon eggs?" he asked the chiefson.

The chiefson looked confused by the question and Carleton realized that he might not know about the eggs since he had not participated in the trip through the dragon's memory. After a quick exchange with the shaman, he answered. "We save children of Nadi Gaman. You stay away."

Gafut gave Carleton's wrist band back to him and returned to the dragon's side. He began collecting the tools and supplies he had been using on the dragon. The fact that she was sleeping peacefully through all of the distractions around her suggested that Gafut must have done something to sedate her. When they had shared minds, he sensed that she trusted the avens, but in her injured state, she had serious concerns about having wyverns and humans so near.

The chiefson waved his hand dismissively. "You go now."

Perry smiled and put an arm around Carleton, leading him away from the aveni camp. "I'm glad everything turned out okay. I had my doubts for a while there."

Carleton agreed that it was good not to be dragon food, but with the immediate threat of death behind him, the terms of his survival were not exactly okay. "It seems I've lost my job again," he said glumly.

Perry patted his back and chuckled. "It's always something with you. You need a more positive outlook. That job at the mine has been nothing but trouble since the beginning, and you just had the experience of a lifetime. I don't pretend to understand what the shaman was up to, but that was one hell of a show."

Given the seriousness of the circumstances, Carleton couldn't help but feel a bit annoyed by Perry's flippant attitude. "I'm sure I would have enjoyed it a lot more if I hadn't thought it was going to end with me being lunch for Nadi Gaman."

They reached Remington, whose coat was still slick with sweat from the sprint to the camp. "See, there you go again." Perry said, untying the horse. "You weren't guilty. Sometimes you gotta have faith that the truth will win out."

Carleton followed Perry as they walked the horse toward the ranch. The path away from the aveni camp followed a wide track the dragon had crushed through the vegetation.

There wasn't much point in arguing with Perry's optimism; the man was right. More importantly, Carleton didn't want to talk about his guilt or innocence. That conversation might lead to a discussion of how he had been coerced in the first place. He might eventually tell Perry about Penelope's manipulations, but not until the time was right.

"Besides," Perry went on, "we got new problems to solve. The avens know the mine has crossed into their territory, they know Bart shot the dragon, and they know dragon eggs are in danger. You may not be a treaty breaker, but Bart sure is, and there's gonna to be hell to pay."

CHAPTER 23

Stone Golem

They were so close to Commonwealth that Perry insisted on visiting the mine and talking to Bart before they returned to the ranch. Carleton tried to talk him out of it, but Perry was adamant.

After his ordeal with the avens, Carleton was tired and stressed. He didn't feel up to having an argument with Bart. He also didn't want to see Penelope again until he'd had time to come to terms with her betrayal.

Perry insisted that a delay was a bad idea. "The avens won't waste any time going after those eggs. Bart needs to pull back or this situation is going to blow up into a war between the miners and the avens."

Carleton hoped it wouldn't come to that because the miners would be caught in the crossfire. They were only following Bart's orders, and Penelope's influence would suppress whatever objections they might have. If any of them were hurt in the conflict, he would be hard-pressed to choose whether Bart or Penelope was more responsible, and charm or no charm, he'd feel partially responsible himself.

By the time they reached the manager's residence, Carleton had walked off some of the strain of his experience with the avens. The short journey also gave him time to work with Perry on what they'd say to Bart. At Carleton's request, Perry agreed to do most of the talking and avoid bringing up the dragon eggs. Bart seemed to think that dragons were vermin, so he'd probably destroy the eggs if he knew they were there.

They found Bart talking to Willie outside the bunkhouse. When Bart saw them coming, he interrupted his conversation, sent Willie on his way, and waved Penelope over from where she was sitting in the shade of the porch while Perry tied Remington to the hitching post. Facing Bart and Penelope with Perry had a distressingly familiar feel to it. Carleton kept a close eye on Penelope's hands, ready to stop her if she reached toward one of her glass casting globes.

Perry laid out the situation. The mine was in violation of the Dragon Mountain Treaty, and because he had shot the dragon, so was Bart. The avens were angry and preparing for action.

"I don't care if they're mad," Bart said, leaning toward Perry to speak right into his face. "I'm following that vein, and I'm protecting my miners. If they're worried about their damned dragon, they should keep it out of my way!"

Perry was unimpressed with Bart's vehemence. "What you're doing is illegal. If you don't back off right now, I'll have no choice but to get a marshal out here to stop you. It's my duty as the aven agent to report treaty violations and prevent the escalation of hostilities."

Carleton watched Penelope's reaction carefully. When Perry laid out his charges, she initially looked alarmed, but her expression had grown more thoughtful as the argument progressed. Carleton worried that her preoccupation might be a prelude to another attempt at charming them, so he was surprised when she laid a hand on Bart's arm to interrupt his response to Perry.

"You don't want a war with the avens," she said. "Maybe you should pull the miners back and put them to work on the second vein that Carleton found. At least until this situation is resolved."

Bart looked down at her hand and shook it off, easing back a step and giving her a narrow-eyed glare. "What are you going on about? There's an exposed wall of ore twenty feet long waiting to be stoped out of that cavern. I'm not going to let it just sit there."

Perry glanced at Carleton with a raised eyebrow. Carleton guessed he was asking if it was time to bring up the subject of the dragon eggs. Carleton subtly shook his head.

Perry pursed his lips for a moment and then nodded his head once, decisively. "That cavern is under aveni land and it's part of the dragon's lair. The avens won't let you continue your mining operations there."

Bart huffed out a derisive laugh. "I'd like to see them try to stop me. We've already blocked the passage that connects that cavern to the dragon's lair. If the little demons want it back, they'll have to dig through a hundred tons of rock."

Perry's face went pale, and he traded glances with Carleton. Carleton had forgotten that Bart was planning to isolate the cavern to prevent the dragon from returning. The miners had apparently wasted no time getting that taken care of. He hoped the eggs had not been damaged in the process. If anything happened to those eggs, negotiating a peaceful settlement with the avens might become impossible.

Distant shouting from the mine entrance up above drew everyone's attention. A wagon started down the access road, its wheels bouncing from the lack of a load as the driver pushed his draft team to a dangerous speed.

"What the hell?" Bart said. He started walking with long strides toward the base of the mountain. After a moment's hesitation, Carleton and Perry started after him with Penelope close behind.

The wagon descended the mountain quickly with its brakes squealing at each switchback. By the time Bart reached the bottom of the road, the wagon had already rounded the last bend.

As he approached Bart, the driver braked hard and reined in his team. Jasper leaped down before the wagon came to a stop.

Carleton had never seen Jasper look so distressed. His eyes were wide and he was shaking. "The mountain's alive!" he exclaimed, pointing upward toward the mine entrance. "And it damn near killed us all."

~

"What are you babbling about?" Bart demanded. He impatiently signaled the wagon driver to turn the wagon around.

Penelope stepped forward and interrupted. "Is anyone hurt?"

Jasper clenched and unclenched his hands, visibly trying to calm himself. "Nay," he answered. "The lads were smart enough to run as soon as the stone golem appeared."

Carleton suppressed the urge to laugh. While studying geomancy, Carleton had learned about many myths and legends related to elemental earth magic. Stone golems were one of those myths. As the story went, they were strong spirits of the earth which a powerful wizard could direct to take humanoid form and do his bidding. Assembled from the earth and stone of their native domain, they were practically invincible and unstoppable. No one—well, no *human*—had seen a golem or attempted to summon one in centuries.

Bart threw up his hands in exasperation. "What in blazes is a stone golem?"

Jasper ignored the question. He rubbed his forehead and mused to himself. "Dragons and now golems. This mine be cursed!"

"Don't be ridiculous," Bart said with a frown. "This is one of the richest mines in the area. The only curse seems to be that I can't get decent help to work it."

Jasper looked up at Bart with an angry glare. "How dare ye. Ye'll not find better crews. We've mucked yer ore and followed yer orders, Father help us. Doing battle with dragons and golems is more than anyone should ask."

Bart seemed to realize he'd gone too far. "You're right," he said, raising one hand in a placating gesture. "I'm as frustrated with the obstacles as you are. Where are the crews now?"

"I was going down to check on Tully's progress when the thing attacked. I got everyone out of the drift, and they're waiting inside the daylight curve."

Carleton was fascinated by the idea of a real stone golem appearing in the mine, but he doubted that was really what they were dealing with. "Can you describe what you saw?" he asked Jasper.

"Aye. I was talking with Tully when the golem stepped into the cavern from the passage we blocked. At first, I thought the backfill was shifting or maybe the dragon was trying to dig through. But then the stones lifted free of the pile in the shape of a huge man."

Bart cast a dubious look at the delvan. "What? That's impossible. The avens were probably tricking you with some kind of illusion."

Jasper shuddered. "The thing that came for us with steps of grinding stone was no illusion. Two men couldn't have lifted the chunk of rock it threw at us. The piece came off the end of its arm and shattered against the wall next to where Tully and I stood. We ran before it could get off another toss."

Bart looked at Carleton. "You know anything about this? Sounds like some kind of earth magic to me. You're supposed to be the expert; how do we destroy it?"

Carleton shook his head, at a loss for a solution. "Until now, I've always believed stone golems were a myth. I've no idea how to destroy it."

Bart exhaled impatiently. "Then I think you have your work cut out for you, wizard. I'm not going to let the avens scare me off with some magical bogeyman. I need to get the miners back to that ore."

"That won't be as easy as ye think," Jasper cautioned. "Ye haven't heard the rest of the story. It didn't stop chasing us at the cavern. It followed us halfway back to the loading stope, backfilling the drift as it went. It will take us a couple of weeks of mucking to get back to that cavern."

Bart's face turned red at the news. "It collapsed the drift? How?"

"I couldn't tell ye," Jasper answered.

Perry interrupted. "You say this golem followed you about halfway down the drift?"

"Aye," confirmed Jasper.

Perry looked at Carleton, and the wizard suddenly knew what he was getting at. "It chased them back to the border line," Carleton concluded.

"That's what I'm thinking," said Perry.

Bart silently fumed for a moment. Penelope watched him closely, her expression hard to read. Her furrowed brow showed concern, but the sharp look in her eyes gave Carleton the impression that she might be planning something.

When Bart finally spoke, his voice had a decisive edge to it. "We can't let the avens think they have the upper hand, so here's what we're going to do. Jasper will get all of the crews working on clearing that drift. Wizard Kazimer will figure out a way to deal with the golem. I want to be back in that cavern by the end of next week."

Perry started to protest, his face clearly showing his outrage.

Bart held up a hand and cut him off. "You do what you have to do, Mr. Aven Agent. My job is to mine that ore, and I'm not going to let a few little demons stop me."

"You're going to have to do it without my help," Carleton declared.

Bart stared at him in surprise. He sent a questioning glance at Penelope, which she ignored. Frowning, he said, "Fine. You've done about all you can for me anyway. You can pick up your final pay on Saturday."

Although Bart's dismissal of his contribution insulted him, Carleton was relieved that the mine manager hadn't tried to argue with him about quitting. The man had probably figured out that Carleton was no longer under Penelope's charm, which made his continued presence more trouble than it was worth.

Meanwhile, Jasper was shaking his head. "The crews won't be too keen on clearing the drift, ye know. Ye weren't chased by that moving pile of rocks like they were. It was an eerie thing to behold."

Bart rolled his eyes. "In other words, they're all up there clinging to each other and shaking like a bunch of old women."

Jasper pressed his lips together in annoyance, but didn't deny the characterization.

Bart sighed and said, "Well, let's go talk to them. One thing I've learned about magic is that it has limits. The shaman who sent that golem against us won't want to do that every day. The little bastards probably think they've scared us off, and I see no reason to tell them otherwise. I'll bet they've cleared off by the time we get back to the cavern."

"What about the dragon?" Jasper asked.

"One thing at a time. Let's go get that ore."

The two men started walking toward the waiting wagon, leaving Carleton and Perry standing with Penelope. Bart didn't immediately notice that she'd stayed behind.

"Do what you have to do," she said quietly to Perry, repeating Bart's words.

When Bart realized that Penelope wasn't following, he stopped and half-turned toward the remaining trio. "Penny, I'd like your help with this," he called.

Glancing at Carleton, Penelope added, "We *all* do what we have to do." She turned and walked away, joining Bart and Jasper.

Perry raised one eyebrow. "You know what that was about?"

Carleton thought he did know, but he wasn't ready to share the information. He shrugged and answered, "Like I told you before, women mystify me."

That time, Perry seemed inclined to agree. "Yeah, I reckon some more than others."

Carleton scratched his head. "Now what?"

Perry turned and started back toward Remington. "Now we get the deputy marshal and put a stop to this mess before it gets any more out of control."

Following close behind, Carleton said, "You know, what bothers me is that Bart doesn't seem too worried about you bringing in the marshal."

"I noticed that," Perry said. "It's a might worrisome, but it's the right place to start. If the deputy marshal in Tombstone won't back me up, I'll try the marshal in Tucson."

"That sounds … time consuming," Carleton said.

Perry glanced over his shoulder as he reached Remington. "I know what you're getting at, and you're right. The avens have made their position clear. If Bart keeps ignoring them, we're looking at a full-blown war with the avens within another two weeks. I'll need to move fast, and I could use your help."

Having seen the power the avens wielded, Carleton didn't want to be anywhere near if war broke out. His association with the mine would undoubtedly count against him, even if he had quit. "Just tell me what you want me to do," he said.

CHAPTER 24

Tombstone

At sunrise the next morning, Carleton returned Perry's wave as he rode Peppy away from Sunrise Ranch. Perry had drawn a map in the dirt and described the shortest route to Tombstone. but still, Carleton had a long day of riding ahead. Nearby Middlemarch Pass would have given him a shorter and quicker route straight through the mountains, but unlike Perry, he couldn't traipse through aveni land. Instead, he took the southern route between the foothills of the Dragon and Mule Mountains, which at least had the advantage of being much less rugged.

Carleton was tired and saddle-sore by the time he reached Tombstone in the late afternoon. At Perry's recommendation, he stopped at the "You and the Horse You Rode In On" hotel and livery. While arranging accommodations for both himself and Peppy, he checked the pistol Perry had loaned him with the desk clerk. Tombstone didn't allow firearms in town, and aggravating local law enforcement would work against his mission of getting their assistance.

Carleton was just as glad to be rid of the gun. He still wasn't good at shooting it, in spite of Perry's tutelage, and the weight of the thing was a constant distraction.

Tombstone was the largest town Carleton had visited since he'd arrived in Arizona. It was impressive in its own way; he'd never seen so many saloons and bordellos in one place. He was pretty sure they outnumbered all other forms of business put together.

Perry had warned him that he'd be arriving in town right as it was starting to wake up. Tombstone drew a crowd of hard-working miners, cowboys, and ranchers from the surrounding countryside. They'd spend most of the night drinking, gambling, and whoring. Free-flowing whiskey, combined with competition for money and women, often resulted in misunderstandings and free overnight lodging in the local jail.

Carleton would have to watch his step.

After being out in the country for so long, Carleton had forgotten how aromatic civilization could be. He stayed up on the wooden boardwalk, which ran in front of the establishments along Allen Street, to avoid the thoroughfares that were paved in horse dung.

He was about a half-block from his destination when Penelope emerged from a doorway several buildings down. He stopped and turned toward a mercantile shop window, feigning interest in the wares displayed there while keeping an eye on her. If she looked his way, he'd have to hope that the other pedestrians on the busy boardwalk would obscure her view of him.

What was she doing here? During his tenure at Commonwealth, he'd noticed that she had disappeared a few times. He'd assumed she'd gone to Pearce or Cochise to do some shopping, but maybe she'd had business in Tombstone instead. Regardless, Carleton had an uneasy feeling that her trip was no coincidence on that particular occasion.

Penelope never did look in his direction. She ducked her head and turned to her right, putting her back to him. She walked quickly down the boardwalk and accepted the hand of a waiting driver who helped her climb into the seat of Bart's carriage. She appeared to be the only passenger. Carleton waited until the carriage rolled away before leaving his position at the shop window.

Walking slowly down the boardwalk, he approached the door she'd exited. It was the marshal's office—the same place he had been trying to find. His uneasiness turned to alarm, and his intuition told him to tread carefully. He hesitated as he reached for the doorknob, but seeing no reason to delay, he pushed the latch and entered the office.

The marshal's office was furnished with a large wooden desk, a few visitors' chairs, and a small safe in one corner. Two jail cells, currently unoccupied, had obviously been added long after the building was constructed, judging by residual evidence of torn-out walls that had been replaced by support posts.

Carleton removed his hat as he entered the room and approached the desk. Deputy Marshal Charles Bodine was busy contemplating a note in his hand. As soon as he looked up and saw his new visitor, he folded the note and stashed it in a drawer.

The marshal had a distinguished look, with a meticulously-groomed handlebar mustache and slicked-back brown hair that curled where it hit his shoulders. His badge glittered on the chest of his buckskin jacket. He assessed Carleton with a sweep of his blue-gray eyes. "What can I do for you?" he asked in a deep voice.

"Good evening, Marshal Bodine. I'm Carleton Kazimer, and I'm here as a representative for Aven Agent Peregrine Maine." Carleton nervously turned the rim of his hat in his hands. "He asked me to deliver a message."

A brief flicker of surprise passed over the marshal's face and his eyes cut toward the door. Carleton kept his expression carefully neutral, although the glance confirmed that Penelope had probably mentioned his impending visit. The marshal was probably disturbed that Penelope had exited his office only moments before his expected visitor had entered.

Adopting a pleasant smile, the marshal said, "And what might that message be?"

Using only the thumb and index finger of his left hand, Carleton lifted the left side of his vest to show the marshal that he was reaching for a note that stuck out of the interior pocket and not for a hidden weapon. As he handed the note to the marshal, the man gave him an appreciative nod.

While the marshal reviewed Perry's complaint against the Commonwealth Mine and Bart McLaury in particular, Carleton wondered what Penelope had said to the man. He dearly wanted to read the note she'd evidently left. Knowing there was little possibility of that happening, he was tempted to see if he could somehow finesse the information from the lawman. But Carleton knew his limitations. A subtle interrogator he was not. He could come right out and ask the marshal about Penelope's business, but he doubted the man would reveal anything useful. Instead, he'd probably inform Penelope that Carleton had been asking about her visit.

"These are some serious charges," the marshal said, laying the note on his desk. "What's your role in this?"

"I'm just the messenger," Carleton answered, but his tone betrayed that there was more and the marshal's narrowed eyes prompted him to expand his statement. "Well, I suppose I'm a witness as well. I worked at the mine until recently and observed the treaty violations firsthand."

The marshal sat back with a doubtful expression. "You don't look delvan to me. How is it that you witnessed these alleged violations?"

The conversation was turning in a direction Carleton hadn't anticipated and didn't much like. It seemed the marshal had decided to interrogate him.

"I'm a geomancer, Marshal. An earth wizard, if you will. Bart McLaury hired me to assist with the mining operations.

I worked closely with the delvan miners and I was present for the incidents mentioned in Agent Maine's letter."

"I see," said the marshal. "You participated in the alleged treaty violations, and now you're out of work. Are you sure this isn't about some personal beef you have with Mr. McLaury? Maybe a little vendetta over getting fired?"

Carleton's face heated. "No, sir. I wasn't fired. I quit because I believe that Mr. McLaury is not only breaking the law, he's endangering the lives of the people who work for him by inciting the avens."

The marshal stared at Carleton for what seemed like a long time, chewing over their conversation. He finally nodded slowly a few times. "All right, Wizard Kazimer. I'll take you at your word for now. If this matter goes to prosecution, the investigation will reveal the truth about your involvement."

The marshal didn't seem to be taking the situation as seriously as Perry had hoped. His wording so far had been full of words like "alleged" and "if." Questioning Carleton's motives so quickly might have been a matter of convenience, or it may have been related to whatever message Penelope had delivered.

"Now, if that's all, I have other business to attend to. Good day, Wizard Kazimer."

Carleton had a bad feeling that the marshal's "other business" would keep him busy for quite some time. "May I ask when Agent Maine should expect your visit to Commonwealth?"

"You can ask, but I don't have an answer for you right now. It will take some doing to clear my schedule and arrange the support I'll need. Bart McLaury isn't known for being cooperative."

Carleton smiled at the characterization. "You'll get no argument from me there, Marshal. Thank you for your time."

Stepping out of the marshal's office onto the busy boardwalk, Carleton inhaled a deep breath and instantly regretted it. Choking on the ripe evening air, he dodged a few oncoming pedestrians and headed back toward his hotel.

Perry had encouraged him to explore the town, suggesting that he might find items that would be useful for his spell casting. He had also hinted that a man who hadn't had the pleasure of a woman for a while might find interesting ways to put some of that hard-earned contract money to use. At the time, Carleton had seriously considered the suggestion, but the heavily perfumed, provocatively dressed women who tried to get his attention on the streets of Tombstone didn't appeal in the slightest. Every one of them paled miserably in comparison to Penelope, not that he could ever hope for a relationship with Penelope. If he found out she was playing him and interfering with the plan to stop Bart, what little friendship they currently shared would be over.

Perry had also asked Carleton to pick up a few small items. Carleton ducked into the first mercantile he encountered so he could satisfy his friend's request, and then, packages in hand, he went back to the hotel.

When hunger forced him back out into the boisterous town, Carleton went to the nearest saloon that offered food. He treated himself to two shots of whiskey to take the edge off the agitation that had been building since his meeting with the marshal. Eating quickly, he left as soon as he could to escape the smoke, curious stares, and rowdy patrons lined up at the bar. Gambling held no interest for him, so he returned to his room at the hotel. The whiskey and food made him drowsy enough to ignore the raucous noise that seeped through the walls.

As soon as it was light enough to travel the next morning, Peppy and a disillusioned Carleton were on the road back to Sunrise Ranch.

~

During the days that followed Carleton's return from Tombstone, he and Perry distracted themselves with work around the ranch. The marshal would either show up or he wouldn't, and it didn't seem like there was anything they could do to hasten his arrival.

After Carleton's description of his interview with Marshal Bodine, Perry seriously considered going over his head to Thomas Betters, the U.S. Marshal in Tucson, but they didn't know for sure that Bodine wasn't going to respond eventually, and it was unlikely that Betters would get there in time even if they could convince him to take action.

Every day that went by, the miners dug closer to the cavern that had started all the trouble. No one knew what to expect when they reached it. Were the dragon eggs still there, or had the avens moved them? Had the stone golem backfilled the entire cavern? Would the dragon be waiting there for the miners? Or perhaps the avens?

In the meantime, Carleton couldn't keep his mind off the eggs. His mind-share with the dragon had left him feeling concerned for them. His involvement with putting them at risk was a constant source of guilt, and he wanted to do something to help protect them.

On Sunday, Perry insisted that they take a break from work and do some target practice. Carleton still wasn't a big fan of firearms, but thanks to Perry, he was becoming a better marksman. He could shoot, reload, and clean Perry's full arsenal, including rifles, shotgun, and pistols. He could even handle Perry's old ball-and-cap Colt Walker six-gun properly.

Perry's shooting range was off the side of the road below the plateau where the ranch was situated. There, they could plink away without frightening the animals or worrying about a stray shot. Most of the bullets they fired ended up in the sand trap behind the targets.

Carleton successfully obliterated three out of six gourds that Perry had lined up for him. He grinned as he took out the earplugs he'd repurposed from his mining work.

Perry returned the grin and patted him on the back. "We'll make a gunfighter out of you yet."

Carleton shook his head in amusement as he ejected the spent brass from the Colt Frontier. He was handing the weapon to Perry when he noticed Flint waving to them from the road. He nudged Perry with his elbow and gestured with a wave for Flint to join them.

After learning that Carleton had quit, Flint had come up to the ranch for a visit. He was worried about how things were going at the mine, and he was disappointed that Carleton would no longer be there to help keep them out of trouble. With Perry's approval, Carleton gave his delvan friend the full story about what was going on, even letting him in on the secret dragon eggs. Flint swore to preserve the secret and promised to keep them informed on what was happening at the mine.

"That's some impressive shooting," Flint commented, tilting his head toward the remaining gourds as he joined them.

"Thanks," Carleton said. "I still can't get them all, but I seem to be doing better."

"Hell, most of the time I can't get them all either," Perry said. He offered the gun to Flint. "Want to give it a try?"

Flint shook his head. "Nay, I've got news to give ye, and then I'll be on me way."

Carleton went on the alert, as did Perry.

"What's up?" Perry asked.

"The crews have been making fast work of mucking out the backfill. They're off today, but at the rate they're going, they'll reach the cavern sometime Tuesday," Flint reported.

"Only two more days?" Carleton interjected.

"Aye," Flint confirmed. "Have ye heard anything from Marshal Bodine?"

Perry shook his head. "Not yet, and it sounds like we're running out of time."

"We have to stop them," Carleton said. Addressing Flint, he asked, "Can't you talk some sense into the other miners? Surely they don't want another fight with the dragon. I won't be there to shield anyone."

Flint shrugged. "I tried. I talked to Jasper about it, but he told me not to make trouble. Bart promises to protect the miners like he did before, even if he has to hire armed guards. That's good enough for Jasper and the crews."

Carleton wondered if Penelope had reneged on her promise to release the miners from the charm. She claimed her magic had been ineffective from the beginning, and delvan stoicism could just as easily explain their pragmatic and fatalistic reaction to the circumstances at the mine. "Don't you think the miners are accepting an awful lot of risk?"

Flint shrugged again. His next words confirmed Carleton's musings. "Mining is risky. If it's not one thing, it's another. The pay at Commonwealth is good, and so far, Bart has kept his word on protecting the crews."

"What about Mag?" Carleton asked.

"No one knew what we were dealing with back then. Yerself didn't even know. Poor Mag was the unlucky one who discovered the danger, and he voluntarily took that risk when he went exploring."

Carleton could tell there was no use appealing to the miners. It wasn't that they didn't care. They were just too accustomed to accepting mortal risk every day, and legalities were the responsibility of their overseers. "Miners mine," Carleton concluded with a resigned shake of his head.

"Aye, that's the truth of it," Flint approved.

"Then it's up to us," Carleton declared.

"But we have no legal standing," Perry objected. "We can't arrest Bart, and we can't force the miners to stop working. We also can't stop the avens from fighting back."

"The whole problem is that the right people aren't talking," Carleton insisted. "If Bart won't go to the avens, then we need to bring the avens to Bart."

Perry gave Carleton an incredulous look. "Have you lost your mind? You've seen how touchy the avens are. Bart has already said there's nothing to negotiate. If we bring those two together now, there will be nothing left but a crater."

Carleton couldn't see any other solution. Something had to be done, and it had to be done quickly. If law enforcement wouldn't help, they'd have to find a way to resolve the dispute themselves. They had been allowing Bart's orneriness to shape the conflict, and if they continued down that path, people and dragons would end up dead.

"Not that long ago, it was your plan to negotiate a settlement," Carleton pointed out.

Perry blinked a couple of times and his voice became defensive. "Sure, but that was before Bart broke the treaty and forced the avens to retaliate. This is now a federal criminal matter that should be turned over to the proper authorities."

"The marshal isn't here," Carleton insisted. "And I doubt he's coming. Bart seems to have more influence than we imagined."

The memory of Penelope stepping out of the marshal's office popped into Carleton's head. *Or at least somebody has influence.*

"As I recall," Carleton said, "you once told me that you got the agent job because you're such a good negotiator." Perry blushed at having his boast turned around on him. "Well, Aven Agent Peregrine Maine, I think it's time for you to do some negotiating."

CHAPTER 25

Standoff

Perry chose the location for the parley carefully. He didn't want either side to have a geographical or psychological advantage. In the end, he picked an open area at the mouth of a canyon that straddled the aveni border not far from the mine.

When Perry invited Bart to the meeting, the mine manager initially refused, saying he had better things to do. Penelope talked him into attending, saying that it wouldn't hurt for him to speak with the avens and find a way to avoid bloodshed. Bart had scoffed, still not willing to credit the avens and their "primitive weapons" as a genuine threat.

The man seemed to have a selective memory. The stone golem could have easily killed several miners if it had collapsed the drift on top of them instead of behind their fleeing backs. Bart had a hard time accepting aveni "hocus-pocus" as something to fear. As for the dragons, they were a pest to be exterminated when they inconvenienced him.

Monday afternoon, Carleton and Perry went to the parley spot an hour early to make sure they arrived before any of the other participants. Right near one of the aveni border markers, Perry set up a tall pole with a white flag tied at the top. The flagpole served two purposes: first, it was a symbol of truce; second, it was the signal Perry always used at the ranch when he wanted to speak to the avens. The chiefson's hunting party could easily spot the invitation from the air, and most of the time they'd honor it.

Not that Perry was taking any chances. After Flint's warning on Sunday, Perry had literally flagged down the avens and invited them to the meeting. During that discussion, he told them he'd use the flagpole to identify the meeting spot.

Looking around with pursed lips, Perry asked Carleton to help him define a neutral space. The two men dragged the heels of their boots through the dirt and placed marker rocks to demarcate a large rectangle. The rectangle was much longer than it was wide, with the long side spanning the aveni border.

"What's the point of the neutral space?" Carleton asked.

"You know as well as I do that both sides will come armed and in force. The last thing I want is two mobs screaming accusations and threats at each other across the border. If they'll agree to it, I want Bart and the chief to face each other unarmed and away from the influence of their supporters. They are the decision makers, so no one else needs to be involved."

"So, everybody stays out of the neutral space except the unarmed representatives," Carleton said. Perry nodded. "Where do you want me?"

"I'll be unarmed, too, and you're my backup. Stand right next to the flagpole outside the neutral space."

Carleton looked down at the gun belt he wore and the pistol that hung at his side. "I feel ridiculous wearing this," he said.

Perry grinned. "Oh, I don't know. It gives you a dangerous air. Folks will think twice about messing with a gunfighter wizard."

"I don't know how I let you talk me into this," Carleton said.

"Don't worry about it," Perry said. "If you need to use that pistol, we're probably all dead anyway."

"Thanks. I feel so much better now."

Several large shadows danced across the desert vegetation nearby and Carleton looked up to see a dozen avens circling the meeting site.

"Looks like our first guests have arrived," Perry said.

Most of the avens landed about fifty yards back from the meeting place. Four of the warriors circled a couple more times before flying off to the nearest high spots where they landed their wyverns and remained mounted.

Chiefson Sulc came toward them, leaving two warriors to watch the wyverns. He stopped at the edge of the rectangle they'd created and inspected it with curiosity.

"We'll meet over there," Perry explained, pointing at the white flagpole. "But only the speakers. The warriors will stay back," he said, waving toward the landscape behind the line. The chiefson nodded his understanding.

"The speakers will leave weapons here," Perry added.

The chiefson considered that, not looking pleased about it. He pointed at the six-guns strapped to Perry's waist. "You have weapons?"

"No, I'll be unarmed, too."

The chiefson accepted the conditions with a nod.

Perry looked around behind the chiefson. "Where's your father, the chief? Are you speaking for him?"

The chiefson shook his head. "Father no fly. This dragon matter. Shaman speak for dragon."

Perry's face creased in confusion. "Okay. Then where's the shaman?"

"Shaman here soon," the chiefson answered cryptically.

Remington's whinny alerted Carleton and Perry of Bart's approach before they heard the clop of horse hooves. Carleton followed his friend to the other side of the rectangle just as

Bart arrived with Jasper, Penelope, Willie, and a half-dozen men Carleton had never seen before.

The new men were a scruffy-looking lot. Their most distinguishing feature was the sheer firepower they displayed. Every man had at least two handguns in plain view and all carried rifles either resting across their arms or in a scabbard attached to their saddle. Bart had brought gunfighters to the negotiation.

Well, at least I don't look so out of place now, Carleton thought. Perry had been prophetic when he said they'd probably be dead if it came to Carleton needing to use his gun.

Bart rode forward until his horse's hooves stepped on the rectangle border. His face split into a grin. "What you got going on here, Agent Maine? Looks like you created us a little playground."

Bart dismounted, and Perry explained the purpose of the rectangle as well as the rules he had in mind for the negotiation.

"Unarmed, you say?" Bart asked. "And I suppose the little demon will leave his weapons behind as well?"

"Yes," Perry answered. "And as mediator, I'll be unarmed too."

Bart looked over his shoulder at the men he'd brought with him and chuckled. "I suppose that'll be fine. I seem to be the lightest on firepower anyway. Except for maybe our wizard friend over there." The gunfighters chuckled at his comment.

When Bart mentioned that Carleton was armed, Penelope did a double take. Her gaze went from the gun at his side to Carleton's eyes. The concern in her expression puzzled him at first. Then he put it together; she thought that wearing the sidearm made him more of a priority target if things turned ugly.

Bart removed his gun belt and looped it over the pommel of his saddle. Perry removed his guns as well, setting them on a rock next to Carleton outside the rectangle. Bart and Perry met next to the flagpole and looked toward the chiefson expectantly.

"Well, where's this shaman I'm supposed to talk to?" Bart asked.

The chiefson gave him an enigmatic smile. "I call him now." The chiefson took something out of his pocket and set it on the ground. He took two long steps backward. The object reflected the morning sun with the luster of a silver coin, but the top surface was convex, like a skipping stone.

Within seconds, the ground started to vibrate and a rumbling noise made the horses shy. The ground under the chiefson's artifact began to bubble upward, and a round-topped column made of stone pebbles rose from the ground.

The gunfighters milled and grumbled to each other. Two had stayed on their horses, but the others were on foot. Only one of them didn't seem frightened by what he was seeing, and he told the others to calm down.

When the rumbling stopped, the column had risen to about five feet. The hundreds of small stones that comprised it fell to the ground like a bead curtain cut from its hangings, revealing Shaman Gafut standing within. The shaman stepped out of the circular pile of stones that encompassed him and took a position next to the chiefson.

"Hell of an entrance," Bart commented to Perry with a rare note of respect in his voice. Judging by Perry's open-mouthed awe, Carleton guessed he'd never seen anything like it either. Carleton knew he'd just witnessed some extremely powerful geomancy, and he dearly wanted to understand how it was done. When he glanced at Penelope to check her reaction to the display, she read the eagerness in his face and responded with an amused smile.

The chiefson spoke to the shaman in their native tongue while gesturing toward the flagpole and the neutral area. Shaman Gafut nodded and waited while the chiefson handed his spear and his knife to one of his warriors. The two crossed into the rectangle and stopped near the flagpole, across from Bart.

Perry started by introducing Bart to the avens and the avens to Bart. Neither side seemed happy to make the other's acquaintance. It was frowns and folded arms all around. Perry was facing a tough crowd.

Carleton's position on the north side of the rectangle put him closest to the conversation, so he was able to hear clearly. To his left, the aveni warriors gathered along the western line. To his right, the gunfighters took up positions that gave them a clear line of sight, seemingly uninterested in what was being said. Of course, they weren't being paid to listen; they were waiting for some kind of signal to defend or attack.

Penelope looked ready to flee at a moment's notice, in spite of Willie's protective presence nearby. She stayed on her horse and frequently cast glances back down the path toward the mine. Carleton had expected Bart to include her in the negotiations, possibly to influence the outcome, although using aeromancy on the avens would be disastrous if it failed and they understood what she'd tried to do.

Carleton didn't blame Penelope for her nervousness. The aveni warriors kept their spears at the ready and had a coiled look about them. The gunfighters feigned boredom, but their eyes flicked toward every tiny movement.

Jasper was the only person present who seemed undisturbed. Once he figured out that he was more or less in the line of fire between the gunfighters and the aveni warriors, he shuffled over to the corner of the rectangle where Penelope and Willie waited and found a rock to sit on.

Meanwhile, Perry launched into his mediation, pausing occasionally to let the chiefson translate for the shaman. "I asked you here to see if we can resolve the conflict that has developed between Commonwealth Mine and the Siri Tan. I'm hoping we can leave here today with a solution that will work for both of you. Let's start by stating what each of you wants from the other side, and we'll negotiate from there. Mr. McLaury, you go first."

Bart shrugged. "All I need is for them to keep the dragons out of our way. If they don't—"

"Stop there, please," Perry interrupted, holding up his hand. "We're just exchanging desired outcomes right now. We'll talk about consequences later."

Bart grunted. "Whatever you want, Agent Maine. This is your circus."

Perry turned to the avens. "Chiefson Sulc, what do the avens want from Mr. McLaury?"

After a short exchange with the shaman, the chiefson answered, "Treaty breaker leave home of Nadi Gaman."

"If I'm hearing right," Bart said, "he's saying we have to stop mining, and that ain't gonna happen."

"This is only a starting point," Perry said. "Now comes the hard part. We have to find a compromise that is acceptable to both parties."

Bart shook his head in exasperation. "You're making this harder than it has to be. The compromise is simple. If the avens move the dragon to a new cave, we won't be invading its home and it won't get hurt."

The chiefson made a chopping motion with his hand. "No. Eggs not move. Nadi Gaman not move."

"What eggs?" Bart asked.

There was no way around it. Perry had to let Bart in on the secret. "The dragon is a female. She has two eggs in the chamber you found. That's why she was protecting it so fiercely."

To Carleton's relief, Bart didn't seem to have much interest in the dragon eggs. "So move them to another chamber."

The chiefson shook his head. "Eggs move, eggs die."

That was new information. Moving the dragon eggs would kill the embryos inside. No wonder the avens hadn't wanted Carleton's help with them.

The chief pointed an accusing finger at Bart. "Mine break treaty."

"The Mining Act says I can follow a vein wherever it leads," Bart argued, "even if that's onto another claim."

"I'm no lawyer," Perry said, "but that's a United States law, and aveni territory is sovereign. The Mining Act doesn't apply."

Bart squared his shoulders and folded his arms. "Like it or not, the avens are part of the United States of America now. When a genuine official of the U.S. government tells me I can't follow my ore under aveni territory, then I'll believe it."

Perry shot a rueful look over his shoulder at Carleton. They had tried to get an official out here to straighten Bart out, but that plan had failed.

Perry waved toward Jasper as he addressed Bart. "Don't you think the delvans should have something to say about this? It's their lives you're putting at risk."

Carleton had wondered about that himself. He had expected both Jasper and Penelope to join Bart in the negotiation.

Bart glanced over at Jasper. "The delvans do what they're paid to do, and that's mine ore. Jasper supervises the miners.

I run the mine. Jasper is here as a witness and because he asked to come."

It was obvious to Carleton that they were getting nowhere. Bart hadn't come to negotiate; he'd come to dictate terms. The fact that he'd brought gunfighters to the parley should have been their first clue.

Then an idea occurred to him that he thought might be acceptable to both sides and salvage his contract at the same time. He cleared his throat to get Perry's attention.

Perry turned. "What is it, Carleton?" The annoyance in his voice betrayed the pressure he must have been feeling.

"I have a suggestion."

Perry took a step toward Carleton, but then seemed to reconsider the idea of leaving the avens and Bart alone.

"Well, out with it, wizard," Bart said.

Perry held up a hand. "Wait. Carleton, leave your gun behind and join us here."

Carleton unbuckled his gun belt and set it next to Perry's.

How could he best word his proposal? Bart was going to resist anything that didn't let him scrape every ounce of ore out of that mine. Carleton was less worried about the avens. Their primary concern seemed to be the dragon, and there was no way Carleton would suggest anything that would put the dragon or her eggs at risk.

Everyone was looking at him expectantly when he lifted his eyes to regard them. The shaman surprised him by giving him a respectful nod, which Carleton returned. Their shared experience with the dragon had forged some kind of understanding between them.

Carleton started with the obvious. "Bart wants as much ore as he can get, and the avens want to protect the dragon and her eggs. There's some debate over whether or not Bart has the right to pursue ore under aveni territory, but if the avens gave him permission, that wouldn't be an issue."

He stopped to let the chiefson translate for the shaman. So far, Bart was listening without protest. That was a good sign.

Carleton continued. "What if we make an arrangement that protects the dragon lair and gives Bart access to the ore under aveni territory?"

"How will we do that?" Bart asked. "You said yourself that those caverns intersect the ore body several times. There's no way to avoid them."

"There is a way," Carleton insisted, "but you'll need my help. I can locate the caverns. I suggest we establish a buffer zone around every cavern. You can mine all the ore that isn't part of a buffer zone."

Bart looked skeptical. "How much buffer zone are we talking about here?"

Perry seemed positively disposed to the idea, but the chiefson looked confused. Perry bent down and drew an ellipse in the dirt, scooping out the center. Pointing to it, he said, "This is a dragon cavern." He made a squiggly line around the outside of the ellipse. "Here is the rock around the cavern." With his fingertips, he scooped out a path next to the squiggly line. "This is the mine." He pointed at the squiggly line and looked up at Chiefson Sulc. "How much rock do we need to protect the cavern?"

The chiefson considered his crude diagram for a moment and then talked to Shaman Gafut. "One hundred paces," he answered.

"A hundred paces," Bart scoffed. "Even if we're talking aveni paces, that's got to be nearly two-hundred feet. There's no way I'm giving up two-hundred feet of ore around every chamber."

"Not all of the material would be ore," Carleton objected.

"You saw that chamber we already found," Bart said. "The ore was part of the wall. Hell, if we have to go two-hundred feet around every chamber, we'll lose more than half the ore body. Nice try, wizard, but your idea isn't going to work."

Perry broke into the exchange. "Not even if the avens break off hostilities and give you permission to dig?"

The chiefson narrowed his eyes and said, "No permission for treaty breaker."

"I don't need permission," Bart retorted.

Their voices had risen during the last part of the exchange, and Bart's final comment was nearly a shout. The aveni warriors and the gunfighters shifted uneasily on their respective sides of the neutral area.

Everyone turned at the sound of more horses approaching from the direction of the mine. Penelope was the only person who didn't appear to be surprised by the interruption. In fact, Carleton thought she looked relieved. Would that turn out to be a good thing or a bad thing?

CHAPTER 26

Agreement

Bart's gunfighters had the first view of the approaching riders. One man tensed and whispered to the leader as he eased toward his horse. Two other men followed suit. The leader ordered them to stay and motioned them to new positions that placed them opposite the oncoming riders. The gunfighters didn't look pleased, but they did as they were told. All three adjusted their bandannas and hats to obscure their faces.

A few moments later, Marshal Bodine came into view, followed by four men on horseback, including a man with a sheriff's badge. The marshal reined up short when he beheld the scene.

Bart's confident grin upon seeing the marshal put Carleton on alert. "Howdy, Marshal," Bart shouted. "Maybe you can put something to rest while you're here."

"I'll be happy to oblige," said the marshal. He dismounted and said something to the sheriff. The sheriff stayed on his horse, as did the posse. They cast suspicious glances at Bart's gunmen.

The marshal trudged over to the mediation group, tipping his hat to Penelope along the way. No one bothered to tell him he was supposed to disarm. His eyes traveled over the small group and then he glanced toward Perry's and Carleton's gun belts resting on the rock. He came to a stop next to them, letting out a harrumph of approval. The man didn't miss much.

The marshal seemed to know everyone who was present. He acknowledged the chiefson and shaman with a nod and they returned the gesture. He and Perry greeted each other. He raised an eyebrow at Carleton but didn't comment.

"Sorry I'm late," he said. "Looks like you decided to start without me."

Carleton didn't like how things were shaping up. Bart was entirely too happy to see the marshal, and it seemed that Penelope had been expecting his arrival. Their reactions suggested that Bart had some influence with the marshal, which didn't bode well for the negotiations.

Carleton should have kept his mouth shut, but he was too frustrated to remain silent. "We were under the impression you weren't interested."

Perry quickly put a restraining hand on Carleton's shoulder. "Sorry, Marshal. We hadn't heard anything from you and we were running out of time."

The marshal leveled a "watch it" glare at Carleton before responding. "It took time to check into your complaint and gather the assistance I needed."

"What complaint?" Bart demanded.

"Tell me what's happened here," the marshal instructed Perry, deflecting Bart's question.

Perry quickly explained how the negotiations had progressed up to that point. He concluded with, "Now we're at a bit of a stalemate."

The marshal pursed his lips and then gave Bart a sidelong glance. "You don't like the wizard's compromise?"

"What does the wizard know?" Bart scoffed. "He gets paid the same no matter how little ore we muck out of there. A lot of money and time has been invested in Commonwealth, and it's my job to see that we get the most out of it."

"Is that why you followed the ore under the aveni border?" asked the marshal.

The question seemed to confuse Bart. "Of course."

"What about the attack on the dragon?"

Bart seemed to recognize that the tenor of the marshal's questions was not necessarily in his favor. His voice took on an edge of defensiveness. "What about it? The beasts are a menace. I got a right to protect my miners."

The marshal narrowed his eyes at Bart. "What made you think the treaty didn't apply to you?"

Bart glanced toward the sheriff and the posse. He straightened his shoulders and gave the marshal a hard look. "This is a new territory, Marshal, and a tough land to wrangle. Rules get bent in the name of progress." He leaned forward, "You know as well as I do that money is power and power bends rules."

The marshal nodded slowly. "Are you suggesting I should hold someone else responsible for your decisions? Someone with money and power?"

Bart clamped his mouth shut and looked at the ground. He took a deep breath and exhaled. "No, Marshal. I'm not suggesting that. I take full responsibility for my own actions."

"I'm sure that's a wise move, Mr. McLaury." The marshal took a pair of handcuffs from his vest pocket and motioned for Bart to turn around. "I'm placing you under arrest for violating the terms of the Dragon Mountain Treaty and endangering national security."

Bart took a hesitant step back, his face turning red. His hand went uselessly to his hip where his gun would have been if he hadn't disarmed. "Those charges are ridiculous, Marshal Bodine, and you know it. You aren't going to lock me up just so you can save face with the avens." He nodded toward his gunmen, and they all drew their weapons. However, they seemed to have trouble picking a target. Guns alternately pointed at the posse, the negotiators, and the aveni warriors.

Marshal Bodine's voice seemed to come from the depths of the earth. His words were strong and clear. "You'd better reconsider your position right now, Mr. McLaury. Resisting arrest and threatening an officer of the law won't help your case."

Bart started backing up toward his gunfighters. "Be reasonable, Marshal. There ain't no case. If you take me in, I'll walk out a free man within hours."

"You're wrong, Bart. You may have friends in high places, but Agent Maine here has stirred up the attention of some powerful folks, too. The United States doesn't want trouble with the avens, and if you had any sense, you wouldn't either."

Bart wasn't listening anymore. He'd turned to run toward his horse, which was near the gunmen. Carleton couldn't understand what the mine manager hoped to accomplish. Even if he escaped, the marshal would simply arrest him at the house later. Was he that sure the mine owners would back him up?

The marshal drew his gun. "Sheriff!" he yelled. "Arrest that man and anyone else who gives you trouble. We'll sort 'em out later."

The sheriff and the posse all drew their guns and a shot was fired. A posse member fell to the ground clutching his shoulder. Everyone, including the negotiators, scattered and ducked behind the nearest available rock as more shots rang out.

Bart had reached his horse and grabbed his pistol before the first gunshot frightened the horse into running. Bart dove behind a rock near his gunmen.

Hiding in a shallow ravine with Perry and the marshal, Carleton assessed the situation. The gunmen were hunkered down opposite the posse. He couldn't see Willie, Jason, or

Penelope, so they must have found cover somewhere. As for the avens … they were still standing by the truce flag!

Perry spotted the problem at nearly the same moment as Carleton. "Chiefson Sulc!" he called, waving for the chiefson and the shaman to join them.

The chiefson shook his head, standing resolute with his arms crossed. Next to him, the shaman was mumbling to himself with his eyes closed. He rubbed two stones together as he chanted.

Perry's face paled. "Uh-oh."

"What's he doing?" the marshal asked.

"Using magic," Carleton answered.

Fortunately, Bart and his gunmen were distracted by the posse, exchanging shots when targets presented themselves. For the moment, they seemed oblivious to the shaman's activity.

Then the ground began to shake. The rumbling seemed to come from everywhere at once. Guns went silent while everyone paused to listen.

A deep grinding and bumping sound echoed off the peaks that bracketed the valley. Everyone glanced up in panic, expecting a landslide, but other than a few rocks that were knocked loose by the quaking, the slopes held steady.

Rhythmic thumps that felt and sounded like underground detonations grew in volume. A moment later, a giant made of stone lurched past the shaman, moving toward Bart and his gunmen. Several seconds of stunned silence passed as the ten-foot golem advanced. It waved an arm, and a chunk of rock hurtled forward, shattering in a spray of rocky shrapnel and dust against the boulder that sheltered two of Bart's gunmen.

Shaken out of their stupor, the gunmen fired at the monster with no effect other than the whining ping of treacherous ricochets.

Bart peered from his hiding place and narrowed his eyes when he spotted the shaman. Carleton didn't have to read Bart's mind to know what he was thinking. Scrambling from his hiding place, Carleton ran toward the chiefson and shaman.

The golem waded toward the gunmen, forcing them back to new positions. A man cried out in pain when one of the stone missiles scored a hit. Bart bravely held his position, pointing his gun toward the shaman and waiting for the golem to give him a clear shot.

Taking in the situation with a glance as he ran, Carleton reached for his wrist band, unsure he'd reach the shaman in time. Skidding to a stop, he activated his shield and oriented himself to face Bart just as the mine manager aimed and pulled the trigger.

Three bullets slammed into Carleton's shield in rapid succession. Deflecting them drained some of his swi, but the bullets were nothing compared to dragon fire. He estimated he could hold off at least another dozen rounds of similar power.

Bart took aim for another shot, and then yelped in pain, dropping his pistol. He went to his knees, clutching his shooting arm to his chest. With their employer out of the fight and the golem closing in, the gunfighters fled the conflict. They fired enough lead over their shoulders to keep the posse pinned down as they retreated deeper into the canyon.

When the gunfire finally subsided, everyone cautiously emerged from their positions. Gafut stopped chanting, and the golem froze for a second before collapsing into a loose pile of stones.

Carleton dropped his shield as Perry ran up to him.

"You okay?" Perry asked.

"I'm fine," Carleton answered. He turned to check on the avens.

Shaman Gafut looked tired but was rallying quickly. Carleton envied the power the aven had displayed in controlling the golem for so long. He would give a lot to learn the secrets of aveni mysticism.

The shaman mumbled a few words to the chiefson, who translated for Carleton. "Shaman say thank you. Bart faster than stone man."

"Glad I could help," Carleton replied with a shallow bow toward the shaman. The chiefson didn't bother translating.

"Hey, take it easy with that!" complained an unfamiliar voice. The gunfighters were returning to the clearing with their hands clasped behind their necks. Six aveni warriors prodded them along, holding spears at their backs. Two more warriors circled overhead on their wyverns. The posse swiftly moved forward and took custody of the gunmen.

Carleton had wondered where the chiefson's underlings had gone during the confrontation. They had apparently flanked the gunfighters and were waiting in ambush when the cowards made a run for it.

"It's not easy to hide from an aveni scout," Perry said with amusement, watching the airborne avens return their wyverns to their hillside perches.

Meanwhile, the marshal had been dealing with Bart. The mine manager's wound had been roughly bandaged and the sheriff was taking him into custody. As the marshal headed back toward the avens, Bart called out, "The investors won't sit still for this. They need me to run the mine."

The marshal raised an eyebrow. "They need *someone* to run the mine. It doesn't have to be you."

Penelope, Willie, and Jacob had returned to the edge of the rectangle. Willie was frowning and shifting from one foot to the other, probably worried about the future of his job at the mine. Penelope clutched an envelope in her hands and repeatedly tilted forward onto the balls of her feet. Jasper stood next to her, watching the proceedings with a grim expression.

Perry waved them over and called out, "I think we can forget about the neutral area. The negotiations are off."

"Oh, I wouldn't say that," the marshal commented.

When Penelope, Willie, and Jasper crossed into the rectangle, the chiefson signaled his own warriors forward.

"I believe you have something of interest for these proceedings," the marshal said, holding out his hand as Penelope arrived at his side.

She handed him the envelope she was carrying. "Yes, Marshal."

The marshal made a show of opening the envelope and unfolding the paper inside. "It says here that, in the event Bart McLaury is unable to continue his duties as mine manager, his responsibilities will be assigned to Foreman Willie Broccius and Mine Supervisor Jasper Underlight." The marshal lowered the paper and looked at Willie and Jasper. "Do you men accept those responsibilities?"

Willie was so shocked that he opened his mouth and no sound came out. He finally managed to nod and say, "Yes, sir. I'll do my best."

Jasper gave Willie a considering look and then nodded. "Aye, we can make that work."

"Good. It's settled then," the marshal said, handing the paper back to Penelope. "You can carry on with your negotiations, Agent Maine." He pointed a finger at Willie and Jasper. "Don't you forget that the dragons and the aveni border are protected by treaty."

Jasper shrugged. "There be nothing to negotiate. We'll have to work the ore that's on our side of the border and be done with it."

Willie dropped his head in disappointment, and then raised it to look at Carleton. "What about the wizard's suggestion? Any chance we can still get in on that deal? Any ore is better than no ore."

Jasper shook his head. "Bart was right. It wouldn't be worth the effort to work two-hundred feet around the chambers of the dragon lair."

The chiefson's earlier words tickled the back of Carleton's mind. The avens had seemed willing to entertain the idea of the mine going under their territory as long as it maintained a buffer of a hundred paces. When Bart had balked at the offer, the chiefson had revoked it by saying *no permission for treaty breaker*. Would the avens be willing to accept new terms from someone other than Bart? Two-hundred feet of buffer did seem rather extreme. If the ore was stoped out and then backfilled carefully, Carleton estimated that fifty feet would be plenty.

"Excuse me," Carleton interrupted. "This is still a negotiation. The avens wanted *Bart* to stay a hundred paces from the lair. Let me see if I can get a better deal."

Carleton took the chief and the shaman aside. Scaling up Perry's idea of using a diagram, he dug a line in the ground with his heel and used his boot to scoop dirt away from one side. Motioning toward the cleared area with both hands, he said, "Dragon lair." The avens nodded their understanding. He walked twenty paces from the lair marker and dug another line with his heel, clearing the opposite side. Motioning again, he said, "Mine." He walked back to a spot about halfway between his marks. "Rock," he declared, with his hands to either side. "Is this enough?"

The chiefson started to translate, but Shaman Gafut stopped him, appearing to understand what Carleton was suggesting. He looked back and forth between the two lines and then paced the distance between them for himself. Carleton counted thirty-two paces to cover the sixty-foot distance, so Bart hadn't been too far off in his estimating.

But the shaman wasn't done. He continued eight more paces for a total of forty. He pointed emphatically toward the ground. Carleton strode over and marked the spot the shaman indicated. "This is enough?" he asked. The shaman nodded.

Carleton rejoined the group at the flag with the avens close behind.

"What do you think?" Carleton asked Jasper. "That's about seventy-five feet."

Jasper considered the distance and nodded. "Aye. That'll do. Does this mean ye're reconsidering yer position at the mine? We can't make this deal without yer wizardry to help us avoid the lair."

Carleton smiled. "Yes, of course."

Willie seemed ecstatic about the unexpected turn of events. He clapped Carleton on the back and said, "You're all right, Wizard Kazimer."

With the marshal's help, Perry presided over the final details of the agreement between Commonwealth Mine and the Siri Tan. The miners would be allowed to follow the ore under aveni territory as long as they respected the agreed-upon dragon-lair buffer zone. To protect the interests of the mine, Carleton's first responsibility would be to make a detailed map of the dragon lair so the miners could continue working in the event that something happened to him.

When the negotiations were complete, the marshal was treated to the jaw-dropping spectacle of Shaman Gafut's departure. The shaman returned to the center of the circular rock pile he'd created upon arrival. He closed his eyes and intoned an incantation. As the sounds spilled from his lips, the stones flowed up around him, forming a column that descended into the desert floor. All that remained was a circle of disturbed soil and the silvery artifact that had been used to summon the shaman earlier. The chiefson slipped the object into a hidden pocket and bid the humans farewell.

While Perry spoke with the marshal about recording the agreement and Jasper conferred with Willie about how they would move forward, Carleton caught Penelope's eye and motioned her aside.

"Nice work, Wizard Kazimer," she said when they were far enough away for a private conversation.

"Thanks," Carleton said. "But I'm starting to think we owe it all to you."

Penelope's soft smile gave away nothing. "Nonsense. All I did was deliver instructions from the investors. You and Perry were the ones who set up the negotiations and made a deal possible."

"Is that who you work for? The investors?"

Penelope tilted her head down, "Now, Carleton, I do believe we've had this conversation. Who I work for is an unwelcome line of inquiry."

Carleton huffed out a breath. "I remember. But I'd like to know who to thank for getting Bart out of my life. You must have been quite … persuasive."

Penelope's eyes grew distant and took on a haunted look. "Not nearly as persuasive as you imagine." Catching herself, she looked down at her hands. "Let's just say Bart's employers concluded that he no longer represented their interests at Commonwealth. I was beginning to think I'd failed to convince the marshal of that."

Finally, Carleton had an explanation for her surreptitious trip to Tombstone. He waited until her ice-blue eyes met his. "I hope one day you can trust me enough to let me in on some of your secrets. I'd like to help you somehow."

"That's kind of you to say," she said, her gaze growing tender. "But I'd not wish my secrets on anyone, least of all you."

Carleton glanced past Penelope to see Perry headed their way. Penelope caught Carleton's look and turned as Perry approached.

"What are you two conspiring about over here?" Perry asked in a jocular tone. He looked back and forth between them, seeming to catch on to the serious atmosphere. "Is everything okay?"

Penelope gave him a bright smile. "Of course it is, Agent Maine. Congratulations on a successful mediation."

Perry grinned. "Why, thank you, ma'am. I can't take much credit, but I'm glad it all worked out in the end."

"You're too modest," Penelope said.

Willie and Jasper were headed back to their horses and were so intent on their conversation that they seemed to have completely forgotten about Penelope. She took a step back and said, "I must be going now. Good day, gentlemen."

Carleton and Perry said their farewells, and Penelope hurried to catch up with Willie and Jasper.

Perry tilted his head in her direction. "What do you think she'll do now that Bart has been taken to jail?"

The question hadn't occurred to Carleton. He'd figured Penelope would continue working at Commonwealth. But his friend was right. The situation at the mine was more settled with Bart gone and an agreement hammered out with the avens. Maybe a facilitator was no longer necessary.

"I don't know," Carleton answered. "I suppose she'll go back to wherever she came from."

Perry gave him a sympathetic look. "That makes you sad, doesn't it? I'm sorry things aren't working out for you two."

"Her and me?" Carleton responded with surprise. Although he had harbored that hope from time to time, the idea sounded foolish when Perry said it straight out. "That's unlikely," he said. "We've become friends, sort of, but I've always known our acquaintance was temporary."

Perry put an arm over Carleton's shoulder and walked him toward their horses. "Whatever you say, Wizard Kazimer. As far as I'm concerned, everything in life is temporary. You should celebrate the good things when they happen." Perry released him and untied Remington.

While Carleton freed Peppy and climbed into the saddle, he concluded that Perry had it right. He forced a grin, discarding the melancholy his conversation with Penelope had caused. "You're a smart man and a good friend, Agent Maine. I think we should go celebrate right now."

CHAPTER 27

Farewell

Two weeks later, Carleton enjoyed a quiet morning with a cup of coffee on the front porch of the ranch house. Perry sat on the opposite side of the old table with his feet up on a bench he'd assembled from scrap wood. The sun angled under the porch roof, warming them and defeating the morning chill.

Carleton reflected on what the weather would be like back in his home town of Baltimore. By that time of year, the trees would have shaken off their last leaves, and gusts of cold, wet sea breeze would be harrying tightly bundled residents from one warm doorway to another. Meanwhile, the temperatures at Sunrise Ranch had finally cooled enough to work outside comfortably all day long.

Perry cleared his throat and broke the companionable silence. "Have you decided what you're going to do when you're done at Commonwealth?"

"Not really." Carleton said. "I could ask for another contract, but who knows where the Guild would send me next. I was starting to like this place."

"The desert does grow on you," Perry agreed with a smile. "You're welcome to work the ranch with me as long as you like. I've been thinking about expanding my peccary operations, but I'd need help to do it."

Carleton enjoyed working on the ranch with Perry, but he couldn't give up on his career as a geomancer. The problem with growing his career through the Guild was that he had to go where the contracts sent him.

His alternatives were to work freelance or find local business for the Guild. Going freelance meant managing his own contracts and building a reputation that wouldn't mean much anywhere else. On the other hand, Guild rates were high, and finding a local patron willing to run a contract through the Guild would be a challenge. A part-time contract that would cost less and leave him time to help Perry might be an easier sell.

"Thanks for the offer," Carleton replied. "We might be able to work something out. I have another week or so of work at Commonwealth, and I might be able to convince Jasper and Willie to keep me on part-time after that. In the meantime, I'll ask around, and I'd appreciate it if you'd do the same. See if anyone in the area needs a geomancer, and we'll go from there."

"No problem," Perry agreed. "With all the mining going on around here, I'm sure we can find more work for you."

The clop of hooves and the appearance of a familiar carriage topping the hill brought both men to their feet. As the carriage approached the house, the driver turned it and came to a stop. He got down and helped Penelope out of the carriage.

Penelope wore a light-blue dress and carried a matching parasol. "Good morning, gentlemen," she said as she approached the porch. "I hope I'm not interrupting anything."

Perry tipped his hat to her. "Not at all, ma'am. Just shooting the breeze. Care to join us?"

"Thank you, but I can't stay long. I wanted to say goodbye and thank both of you one last time for your help."

Perry bowed and said, "It was my duty and my pleasure, ma'am."

Penelope giggled and covered her mouth with a gloved hand. She shook her head and said, "I'll miss your charming ways, Mr. Maine."

"Where will you go?" Carleton asked. He hoped his disappointment that she was leaving wasn't revealed in his voice.

"Tombstone, for now. I've been called to testify in front of the grand jury at Bart's trial. Marshal Bodine will be testifying as well, and with the statements gathered from you, Perry, and others, I don't think Bart is going to escape justice."

Perry raised an eyebrow. "It seems you might have had something to do with that turn of events."

Penelope tilted her head in admission. "I did what I could." Looking at Carleton, she added, "I wish I could have done better."

"I guess Bart had us all fooled," Carleton said with a shrug.

Penelope seemed to get the message that Carleton had kept her secret from Perry. She bestowed one of her dazzling smiles on him and said, "I appreciate your generous interpretation of my actions."

Penelope glanced up at the sun. "Well, I must be going. It's a long ride to Tombstone."

The two men followed her to the carriage, and Carleton gave her a hand up. Her gloved hand squeezed his in thanks as she sat down. His throat tightened when he considered that he might be looking into those amazing ice-blue eyes for the last time, and he didn't trust his voice enough to say goodbye right then.

"Have a safe journey," Perry said.

"Thank you, Perry. Good luck to you both."

Swallowing his sadness, Carleton smiled as brightly as he could and tipped his bowler to her one last time. "Fare thee well, Mrs. Cartwright."

Penelope's eyes searched his face, and he was sure she could read all of the feelings he was trying to hide. She tilted her head to the side, as if considering a proposal, and then she smiled. "Until we meet again, Wizard Kazimer."

The driver flipped his reins and the carriage rolled away from the house and headed back down the road toward the valley. The two men sipped their coffee as they watched the carriage leave.

Carleton turned to Perry and discovered an amused smirk on his friend's face.

"What?" Carleton demanded.

"That sounded a lot like a promise to me," he answered.

"Maybe," Carleton replied. He turned for one last look, but the carriage had already disappeared over the hill. "I hope you're right."

Glossary of Terms

Adit: An underground passage that is open to air at only one end. Compare to tunnel

Aven: A species of sapient humanoid indigenous to the mountains of North America. They are much smaller than humans, typically slight of build, and have a dusky brown complexion

Big Fifty: Nickname for the Sharps .50 caliber buffalo rifle

Calico: Western slang term for a woman.

Catalyst: A physical component, often of biological origin, that relates to the desired manifestation of a spell

Corned: Western slang term for being drunk

Crosscut: A horizontal mine passage that cuts through the ore body perpendicular to a drift

Delvan: An albino, subterranean species of sapient humanoid. On average, they are shorter and stockier than humans

Dove (or "Soiled dove"): Western slang term for a prostitute

Drift: A horizontal mine passage that follows an edge of the ore body

Face: The surface of the ore body where the miners are currently extracting ore

Fluvium Terra: A current of wild earth magic that geomancers can use to partially replenish their swi reserves

Gangue: The valueless material that surrounds ore

Head-wall: The top wall or "ceiling" of an underground passage

Imprint: To enchant a physical object with a specific magical spell, allowing a wizard to use the object to cast the spell without the need for catalysts or an incantation

Quad: A common four-bedroom design for an underground series of connected chambers where delvan miners live

Shaft: A vertical mine passage

Silk: Western slang term for barbed wire fencing

Siri Tan: An aven tribe that lives in the Dragon Mountains

Stope: A cavern created by the excavation of ore

Swi: A magical energy force generated by all life forms. Excess swi gathers into streams known as fluvia, which flow throughout the world and concentrate into vortexes. Wizards draw upon their own swi reserves to power spells that alter or shape the physical world.

Transmutation: The consumption of a physical catalyst that reinforces the manifestation of a magical spell

Tunnel: An underground passage that is open to air at both ends. Compare to adit.

Vortex: A confluence of fluvia that pools and redistributes swi, creating a balancing effect on the concentration of swi throughout the local region

Thank You for Reading

Thank you for dedicating some of your reading time to *Geomancer's Bargain*. I hope you enjoyed the adventures of Carleton and Perry and that you look forward to more tales of the Western Geomancer.

If you would like to be notified by email when I release a new book, please subscribe to the New Releases list at my blog: www.DanielRMarvello.com/releases. I only use the list for release announcements, and you may unsubscribe at any time.

I know that not everyone likes to write book reviews, but if you are willing to spare the time to write a sentence or two about what you thought of *Geomancer's Bargain*, I encourage you to post a review at your favorite book vendor site or recommend the story to your social networking friends.

I love hearing from fans. If you would like to share your thoughts with me privately, you can reach me through the contact page on my blog: DanielRMarvello.com/contact. I look forward to meeting you.

Happy reading,
Daniel R. Marvello

Acknowledgements

My thanks go out to my readers and my family for supporting my writing career. I couldn't have done it without you.

Thanks also to my beta readers, who helped me make *Geomancer's Bargain* a better book than it would have been without their feedback. I sincerely appreciate their time and effort:

- Susan Daffron (author of the Alpine Grove Romantic Comedy series)
- Becca Mills (author of the Emanations series)
- Nancy Brashear (contributing author of the *Grimm & Grimmer Volume Two* anthology)
- Paul Sheriff (author of the PDSA programming series)
- Ken Rahmoeller
- Alan Vryhof

ABOUT THE AUTHOR

Daniel R. Marvello writes magical fantasy adventure stories. He lives in a log home deep in the forest of the North Idaho panhandle with his wife of twenty-plus years and a small support staff of Samoyeds. His professional background is in database and software development as well as technical writing.

Daniel's fiction writing was inspired by his love for reading magical fantasy and his years of enjoying fantasy role-playing games. His fiction works include The Vaetra Chronicles, a swords & sorcery adventure series, The Ternion Order, a contemporary paranormal fantasy series, and The Western Geomancer, a western fantasy adventure series.

Visit Daniel's blog at: www.DanielRMarvello.com

Books by Daniel R. Marvello

The Vaetra Chronicles

- *Vaetra Unveiled*
- *Vaetra Untrained*
- *Vaetra Unleashed*

Find out more at www.vaetra.com

The Ternion Order

First Moon